BRINGERS OF DEATH

As if realising that it was being watched, the figure turned. Its mask-like face bore a pair of red, glowering eyes, reminding Brael of the bloody malevolence in the invaders' gaze. On its chest was displayed a pair of spread wings that Brael had seen before: on the wall-hanging in the Sanctum of the Temple of the Holy Varks. With a shock that almost unmanned him, Brael realised that he was standing before a star god. – *from* **Xenocide** *by Simon Jowett*

Haldane's Terminator armour hadn't been hacked apart, it had been hacked *open*. The body of the Wolf Lord was nowhere to be seen. Tears of rage coursed freely down Kjarl's face. 'What have they done with our lord?'

'The orks have taken him. They must mean to give him as a trophy to their leader,' Skaflock replied, biting back his rage. 'A wolf lord's head would be a tremendous prize for an ambitious warboss like Skargutz.'

'Then it's a blood feud, by Russ!' – *from* **Even Unto Death** *by Mike Lee*

In the nightmare world of the 41st millennium, humanity is locked in a desperate struggle for survival against a relentless tide of aliens. Read tales of heroism and valour in this action-packed selection of savage science fiction set in the gothic future world of Warhammer 40,000.

More Warhammer 40,000 from the Black Library

• WARHAMMER 40,000 SHORT STORIES •

WHAT PRICE VICTORY
eds. Marc Gascoigne & Christian Dunn

• GAUNT'S GHOSTS •
by Dan Abnett

The Founding
FIRST & ONLY
GHOSTMAKER • NECROPOLIS
The Saint
HONOUR GUARD • THE GUNS OF TANITH
STRAIGHT SILVER • SABBAT MARTYR
The Lost
TRAITOR GENERAL

• THE ULTRAMARINES SERIES •
by Graham McNeill

NIGHTBRINGER
WARRIORS OF ULTRAMAR • DEAD SKY, BLACK SUN

• CAIPHAS CAIN •
by Sandy Mitchell
FOR THE EMPEROR
CAVES OF ICE
THE TRAITOR'S HAND

• OTHER WARHAMMER 40,000 NOVELS •

DAWN OF WAR
C S Goto

WARHAMMER 40,000 STORIES

BRINGERS OF DEATH

Edited by
Marc Gascoigne
& Christian Dunn

A BLACK LIBRARY PUBLICATION

First published in Great Britain in 2005 by
BL Publishing,
Games Workshop Ltd.,
Willow Road, Nottingham,
NG7 2WS, UK.

10 9 8 7 6 5 4 3 2 1

Cover illustration by Neil Roberts.

A CIP record for this book is available from the British Library.

ISBN13: 978 1 84416 232 1
ISBN10: 1 84416 232 X

Distributed in the US by Simon & Schuster
1230 Avenue of the Americas, New York, NY 10020.

Printed and bound in Great Britain by
Bookmarque, Surrey, UK.

See the Black Library on the Internet at
www.blacklibrary.com

Find out more about Games Workshop
and the world of Warhammer 40,000 at
www.games-workshop.com

IT IS THE 41st millennium. For more than a hundred centuries the Emperor has sat immobile on the Golden Throne of Earth. He is the master of mankind by the will of the gods, and master of a million worlds by the might of his inexhaustible armies. He is a rotting carcass writhing invisibly with power from the Dark Age of Technology. He is the Carrion Lord of the Imperium for whom a thousand souls are sacrificed every day, so that he may never truly die.

YET EVEN IN his deathless state, the Emperor continues his eternal vigilance. Mighty battlefleets cross the daemon-infested miasma of the warp, the only route between distant stars, their way lit by the Astronomican, the psychic manifestation of the Emperor's will. Vast armies give battle in His name on uncounted worlds. Greatest amongst his soldiers are the Adeptus Astartes, the Space Marines, bio-engineered super-warriors. Their comrades in arms are legion: the Imperial Guard and countless planetary defence forces, the ever-vigilant Inquisition and the tech-priests of the Adeptus Mechanicus to name only a few. But for all their multitudes, they are barely enough to hold off the ever-present threat from aliens, heretics, mutants – and worse.

TO BE A man in such times is to be one amongst untold billions. It is to live in the cruellest and most bloody regime imaginable. These are the tales of those times. Forget the power of technology and science, for so much has been forgotten, never to be re-learned. Forget the promise of progress and understanding, for in the grim dark future there is only war. There is no peace amongst the stars, only an eternity of carnage and slaughter, and the laughter of thirsting gods.

CONTENTS

Even Unto Death

Mike Lee

THE WOLF SCOUTS flew like spectres down the dark, tangled paths of the forest, their heightened senses keen as a razor's edge. Red moonlight shone along the edges of their blades, and death followed in their wake.

Guttural howls and roaring bursts of gunfire rent the night air all around them, echoing off the boles of the huge trees. The orks were everywhere, boiling up from hidden tunnels like a swarm of ants and crashing through the undergrowth in search of the Space Wolves. With every passing moment the cacophony of noise seemed to draw more tightly around the small pack of Space Marines, like a shrinking noose. Skaflock Sightblinder tightened his grip on his power sword and led the Wolf Scouts onward, racing for the landing zone some fifteen kilometres to the east.

Ork raiders had been terrorizing the worlds of the Volturna sector since the end of the Second Battle of Armageddon, slaughtering tens of thousands of the

Emperor's faithful and putting entire continents to the torch. Their leader, a warlord known as Skargutz the Render, was as cunning as he was cruel. He never lingered too long on any world, pulling back his forces and retreating into the void before help could arrive. The Imperial Navy was left to chase shadows, and with every successful raid the warlord's reputation – and his warband – grew in stature. When the orks struck three systems in as many years, the sector governor appealed to the Space Wolves for aid. A rapid strike team was assembled and slipped stealthily into the sector. Fast escorts patrolled likely targets, waiting for the call to action. Skaflock and his men had been on one such frigate, the *Blood Eagle*, when astropaths on the forge world of Cambion reported that they were under attack. They and nearly a dozen other small packs of scouts had been unleashed onto the world via drop pods, to pinpoint enemy positions for the lightning assault to come. The scouts had slipped close to scores of landing sites and ork firebases, leaving behind remote-activated designator beacons that would allow the fleet to unleash a devastating initial bombardment within moments of arrival.

The operation had gone according to plan, right up to the point the fleet reached orbit and the initial assault wave began its drop. Then everything went to hell.

The night air trembled beneath the roar of huge turbojets as a Thunderhawk gunship made a low-altitude pass over the forest, but the assault craft held its fire, unable to tell friend from foe in the darkness below. Skaflock bit back a savage curse and tried his vox-caster again, but every channel was blanketed in a searing screech of manufactured noise. He had little doubt that the fleet couldn't pick up the designator beacons through the intense vox jamming, it was even possible that their surveyors were blind as well. He couldn't reach the fleet, much less the assault force his team was supposed to link up with; everyone had been cut off. Instead of catching the ork raiders unawares, they had stepped into a trap.

How, Skaflock's thoughts raged? How could we have been so blind?

The game trail the Wolf Scouts were following angled downwards into a narrow, twisting gully split by a shallow stream. With the wind at their backs and the thunder of the gunship passing overhead, the Space Wolves had no warning as they leapt into the gully and found themselves in the midst of an ork hunting party.

For a moment the orks didn't realize who had fallen in amongst them in the darkness. The hesitation was fatal. Skaflock's nerves sang with bloodlust and adrenaline – to him and the rest of the Wolves it was as though the greenskin raiders were moving in slow motion. Without breaking his stride the Space Wolf decapitated two orks with a single sweep of his blade and buried his armoured shoulder into the chest of a third with bone-crushing force. The air was filled with startled cries and shrieks of pain as the rest of the pack joined the fray, and suddenly the panicked orks were shooting and chopping at anything that moved.

Two heavy ork rounds flattened against Skaflock's power armour. As a member of the great company's Wolf Guard he was better protected than the scouts under his command, and the impacts barely fazed him. Blood sizzled off the power sword's energy field as he leapt at a cluster of orks further down the gully. The first of the greenskins raised a crude axe, aiming a blow at Skaflock's head, but the Space Marine ducked beneath the swing and cut the raider in two. Before the body had hit the ground Skaflock was upon the second ork, smashing his bolt pistol across the raider's knobbly skull and stabbing it through the chest. The ork pitched forward with a moan – doubling up on the searing blade and trapping it with its death throes.

Skaflock leant against the ork, trying to push it off the blade and narrowly avoided the third greenskin's swing. The crude axe glanced off his right shoulder plate and opened a long, ragged cut on the back of his unprotected neck. A second blow bit into his side, driving the axe's chisel point through the breastplate and into the flesh beneath. Baring his teeth at the pain, Skaflock spun on his heel, tearing his sword free and bringing the blade around in a glowing arc that separated the ork's head from its shoulders. For a few heartbeats the body remained upright, steam rising from the cauterized stump of its neck, then the axe tumbled from nerveless fingers and the corpse pitched over onto the ground.

Within moments, the battle was over. The six Wolf Scouts under Skaflock's command were veterans of more than a dozen campaigns, as skilled with sword and axe as they were with stealth and guile. Nearly two dozen orks lay dead or dying in the gully, staining the stream with their blood. As Skaflock watched, Gunnar Dragonbane, a giant of a man even by Space Marine standards, sent the last of the orks sprawling with a mighty sweep of his axe.

The greenskin landed in a heap, then rolled over onto its back, a grenade clenched in each bloodstained hand. Without thinking, Gunnar brought up his bolt pistol and shot the ork through the head.

Skaflock snarled as the distinctive *crack* of the bolt pistol echoed through the trees. 'I said no shooting!' he cried. As if in answer, the forest erupted in eager cries as the orks sought out the source of the gunshot.

Gunnar let out a rumbling growl, spitting a pair of shiny black pits into the crimson-tinged stream. The huge scout had a habit of chewing lich-berries; how he kept himself supplied on the long missions off Fenris was a mystery to everyone in the pack. A single berry was poisonous enough to kill a normal human in ten agony-filled seconds. Gunnar claimed the taste improved his disposition. 'Let them come,' he snarled, hefting his axe. 'We've plenty of cover and darkness on our side. We should be hunting *them*, not the other way around.'

'We're not here to hunt orks, Gunnar!' Skaflock snapped. 'We've got to link up with the assault team and guide them off the landing zone to a more defensible position – provided we aren't overrun by ork patrols in the meantime. Now, move out.' Without waiting for an answer, the Wolf Guard leader broke into a run, leaving the scouts to fall in as he sped on.

The orks were right on their heels. Skaflock heard the greenskins stumble into the gully moments behind them, and then the chase was on. Bursts of wild gunfire tore through the forest around them, kicking up plumes of dirt or blowing branches apart in showers of splinters. The Wolf Guard increased his speed, pushing his augmented muscles to the limit. Only his enhanced eyesight and agility allowed him to dodge the treacherous roots and low-hanging branches that lay in his path. Slowly but surely, the Wolf Scouts began to pull away from their pursuers, melting into the darkness like shadows.

THE SOUNDS OF battle called to the Space Wolves like a siren song, growing in intensity. Every few moments Skaflock closed his eyes and focused all of his concentration on the maelstrom of noise, picking out the distinctive notes of different weapons with a practiced ear: storm bolters, boltguns, plasma weapons and the distinctive hammering of crude ork guns.

After fifteen minutes the sounds of the Imperial weapons began to falter; Skaflock bared his fangs in a soundless snarl and drove himself on. Two minutes later he could no longer hear any plasma weapons being fired. Four minutes after that all he could hear were bolters pounding in rapid-fire mode. Then slowly, minute by minute, the bolter fire dwindled away to nothing.

Not long afterwards the wind shifted, blowing from the north-east, and they could smell the blood on the air. The woods had grown silent. Skaflock abandoned all pretence of stealth for the last two kilometres, breaking into a sprint and praying to Russ that his senses had somehow deceived him.

The Wolf Scouts charged headlong into the broad meadow they'd designated as the assault team's drop zone. The gently sloping, grassy field was now a wasteland of mud, ravaged flesh and spilled blood. The black silhouettes of the drop pods reared like tilted gravestones in the crimson moonlight, wreathed in plumes of greasy smoke from the blazing hulls of ork battlewagons.

The dead lay everywhere. Skaflock's mind reeled at the slaughter. The orks had struck from three sides, charging right into the exhaust flames of the drop pods as they settled to the ground. The Space Wolf packs had been cut off from one another even before the drop ramps opened.

The rest of the pack gathered around their leader, staring bleakly at the scene of carnage. Hogun stepped forward, shaking his head mournfully. 'It's a disaster,' he whispered, his voice bleak.

'It's a defeat,' Skaflock said flatly. 'The orks have turned the tables on us for now, but that's the way of war. We've seen worse, Hogun. All of us have.'

'Skaflock's right,' Gunnar said. The expression on his face was bitter, but he nodded solemnly. 'We've been through harder scrapes than this one and won out in the end. We'll just fade back to the mountains and wait for the rest of the company–'

Before the Wolf Guard could finish, the night air trembled with a distant howl of rage and pain that echoed among the derelict drop pods.

As one, the veteran scouts looked to their leader. Skaflock flashed a rapid set of hand signals and the pack fanned out into skirmish order, sweeping silently towards the source of the noise.

The howl came from the far side of the drop zone. As the scouts crept closer, Skaflock caught sight of a dozen Space Wolves – Blood Claws, judging by their youthful features and the markings on their bloodstained armour. They stumbled and staggered through the piled corpses, flinging green-skinned bodies left and right as they searched frantically among the dead. Many of the young Marines had removed their helmets, and their faces were twisted with grief.

Skaflock waved the scouts to a halt and stepped forward. 'Well met, wolf brothers,' he called out. 'We feared there were no survivors.'

Heads darted in Skaflock's direction. Several growled, showing their teeth. One Blood Claw in particular, who had been crouched beside a pile of corpses, rose to his feet. He was tall, and pale with rage, a still-healing gash running from high on his right temple diagonally down into his blood-matted beard. His bolt pistol was holstered, but the deactivated power fist covering his right hand clenched threateningly as he glared at Skaflock and his pack.

The Blood Claw took a step towards the Wolf Scouts. 'All too few,' he snarled, 'thanks to the likes of *you!*' The words dissolved into a bestial roar as the Space Wolf lunged at Skaflock, his eyes burning with hate. The sudden attack caught the scout leader unawares. Before he could react the Blood Claw closed the distance between them and smote Skaflock on the breastplate of his armour with a sound like a hammer against a bell. The Wolf Scout went sprawling, stunned by the impact. Had the power fist's field been active his chest would have been crushed like an egg.

The red-haired Space Wolf pounced on Skaflock in an instant, knocking him back against the ground. 'Cowards!' he roared, nearly berserk with fury.

Pinned beneath the Blood Claw's bulk, Skaflock barely rolled aside as the Marine's huge fist smashed into the mud mere centimetres from his head. 'Did you slink out of the woods to view your handiwork, or to pick over the bodies of the dead like carrion crows?'

Skaflock felt the Blood Claw's left hand close around his throat. Surprise gave way to a killing rage, rising like a black tide in his chest. Unbidden, his hand tightened on the hilt of his power sword, thumb reaching for the activation switch.

'Remember your oaths, men of Fenris! Russ cannot abide a kinslayer, and the Emperor's eyes are upon you!'

The shout came from the shadow of one of the drop pods, ringed with the bodies of huge, armoured orks. Recognition struck Skaflock like a hammer blow, but it was the Blood Claw who spoke the name first.

'Rothgar!' The young Marine scrambled to his feet, heedless of the power sword pointed at his chest.

The great company's wolf priest stepped slowly into the moonlight. At once, Skaflock could see that the priest was very gravely injured. Rothgar's Terminator suit was rent in half a dozen places, and the jagged tip of a dead ork's power claw jutted from his chest. His face was deathly white, and drops of red glistened in his grey beard. It was a testament to the wolf priest's legendary prowess that he lived at all.

'Well met, Sightblinder,' Rothgar said, showing bloodslicked teeth. 'Late to the battlefield, thank the primarch. What is your report?'

'We've been lured into a trap,' he said simply. 'Once the assault teams began their descent the damned orks started jamming all the vox frequencies somehow.' The Wolf Scout bit back a curse. 'You and these Blood Claws look to be all that's left from the team that landed here.'

'Our pod suffered a malfunction on the way down and we landed some ten kilometres north of the drop zone,' the red-haired Blood Claw said. 'The woods were crawling with ork patrols. We had to fight every step of the way to make it here. Two of our brothers and our Wolf Guard leader were slain.'

'The orks had more time to scout the area than we did. If we could find the best drop zones in each sector, so could they,' Skaflock said. 'But I've never known a greenskin to show such patience and forethought. There's more at work here than meets the eye.'

Rothgar's eyes narrowed conspiratorially. 'This Skargutz has ambitions, I think. He's no Ghazghkull, but he's no mere warboss, either. I think he's got his sights set on uniting the ork warbands in this sector under his banner. If he can prove to them that he can strike anywhere he wants *and* get the best of any force the Imperium can throw at him, they'll join his mob without hesitation.'

'And now that he's bloodied us, he'll pull out of Cambion with whatever plunder he's gathered and start rousing the other warbands.' It was a clever move, as much as it galled Skaflock to admit it.

Skaflock forced his anger and guilt aside and tried to find a way to salvage the situation. 'All right,' he said, addressing the wolf priest. 'The orks have us cut off for now, but our fleet isn't going to sit idle. With every pass they make over the planet their surveyors will have a clearer picture of where the ork landing sites are hidden. The orks can't keep this jamming up forever – they need the vox channels to coordinate themselves almost as much as we do. Most likely they will wait until they think the power cells on our designator beacons have run dry, then they'll begin their pullout. In the meantime, Kjarl here can watch over you at one of our campsites while my pack and I locate the main ork camp. When the jamming lifts, we can contact Lord Haldane and coordinate a counter strike before Skargutz can escape.'

Kjarl shook his head in disgust. 'Have you no idea what's happened?'

'How could he?' Rothgar said darkly. When he turned to Skaflock, his expression was even more pained than before. 'Have you ever known Haldane Ironhammer to let another lead an assault in his place? He dropped with us in the first wave, lad. Your lord lies somewhere among the fallen.'

LORD HALDANE AND his Wolf Guard had made their stand on a low hillock just to the side of their drop pod. They'd fought like wolves at bay, like heroes of old, but one by one they had been overcome.

Haldane's Terminator armour hadn't been hacked apart, as Skaflock had expected. It had been hacked *open*. The body of the wolf lord was nowhere to be seen.

Tears of rage coursed freely down Kjarl's face. 'What have they done with our lord?'

The Space Wolves parted as Rothgar moved slowly and painfully among them. The pain in his eyes as he surveyed the scene had nothing to do with his injuries. 'They have taken him,' he said hoarsely.

'Why?' Kjarl said.

'The orks must mean to give him as a trophy to their leader,' Skaflock replied, biting back his rage. 'A wolf lord's head would be a tremendous prize for an ambitious warboss like Skargutz.'

'Then it's a blood feud, by Russ!' Kjarl raised his fist and howled a challenge to the sky. The rest of the

Blood Claws followed suit, the intensity of their cries raising the hairs on the back of Skaflock's neck.

'The filthy greenskins have defiled our lord.' Kjarl roared. He turned to Rothgar. 'Hear me, priest, I swear that I and my pack will find Lord Haldane and reclaim the honour of our company, and woe to any ork that steps in our way.'

'Don't be a fool,' Skaflock said coldly. 'You won't get more than a kilometre before the orks kill you.'

The Blood Claws snarled in wordless anger. Kjarl turned on the scout leader, his power fist raised. 'Keep your gutless bleating to yourself,' he snarled. 'This is a matter of honour – something you clearly know little about.'

Skaflock advanced on the Blood Claw. 'I know that you've been on this planet less than an hour, and I've been here for three months. I know approximately how many orks there are in this sector. I know their tactics, their equipment, the location of their bases and the routes they're likely to take. I know *exactly* what your chances are, charging about on an ork-held world and lashing out at every foe that presents itself.'

The vehemence in Skaflock's voice took Kjarl aback for a moment. 'What would you have us do then? Cower in the bushes and let them get away with this? What about your duty to Haldane?'

'Don't lecture me about my duty, whelp,' Skaflock said darkly. Meeting Rothgar's eye, he knelt by Haldane's armour and solemnly took up the wolf lord's axe. 'If we hope to reclaim Haldane's body we will have to swallow our anger and put our lord's honour before our own.' He raised the axe before the wolf priest. 'I swear on this axe that I will find Haldane and do what must be done.'

The wolf priest held Skaflock's gaze for a long moment, and then Rothgar nodded slowly. 'I hear you,

Skaflock Sightblinder,' he said, 'and I hold you to your oath.'

'And *I* swear,' Kjarl hissed, 'to tear your head from your shoulders if you fail.'

Skaflock grinned mirthlessly. 'If I fail, I doubt you'll have the chance, but so be it,' he said. 'For now, you and your men gather weapons and ammunition from the dead: flamers, grenades and spare bolt pistol rounds.'

Kjarl glared at the wolf scout, but beneath the forbidding gaze of the wolf priest he swallowed his pride. 'We will not be long,' he growled, and issued orders to his pack.

Skaflock turned to Rothgar, but the wolf priest raised a gauntleted hand. 'I will abide here, Sightblinder. Do not concern yourself about me. Russ knows I've survived worse than this.' With his other hand he drew the Fang of Morkai from his belt. 'Whatever else, I still have my duty to the dead.'

'As do we, Rothgar. As do we.'

HALDANE'S BLOOD MADE his scent easy to follow. Even where countless ork feet had trampled across the wolf lord's trail, Hogun's sharp eyes picked out dark spots of crimson to mark where their fallen leader had gone.

Skaflock had assigned a pair of Blood Claws to each scout, taking Kjarl and another young Blood Claw for himself. After several kilometres the trail led out of the woods and down into a narrow, twisting valley dominated by isolated stands of stunted, twisted trees. Here the ork trail was easy to follow, and Skaflock knew at once where they were headed.

'There's a firebase up ahead,' he said to Kjarl as they loped stealthily along the valley floor. 'A small one. We scouted it out a couple of weeks ago. It's probably where they're staging all of the patrols in this sector, so there will likely be a lot of traffic. I expect the orks carrying Haldane will commandeer a vehicle there to carry their trophy to Skargutz.'

Kjarl glared resentfully at Skaflock. 'We'll see,' he said darkly.

Half a kilometre from the firebase Skaflock waved the scouts off the trail, following a path that led to higher ground and offered a commanding view of the ork encampment. Hogun and Kjarl lay to either side of Skaflock as he scanned the firebase from a stony ledge using his magnoculars.

'No sign of Haldane. If he was still there the orks would be showing off the body,' Skaflock said, passing the magnoculars to Hogun. 'There is something interesting though, a convoy of large trucks unloading fresh troops. And I don't recognize their clan markings.'

'What does this have to do with Haldane?' Kjarl hissed impatiently.

'This sector has the largest number of major ork landing sites on the planet,' Skaflock explained, 'so we always suspected that Skargutz himself was somewhere nearby. We never could find him, though. At the time, we thought that was pretty strange, but now it's clear they must have set up a hidden base to conceal the vox jammers and shelter the bulk of their reserve troops from the initial bombardment.' The Wolf Guard studied the ork trucks thoughtfully. 'I'll bet he's still there, waiting for word that the ambush was successful, and those trucks will lead us right to him.'

Kjarl let out a snort. 'And how do you expect the trucks to get us anywhere once we've killed the drivers?'

Skaflock frowned. 'Killed the drivers?'

'You don't expect they'll survive once we've stormed the base, do you?'

'We aren't storming the base, Kjarl. We're sneaking onto those vehicles as they head back to their base.'

'*Sneaking*.' Kjarl's lip curled in distaste. 'Cowering like a craven is more like. This is not the way the sons of Russ are meant to behave.'

'I won't speak for you, Blood Claw, but I'll behave any way I must if it gets me one step closer to my goal. And so will you, so long as I'm in command.' Skaflock's stare was hard as adamantine. 'Tell your men we're going to *sneak* down to the firebase's northern gate. Pistols will be holstered and flamers doused. Combat will be avoided at all costs. Understood?'

'Understood,' Kjarl said contemptuously, and slid down the slope to where the rest of the group waited.

Hogun watched the young Space Wolf go. 'A good thumping would knock sense into that lad,' he muttered.

'No time for that now. I want you to round up our melta bombs and set up a diversion on the southern end of that base.'

'Good as done,' Hogun said, handing back the magnoculars and heading down the slope.

Skaflock gathered the Space Marines and made for the road north of the firebase in a single, widely spaced group. The Space Wolves reached the dirt road almost a kilometre north of the base, then began working south until they were within less than a hundred metres of the base's crude gate. There they separated into their three-man teams and settled into cover near the road's edge.

The firebase itself was simple and rugged. An irregular perimeter of packed earthen ramparts five metres high was topped with razor wire and littered with small mines. Rough, uneven watchtowers composed of scrap metal and cannibalized shipping containers rose behind the ramparts, sprouting a lethal assortment of heavy guns and wandering searchlights. The noise within the earthen walls was tremendous, a discordant roar of shouting voices, revving engines, machine tools and occasional bursts of gunfire.

Barely a few minutes after the Space Wolves had settled into place, Hogun seemed to materialize out of the darkness at Skaflock's elbow. 'Three minutes,' he reported, then went to take his place along the line.

Kjarl eyed the ork base expectantly. 'What now?'

'When the bombs go off, the orks will think they're under attack. I expect that whoever is running that mob in there is going to send the trucks back to Skargutz for more troops.'

Before Kjarl could reply a string of blue-white flashes ran along the base's southern perimeter, followed by the sharp *crack* of the melta charges. Streams of wild tracer fire fanned and corkscrewed into the air. 'Get ready,' Skaflock called to the Marines.

Within minutes, the scrap metal gate at the northern entrance was pulled back with a tortured shriek of twisted metal, and eight huge ork trucks lumbered onto the road in a billowing cloud of blue-black exhaust.

Skaflock turned to Kjarl. 'We'll wait for the last three trucks, then I'll give the signal–'

The Wolf Scout's instructions were cut short as a stream of heavy ork rounds whipsawed through the air over his head. Skaflock's heart clenched as he ducked his head and stole a look at the firebase to his left.

The watchtowers had somehow spotted the three Space Marines at the far end of the line. Searchlights transfixed the Space Wolves from three separate directions, and the orks in the towers opened fire with every weapon they had. Skaflock watched as one of the Wolf Scouts rose to a crouch and drew his bolt pistol in a single, fluid motion. He snapped off two quick shots, destroying two of the searchlights in a shower of sparks, but as he pivoted to fire at the third a burst from an ork gun blew his head apart in a shower of blood and bone. The two Blood Claws leapt to their feet as one, drawing their weapons and charging at the enemy encampment.

'No,' Kjarl roared, surging to his feet. Skaflock tackled him before he was fully upright.

'Stand your ground,' Skaflock cried, shouting into the maelstrom.

'My men–'

'Your men are already dead, Kjarl,' Skaflock said. At the firebase the Blood Claws had made it into cover beneath the reach of the guns, but a mob of orks was already charging from the gates, their crude axes held high. 'You can either die alongside them or remember your obligation to your lord. Which will it be?'

With a wordless snarl Kjarl shoved Skaflock away and readied himself to move.

The last three ork trucks were coming up fast. Skaflock gauged speed and distance, then shouted 'Now,' and bolted for the road.

The Space Wolves rose in a ragged line and rushed at the ork transports, leaping for struts and flanges on their armoured flanks. Kjarl landed easily to Skaflock's right, both men glaring balefully back at the firebase dwindling in the distance.

THE ORK TRUCKS roared along dirt roads and broken trails for nearly two hours, then abruptly turned onto an old, sharply sloping roadway littered with rocks and debris. The small convoy climbed steadily up the side of a mountain for several minutes, then turned suddenly into the mountainside itself. The trucks' huge engines thundered in the tight confines of the tunnel as the convoy descended deep into the bowels of the mountain. The vehicles finally came to a stop in a cavernous, dimly lit chamber reeking of exhaust fumes and echoing with the bedlam of an ork warband at work.

Skaflock slowly eased himself from the truck's undercarriage and lowered himself to the ground. Peering left and right, he could see that the ork trucks had been driven into an enormous staging area crowded with other vehicles, piles of crates and gangs of grease-stained gretchin mechanics. Illumination in the cavernous space was poor, creating dark alleys between stacked crates and pools of shadow cast by the looming vehicles. Skaflock rolled out from under the truck to the right and dashed into cover between two stacks of looted shipping containers. The Wolf Guard kept moving, trusting that his brothers would track his scent as he worked his way towards the edge of the broad cavern.

Dark shapes emerged from the shadows, weapons held ready. Kjarl was the first to reach Skaflock, his eyes searching the shadows. 'Where are we?'

'We're in an old mine, somewhere south of the landing zone,' Skaflock said. 'There's scores of them honeycombing the mountains in this region. The orks are probably tapping the mine's abandoned reactors to power their jamming system.' The Wolf Guard sought out Hogun. 'Do you have the scent?'

The scout nodded. 'His blood's like a beacon. Not much further to go, I think.'

'All right.' To the assembled Marines, Skaflock said, 'Stick to your teams. No shooting until I give the signal. Hogun, you're on point. Gunnar, cover the rear. Move out.'

Moving quickly and quietly the Space Wolves made their way around the perimeter of the cavern and down a rough-hewn passage running deeper into the side of the mountain. Few of the mine's lamps still functioned, and the darkness served them well in the wide tunnels. They passed numerous side passages, abandoned lifts and galleries; on several occasions the Space Marines had to find an alternative route to avoid mobs of orks along their path. Each time Hogun led them unerringly back on track.

This sector of the mine had been given over to offices and dormitories for the indentured miners who once laboured in the tunnels below. Up ahead, the Space Wolves began to hear the raucous sounds of a celebration, and Skaflock felt a cold, black rage welling up in his heart.

The passageway ahead ended in a broad double doorway, opening onto a huge rectangular space carved from the living rock. Once it had served as a dining hall for the miners, but now it was packed with orks feasting on the plunder of Cambion. Several hundred greenskins tore at haunches of bloody meat and drank from steel casks of ale, roaring drunken boasts of their fighting skill.

The far end of the chamber was given over to a raised dais, where priests of the Ecclesiarchy once exhorted the faithful as they took their meals. Now it supported a crude throne of black iron, where an enormous, armoured ork sat, surrounded by his bodyguard.

A man's bloody body lay at the foot of the throne, wearing only the black undergarment of a Space Marine. As the Space Wolves watched, Skargutz the Render laid an armoured boot on Haldane's dead chest, like a hunter posing with his prize.

The Marines made not a single sound, but Skaflock could feel the fury seething from them like heat from a forge. Kjarl's eyes were fixed on Skargutz, his fangs bared. 'Here it ends,' he said, his power fist crackling into life.

Skaflock nodded solemnly. 'The time for stealth is done at last,' he said, slipping into the tongue of their homeland. 'Now is the time for broken swords and splintered shields, for red ruin and the woeful song of steel. Haldane's eyes are upon us; his honour lies in our hands. Let no man falter until the deed is done.'

Raising Haldane's frost axe high, Skaflock charged through the doorway, and suddenly the hall was filled with the howl of Space Wolves.

The orks nearest the doorway stared in shock at the sudden appearance of the Space Marines. Skaflock leapt forward, swinging the frost axe in a wide arc and carving through the torsos of the three greenskins before him. Grenades flew overhead and bolt pistol shells tore through the packed ranks of orks. With an angry hiss, a half-dozen streams of liquid fire immolated scores of shrieking greenskins; their grenades and ammunition detonated in the heat, adding to the carnage.

An ork clambered over a table wielding an axe and Skaflock shot it in the face. The range was so close the mass-reactive shell had no time to arm, blowing the greenskin's head apart and bursting in the chest of the ork behind. Another of the foul creatures charged him from the right; the Wolf Scout ducked under the greenskin's wild swing and cut the ork's legs out from under it with a backhanded stroke of the axe.

Pandemonium swept the hall. The greenskin mob recoiled from the fire and slaughter around the doorway, many shooting wildly into the backs of those who tried to put up a fight. A heavy bullet smashed into Skaflock's shoulder, cannoning off his armour and half-spinning him around, but the impact barely halted his headlong charge. The orks gave way before him, those that did not move fast enough were shot point-blank or split like a melon by a stroke of the axe. Dimly, Skaflock was aware of Kjarl close by his side, protecting his flanks and firing bolt pistol shells into the retreating mob.

Suddenly the ork retreat stopped, surged backwards, then parted like a wave, and Skaflock found himself face-to-face with Skargutz's bodyguard.

With a roar, the armoured orks opened fire at the oncoming Space Wolves. Two more rounds smashed into Skaflock's chest, flattening against his breastplate, and men screamed behind him as more bullets found their mark. Skaflock raised his bolt pistol and fired at an approaching bodyguard, but the shells bounced harmlessly off the ork's armoured skull. Then the two sides crashed into one another and all semblance of order dissolved into a chaotic melee.

Skaflock leapt at the bodyguard before him, swinging the frost axe at the ork's claw-tipped arm. The keen blade sheared through the metal joint and the flesh beneath, severing the arm at the elbow in a fountain of blood. The ork bellowed in pain and the Wolf Scout put a bolt pistol shell into its gaping maw, blowing out the back of its skull. He ducked around the armoured form as it toppled to the ground, only to be struck in the chest by a blow that drove the air from his lungs and racked him with searing waves of agony. Skaflock fell to the ground, convulsing in pain as a lithe, black-armoured form stepped over him, levelling a long-barrelled pistol at his head. The alien's face was hidden behind a helmet shaped like a leering skull. Its black, chitinous armour was painted with runes of clotted gore, and squares of expertly flensed skin flapped like parchment from fine hooks hung about its waist. A detached part of Skaflock's mind recognized the scraps of flesh as the skinned faces of human children.

The Wolf Guard's mind reeled. A dark eldar? Here? He'd heard tales of exiles from the hidden world of Commorragh offering their skills to warlords in exchange for plunder – usually paid in living flesh for the sadistic xenos to sate their lusts upon. Skaflock realised now where Skargutz had got his powerful jamming devices from, and was horrified to think of how many innocent lives the foul xenos would claim in return.

'You offer me such poor sport,' the dark eldar said. The words came out as a liquid rasp, bubbling wetly from mutilated lungs. The xenos lashed the air with a long, barbed whip of darkly glimmering steel. 'But fear not. You shall have many opportunities to entertain me in the months to come.'

Suddenly the air around the dark eldar shimmered as a flurry of bolt pistol shells streaked at his head and chest – and vanished as if swallowed by the void. From out of the raging melee Hogun and six Blood Claws rushed at the xenos warrior, bloodied chainswords held high.

The alien slipped among the Space Wolves like quicksilver, lashing with his barbed whip. One viper-like blow was enough to paralyze a Space Marine with waves of pain, a second strike shredded the nerves and brought agonizing death. Three Blood Claws died without landing a single blow, the rest hurled themselves at the dark eldar, aiming a flurry of blows at the alien that would have ripped a mere human into tatters. Yet for all their speed and skill, the dark eldar dodged their blows with ease, or absorbed them with his powerful force field. Hogun emptied his bolt pistol at the alien's head, each shell swallowed up by the warrior's eldritch defences. The dark eldar casually pointed his pistol at the Wolf Scout's head and shot him through the eye. One of the Blood Claws leapt at the dark eldar with a roar and the alien spun effortlessly away from the attack. Faster than the eye could follow, the alien's whip struck once, twice, and the Space Wolf died in midswing.

With an effort of will, Skaflock forced his traumatized muscles to work, raising his own pistol and squeezing off shot after shot as the dark eldar's whip took another Blood Claw in the throat. Each round disappeared like all the rest – until suddenly an actinic flash obscured the alien and a sound like a thunderclap rang out as his force field finally overloaded. The dark eldar staggered, and the Wolf Scout saw a ragged hole in the breastplate of his armour.

The dark eldar let out a shriek of fury and a bubbling stream of curses – and then Kjarl seemed to materialize behind the alien, seizing its helmet in his power fist and tearing the alien's head from his armoured shoulders.

Skaflock rolled onto his side and tried to push himself to his feet. His muscles twitched and spasmed from the effects of the whip, and bursts of intense pain rippled through his chest. Then a huge fist closed on his arm and pulled him upright. 'No... faltering... yet,' Kjarl said breathlessly, flashing a wolfish grin. His armour was pierced in a dozen places and streaked with blood and gore, but his eyes were fierce and bright.

The Wolf Scout forced his eyes to focus and take in the scene around him. Over half the hall was ablaze, and the dead lay in heaps from the doorway to the dais. At the foot of his throne, Skargutz and a handful of orks fought the battered remnant of Skaflock's band. As he watched, Gunnar decapitated an ork with a stroke of his chainsword then darted in to strike at Skargutz's knee. Sparks flew as the sword's razor-edged teeth glanced off the armoured joint. The scout leapt back for another strike, but not quite fast enough. The warboss's power claw caught Gunnar in mid-leap, slicing the Space Marine in two.

Skaflock roared in rage and anguish, pushing away from Kjarl and staggering towards Skargutz, gaining speed with each painful step. His bolt pistol thundered and bucked in his hand; two orks fell with gaping holes in their chests and a third round punched a bloody hole through the warboss's leg before the ammunition ran out. He tossed the empty pistol aside and gripped the frost axe with both hands. 'Skargutz the Render, your end is upon you,' he cried. 'You have dared the righteous wrath of the Allfather, and now there will be a reckoning.'

The warboss spun with surprising speed, scattering two Marines with a sweep of his claw. Skaflock leapt forward, rolling between the ork's massive legs, then rose to a crouch and sliced across the back of the warboss's knees. Pistons and hydraulic lines burst; joints and muscles failed, and Skargutz toppled with a crash. The huge ork tried to twist onto his side and lash backwards with his claw, but Kjarl caught its bloodied blades in his power fist. For a moment both warriors struggled, neither gaining ground on the other until, with a shriek of tortured metal, the power claw gave way in a shower of sparks.

Skaflock leapt forward, raising the frost axe high in a two-handed grip. 'When Morkai's kin drag your soul past the Hall of Heroes, tell them it was Haldane Ironhammer's axe that slew you!' The ork's snarl was cut short as the frost axe fell and the warboss's head bounced across the dais to stop at the dead wolf lord's feet.

Kjarl looked down at the dead warboss, his shoulders heaving with exertion. 'It is done.'

'Not quite yet,' Skaflock said. He gestured to the surviving Space Wolves, a single scout and two Blood Claws. 'Go and stand watch at the door.' Then, to Kjarl: 'Let us clear a table to place our lord upon, and lay the bodies of his foes at his feet.'

They pulled a table onto the dais and laid Haldane upon it, and piled his dead foes around him. As Kjarl laid the body of the dark eldar on the pile, he suddenly frowned. 'What's this?'

Skaflock watched the Blood Claw pull a small, silvery object from the alien's belt. A pale cobalt light gleamed on its surface. 'Some kind of control box?' he suggested.

'Perhaps,' Kjarl said, and crushed it in his fist. Suddenly the Blood Claw tensed, his hand going to his ear. 'Static!' he said. 'I can hear static on my vox-bead! That box must have controlled the vox jammers.'

One of the Blood Claws called from the doorway. 'The greenskins are massing at the end of the corridor. They'll be on us in minutes.'

Thinking quickly, Skaflock started digging through his carry-bags. He still had three designator beacons that the scouts hadn't found time to deploy. 'A few minutes are all we need,' he said, laying out the beacons and pressing their activation runes. 'Soon this whole base will be a pyre for our lord, and the end of the ork invasion of Cambion.'

As he worked, a shadow fell over the Wolf Guard. Skaflock glanced up to see Kjarl watching him appraisingly. After a moment the Blood Claw steeled himself and said, 'It appears I misjudged you, Skaflock. You're a braver man than I gave you credit for, and a true son of Russ.'

Skaflock grinned and raised his hand in a weary salute. 'And you fought well, Kjarl Grimblood. I owe you my life. I expect the skalds will sing of your deeds for years to come.'

'So do I, by Russ.' Kjarl said with a smile. 'Speaking of which – I don't suppose you've got a plan for getting us out of here?' Nearly the entire chamber was ablaze, the rock walls running with streams of jellied fire. The heat and smoke was beginning to affect even the Space Wolves' enhanced endurance.

Skaflock grinned. 'Listen.' Beyond the high ceiling came distant, heavy beats, like the pounding of a massive drum. Each one was louder than the one before. 'Bombardment rounds,' the Wolf Guard said.

From the doorway, one of the Space Wolves let out a yell. 'The orks are retreating.'

'I doubt they want to get buried alive any more than we do,' Skaflock said. He glanced at Kjarl. 'Ready?'

Kjarl's eyes widened. 'You want to fight your way through a horde of panicked orks and out into the middle of an *orbital bombardment*?'

'Of course.' Skaflock raised the frost axe. 'I'd rather take my chances with the bombardment than risk Rothgar's fury if I failed to return this. He'd curse my soul until the end of time!'

Kjarl Grimblood threw back his head and roared with laughter. 'Lead on, brother,' he said, clapping Skaflock on the shoulder. And with a last salute to their fallen lord the Space Wolves charged after the fleeing orks, filling the air with their bone-chilling howls.

RED REWARD

Mitchel Scanlon

THEY HAD COME upon the body by chance. Buried in frozen mud, it had been found by two Guardsmen as they hurried to resurrect the fallen wall of a firing trench in the lull between ork attacks. But for the man whose remains now lay at their feet there would be no such resurrection, only reburial in some less vigorously contested section of the city, with just a battered set of dog-tags to give name to the dead.

'It's Rakale, sergeant,' Trooper Davir had said, standing over the body that was still half-concealed in the mud of the trench floor. 'Or that's what his tags say at least. Now his own mother wouldn't recognise him.'

Even from the lip of the trench wall above them, Chelkar could see what Davir meant. Rakale's face was only a memory now, his features reduced to a gruesome flattened smear marked with the striated imprint of the thing that had killed him.

'It could only have been an ork tank,' ventured the hulking Guardsman to Davir's side. 'An ork battle truck. Look, you can see the marks of its tracks on his face. Or what's left of it. It must have rolled over the trench while Rakale lay underneath. Then the trench wall collapsed and the poor bastard was crushed. He would have seen it coming, too. A bad way to die.'

'Bad way to die, my arse,' Davir spat, flat ugly features alive with sudden anger. 'You know a good way, Bulaven? We're all poor bastards. And whether we die with throats cut, heads blown off, or crushed like Rakale here is beside the point. It's all the same in the end.'

'Phh. If you feel that way about it, why don't you end it all now, you stunted idiot?' Bulaven rumbled back. 'Put yourself out of all our miseries.'

'Because, my fat friend, it is a well-known fact that the average ork couldn't hit its own arse with both hands and a guided missile. While I – as you so charmingly put it – am a "stunted idiot", a small target. One who confidently expects to outlive you all, I might add. Especially you, Bulaven. A blind man with a thrown rock and the palsy would be hard-pressed to miss your broad and capacious backside.'

'Enough,' Chelkar said, with just enough quiet force to let the squabbling pair know he meant it. 'I want a four-man detail to move the body and bury it by the old plasteel works. Davir, Bulaven: you have both just volunteered. You may choose the others yourselves. And before I hear anyone complain about how hard the ground is, I want you to remember something: Rakale was one of our own.'

Without another word, two more Guardsmen jumped into the trench to join those already there. Then, with as much reverence as was practicable given the conditions, all four set about the delicate task of extricating Rakale's remains from the mud. Occasionally a spade-head would strike a particularly hard-packed knot of earth, the impact shivering painfully up the handle to the hands of the digger. Then there might come a muffled curse, but for the most part they worked in silence. Four men, mindful of their duty to a fallen comrade and the code between all the defenders of this battle-scarred city: *We bury our dead.*

But by then Chelkar had already turned away to supervise repairs to another part of the company's defences. The last attack had been a bad one. Twelve men dead – thirteen counting Rakale. And, with the remorseless logic of this place, Chelkar fully expected the next attack to be harder and more ferocious still. It was the way of things here. In the city of Broucheroc a man could rely on one thing at least: each new day would be worse than the last.

For a moment, casting tired eyes over the wearingly familiar landscape around him, Chelkar found himself distracted. Before him lay no-man's-land: a great grey expanse of frozen mud and mounds of rubble, punctuated here and there by the fire-blackened silhouettes of dead ork vehicles. Behind him lay Broucheroc itself: an endless, seemingly all but abandoned cityscape of ruined and burned-out buildings. A ghost town, thought Chelkar, and we are its ghosts.

'Sergeant?'

Turning, Chelkar saw Corporal Grishen hurrying towards him from the comms-dugout, four unfamiliar Guardsmen trailing in his wake like black-coated vultures. He did not need to see the crossed-swords-and-prayer-beads insignia at their collars to know who they were: Kessrian Guard. Or to know their arrival here could only mean trouble.

'What is it, Grishen?'

Plainly discomfited, as though struggling to find the words, Grishen paused before answering. Behind him, the Kessrians stood in a rigid line with hellguns held at waist-level, safeties off. Though not normally given to nerves, Chelkar could not help but feel a certain unease to see the muzzles of their guns pointing his way.

'We have received a message from Sector Command, sergeant,' Grishen said, fidgeting as he spoke. 'Well, two messages actually. The first is a communiqué forwarded from General Headquarters, a thought for the day, to improve the morale of the troops. The message reads: "It is better to die for the Emperor than to live for yourself"'.

'I am sure the men will find that very comforting, Grishen,' Chelkar said, doing his best to keep any trace of sarcasm from creeping into his voice. 'And the second message?'

'The second message is from Commissar Valk at Sector Command,' Grishen replied, lowering his eyes as though suddenly noticing something of interest in the mud. 'It instructs that you are to be disarmed and placed under arrest on charges of heresy and treason. These men have been sent to escort you to Sector Command for interrogation. And sergeant? They have orders to shoot to kill should you try to resist.'

Yes. The guns were pointed his way all right.

HERE, IN THE rubble-strewn streets behind the front lines, amid the warrens of ruined tenements that once used to house the city's workers, Chelkar could see some signs of life at least. No, life was too strong a word. There was movement: weary Guardsmen huddled round braziers for warmth, militia auxiliaries dispiritedly hauling supplies, even the occasional feral child hunting rats. But it was all no more than the last twitching spasms of a vast and dying corpse. Had every man, woman and child still alive in Broucheroc gathered in the central square, no one could have mistaken it for anything other than what it was. A gathering of the dead, like grimy-faced shades, who refused to face reality.

They were ghosts, these people. Ghosts with pulses perhaps, still able to love and laugh – even bear children – but ghosts just the same. They, and their city, lived only through some quirk of borrowed time. One day the big push would come and Broucheroc would fall. Then, whether by the orks or at their own leaders' decree, these people would join all those who had gone to their deaths from this city before them. Although Chelkar was forced to admit that even these ghosts probably had one advantage over him. They, at least, might live to see tomorrow.

His captors had stopped short of putting his legs in irons. That was something. But Chelkar knew better than to see it as any great cause for hope. It was a practical matter, they would have to walk to Sector Command. And, if his escorts did not want to carry him, his legs would need to be left unfettered.

Not his hands, though. There, the Kessrians had followed regulations to the letter. It was a new experience, walking these debris-choked alleyways with hands manacled behind him. Already he had suffered several bruisingly abrupt encounters with what the propagandists liked to call 'the sacred ground of Broucheroc'. Enough to learn that the frozen soil was every bit as impregnable to the sudden impact of a human face as to the blade of an entrenching tool. But even the taste of his own blood, and the painful awareness that he had probably broken his nose three falls back, was not the worst of it.

Chelkar felt naked. He had been a Guardsmen seventeen years, the last ten spent bottled up in this damned city by the orks. Long enough to know there was no easier way to get killed than to be wandering around unarmed in the middle of a war zone. Your gun is your life; lose one and you'll soon lose the other. It was a lesson every Guardsman lived or died by. A lesson Chelkar had learned as a snot-nosed recruit on his first day of training, courtesy of a kick up the arse from his drill instructor's boot by way of emphasis. A kick that had probably saved his life a hundred times since. In the last seventeen years, whether he ate, slept, washed – even in the latrines – his shotgun, hellpistol and knife had been his constant companions. Now, without them, Chelkar knew what it was to lose a limb. He felt a sense of incompleteness, a phantom itch, impossible to scratch.

'Get up, damn you!' one of the Kessrians barked, hauling Chelkar painfully up by the arms in the wake of yet another fall. 'And next time, be more careful where you put your feet,' he added, apparently convinced this constant headbutting of the ground could only be some act of ill-conceived defiance.

Other than that, and the occasional sharp dig of a gun muzzle against his back, his escorts seemed disinclined to converse. What contact Chelkar had had with Kessrians in the past convinced him this was more blessing than curse. They were humourless fanatics, dour even by the standards of Broucheroc – where to live at all was to live with the threatening weight of despair constantly at your shoulder. Some men succumbed to it, ending their days with the barrel of their own lasguns clenched between their teeth. Others sought refuge in false hopes, gallows humour, or a simple dogged refusal to die. But not the Kessrians. They were devoted to the Imperial creed, and lived with all the mean smugness of men who believed they need only follow orders and, come death, they would sit with their Emperor in paradise.

Though perhaps there was a subtle wisdom in their piety. Counted the most loyal troops in all Broucheroc, they had been detached to the permanent service of the city's commissars, while more 'suspect' troops, like Chelkar and his men, suffered the brunt of the fighting. Still, their silence was a mercy. He might have to endure the Kessrians taking him to the gallows, but he saw no good reason why they should be allowed to try and bore him to death first.

'Keep close,' one of the Kessrians said. 'If you run, we will shoot.'

For a moment Chelkar wondered why the man thought it necessary to state the obvious. Then, even with his nose broken, he could smell the stench of burning ork flesh and knew the corpse-pyres were close. They turned a corner, heading up towards a low hill whose summit was shrouded in an acrid haze of smoke. He did not need to see through it to know what they would find at the top. The corpse-pyres: great burning mounds of dead greenskin bodies dragged here from every corner of the city. Through the smog Chelkar could see the outlines of perhaps half-a-dozen such pyres, each containing a hundred alien corpses or more. And for every mound he could see, a dozen other pyres would be hidden in the smoke. As many as ten thousand orks might lie burning here, but they were no more than drops in the ocean. For every ork on that hill, a thousand more waited outside the city.

Once this would have smelled like victory to me, Chelkar thought. *I am past such delusions now.*

It was a tradition started in the first days of the siege. Every morning Guardsmen armed with long hooks would collect the orks killed in the previous day's fighting, drag them up the hill, stack them in great mounds, douse them in promethium, then set them alight. At first, it had been done to prevent disease: this city manufactured so many corpses that they could not all be left to rot in the streets. Then someone – a commissar, most likely – had proclaimed the corpse-pyres were more than just an act of hygiene. Broucheroc was sacred ground, he said, sanctified by the blood of all the heroes who had died defending it. And to bury even a single alien here would be to dishonour that sacrifice. Only heroes were worthy to be buried in Broucheroc; the bodies of the alien scum must always be burned, both to preserve this sacred soil from their taint, and so the orks outside the city would see the smoke rising on the wind and know what awaited them.

So went the dogma, anyway. Chelkar could not help but reflect how ten years of corpse-burnings had done little to dissuade the orks thus far. But there was a certain symmetry to it. Broucheroc had once been one huge refinery, where crude from the oilfields further south was brought to be refined into fuel. Even now, the city sat on billions of barrels' worth of promethium in massive underground storage tanks. That was why the orks were here: without fuel to feed their armour, their assault elsewhere on the planet had been brought grinding to a halt. They were here for the promethium. And, thanks to the inspiration of some long-dead commissar, every ork that died here got some small taste of the stuff.

They were at the summit now, the air about them thick with smoke and drifting fragments of ash. Eyes watering, almost retching from the stench, Chelkar could see ghostly figures moving through the haze, as masked Guardsmen worked to add more orks to the fires. The heat was stifling; he was sweating under his greatcoat. Here, in the warmest spot in all of Broucheroc, the city seemed even more like hell. Then he felt a stern hand suddenly grip his shoulder, as though his escorts were afraid they might lose him. But they were wrong to think he might run. Where could he go? Between Broucheroc and the orks, there was no escape.

For better or for worse, Chelkar would have to put his faith in Imperial justice.

HE WAS COVERED IN bruises and every part of his body ached. On arrival at Sector Command, Chelkar had been delivered to the custody of two new Guardsmen who had promptly taken him to a cell, stripped him naked, then beaten him bloody with fist and club. Softening him up, they had called it. Groin, stomach, kidneys – especially his kidneys – they had done their work so well Chelkar had no doubt he would be in tremendous pain for a week. Always assuming that they let him live that long.

Now, he lay prone on the stone floor of another room, waiting for Commissar Valk to acknowledge his existence. A thin man, with thin lips and nose, the commissar sat at a desk at the other end of the room, eyes glued to the display screen of the data-slate he held in his long thin hands. Silent minutes passed as the commissar kept reading. Then, without raising his eyes from the screen, he spoke in a voice every bit as thin as his lips and nose and hands.

'Bring the prisoner a chair.'

The guards complied, dragging a chair to the middle of the room, propping Chelkar up in it with a hand on each shoulder. But still, the commissar did not so much as glance his way. Instead, keeping his eyes on the data-slate, he leaned back in his chair and began to read aloud.

'Eugin Chelkar. Sergeant, 902nd Vardan Rifles, with service in the Mursk Campaign, Bandar Majoris, the Solnar Restoration and, most recently, Broucheroc. Decorated six times, including the Emperor's Star with Galaxy Cluster, presented for extraordinary bravery in the face of the enemy. Though never convicted, you have also faced disciplinary proceedings six times in the past on charges ranging from insubordination to failure to salute an officer. You would seem a remarkable study in contrasts, sergeant. I wonder, which is the real Eugin Chelkar: the hero or the malcontent?'

With that, Valk finally looked his way. But Chelkar stayed silent. The time for expressions of love and loyalty to the Emperor would come later. For now, better to hold his peace until he knew the substance of the charges against him.

For a moment, the commissar stared at him with cold piercing eyes, the smallest touch of a graveyard smile twitching at the corners of his lips. Valk turned away then pulled open the bottom drawer of his desk. He lifted out a vox-recorder. Setting it on his desk, Valk fussed for long seconds, ensuring the recording spools were aligned and the long wire of the vox-receiver properly connected. Then, pressing a stud to set the device working, he turned back to Chelkar once more.

'There now, sergeant, I see no reason to delay the start of these proceedings any further. Speaking clearly, and being careful not to leave anything out, I want you to tell me all about your dealings with one Lieutenant Lorannus...'

CHELKAR SLEPT A deep and even sleep. A sleep untouched by dream or nightmare. He slept, cocooned in blessed moments of peace. Then, he heard Corporal Grishen's urgent voice in his ear and knew his sleep was done.

'Sergeant! A message from Sector Command! Auspex has picked up an object falling to earth in the northwest quadrant of the sky. A drop-pod, sir!'

With a start Chelkar awoke to the darkness of the barracks dugout, Grishen's voice buzzing insistently in his comm-link's earpiece. He dragged himself from his bunk, then, after grabbing his shotgun, helmet and greatcoat, he stepped blinking into the grey light of dawn outside.

Although still half-asleep, what came next was second nature. Half-crouched, keeping to cover as best he could, he ran zig-zag across the open ground between the dugout and the forwardmost trench. Upon reaching the safety of the trench, he found Davir and Bulaven waiting within.

'I don't see anything,' Bulaven said, squinting up at the sky.

'The pod is still too far away, pigbrain,' Davir replied, perched on a stack of empty ammunition boxes. 'And anyway, the corporal said north-west quadrant: you are looking at the wrong part of the sky.'

Bulaven made some unpleasant comment about Davir's parentage, but Chelkar ignored them. Had he even wanted to follow the progress of yet another of their endless disputes, now was not the time. Not with Grishen's excited tones still pulsing in his ear.

'It is one of ours, sergeant – Command is sure of it! We are awaiting verification as to its contents, but auspex has it on a vertical bearing of forty-nine degrees – I say four nine degrees. You should be able to see it soon.'

Raising his field glasses, Chelkar scanned the foreboding heavens. There, he saw it. A black speck, haloed by flame. A drop-pod, all right, and it was headed their way.

'Perhaps it is a relief force,' Bulaven said, his usually booming voice now an awed whisper. 'A space-borne assault, to destroy the orks and break the siege.'

'With a single drop-pod?' Davir sneered. 'I find such stupidity surprising even from you, Bulaven. Most likely some distant bureaucrat has decided to send us a supply pod to reassure us we have not been forgotten. Something remarkably useless no doubt: insect repellent, or paperclips. Remember when they sent us a whole drop-pod full of prophylactics? I never could decide whether they wanted us to use them as barrage balloons, or simply thought the orks must have a morbid fear of rubber. Still, whatever is inside this one, I shall be content so long as the bastards have aimed it right and it doesn't land on top of us.'

The pod was closer now and visible to the naked eye. With a tail of fire streaming behind it, it looked like a comet. Glancing at the network of trenches and fox-holes around him, Chelkar could see dozens of fur-shrouded helmets peering over parapets as every man in the company craned their heads up towards the sky, every one seeing in this man-made comet some different portent, whether for good or ill. All but Chelkar. He had lost his faith in portents some time back.

'You are an evil runt, Davir,' Bulaven growled petulantly. 'It would kill you, wouldn't it, to leave a man's hopes intact?'

'I'm doing you a favour, Bulaven,' Davir shrugged. 'Hope is a bitch with bloody claws. Still, if you must hope for something, hope the greenskins never develop a fatseeking missile. If they do, you're f–'

'Sergeant! We have verification!' screeched Grishen in his ear, so excited now that the top end of his voice became a squealing squall of static. 'They're reinforcements! Command says the drop-pod is full of troops!'

'Thank Command for the good news, Grishen,' Chelkar said into his comm-link mouthpiece. 'But advise them they may wish to post more men on gravedigging detail. The pod looks set to land smack in the middle of no-man's-land.'

The pod fell closer, and with every metre a roar grew louder. It was big now, so big Chelkar could pick out the design of the Imperial Eagle embossed on its side. An eagle wreathed in flames, and about to land right under the ork guns.

'Take cover!' he screamed.

There came a deafening boom and the whoosh of air as the shockwave passed overhead. The ground quaked. As the tremors subsided, Chelkar stuck his head back over the parapet. He saw no sign of casualties amongst his men. The pod had landed so far away the tidal wave of uprooted earth and stone had fallen short of their lines. Ahead, Chelkar could see it half-buried in a newly-created crater, steam rising from the rapidly cooling hull. For a moment there was silence, the air itself seemingly as frozen as the ground underfoot. Then, the orks opened up with everything they had, and the apocalypse began.

Bullets, rockets, shells – even the occasional energy beam – fell roaring all about the pod, turning the ground around it into a churning sea of leaping soil. As ever, ork marksmanship was appalling, so far they had not even come close to hitting their target. But given the sheer volume of fire, it was only a matter of time.

'Sergeant!' Grishen screamed through the static. 'I have Battery Command on the line. Permission to request artillery counter-fire?'

'Negative, Grishen. Their marksmanship is every bit as bad as the orks'. We must give those poor bastards out there a chance at least. I want you to take a range estimation on the centre of no-man's-land and await my instructions.'

Out in no-man's-land, the pod doors opened, disgorging shaken Guardsmen. Seemingly leaderless, confused to find themselves delivered into the middle of a firefight, they milled uncertainly in the shadow of the pod, heads moving as hundreds of eyes scanned hopelessly in search of more permanent refuge. Though Chelkar had long since come to believe the absurdities of this city could no longer surprise him, even he was taken aback by the sight of the new arrivals' uniforms.

'There must be a shortage of paperclips and prophylactics,' Davir said. 'Now they are sending us painted lambs to the slaughter.'

They looked like toy soldiers. Several hundred Guardsmen standing all but doomed in the middle of no-man's-land, each wearing a powder-blue monstrosity of a uniform, festooned with a dazzling array of gold braids and epaulettes, and topped with a tall pillbox hat bearing what appeared to be a feather. Toy soldiers, delivered into the most coverless section of no-man's-land: an empty wasteland that, for them, might as well have been in hell. Still, toy soldiers or not, Chelkar could only hope they knew how to run.

'Targeteer makes the range six hundred metres, sergeant. Awaiting your instructions.'

'Keep the line to Battery Command open, Grishen. At the command mark I want you to give them that range and tell them to hit it with everything they've got. Confirm.'

'Six hundred metres, sergeant. With everything they've got. At the command mark.'

'All other troops: at the command "fire" I want suppression fire aimed at the ork lines. You have my command. Fire!'

From every foxhole and trench, the company opened up with lasgun, missile and mortar. At this range the chances of hitting anything were slim, but all Chelkar wanted was to encourage the orks to keep their heads down long enough for the new arrivals to escape. The only problem was that, so far, the toy soldiers showed no sign of moving.

A shell rebounded off the hull of the pod as the ork gunners finally found their range. Seeing two of their own cut down by shrapnel, the toy soldiers finally seemed to get the message. They began to run towards the human lines, legs carrying them with a speed born of desperation as bullets and shells flew all around them. Six hundred metres to go, and men fell and died in great waves, bodies pierced by shrapnel and bullets, or else just ripped to bloody pieces by blasts. Four hundred metres now, and already more than half were dead.

'Give me smoke!' Chelkar yelled into his comm-link. 'I want smoke now!'

In answer there came a flurry of grenades and mortar fire, and in seconds all Chelkar could see before him was a drifting white wall of smoke. A desperate gambit. If the toy soldiers could reach the cover of the smoke they might survive. But the same smoke cloud could offer cover to the orks as well.

'Sergeant, auspex reads movement in the ork lines. They are advancing into no-man's-land! The line to Battery Command is open and ready, sergeant, let me give the order!'

'You have your instructions, Grishen. Wait.'

There. Finally. He could see human figures emerging through the fog of smoke. Five. Six. Eight. Perhaps no more than two-dozen men left from hundreds, stumbling gratefully to safety at last.

'Sergeant! Auspex reads a large ork force moving towards us on foot! You must let me order the bombardment! There are thousands–'

Chelkar was about to give the order, his lips moving to frame the words, when he saw something that set him cursing in disbelief. There, amid the smoke, he saw the figure of a single remaining soldier. A last straggler who, spurning the chance to run for cover, turned instead to fire his laspistol towards the unseen horde of approaching orks hidden somewhere in the smoke cloud behind him. A fool, who probably deserved everything that was coming.

'You have my command, Grishen!' Chelkar yelled, already out of the trench and running. 'Mark!'

Half a dozen footsteps, and already in the distant air above him the scream of falling shells could be heard. A dozen, two-dozen steps, and the screaming grew louder. Reaching the man, Chelkar grabbed him by the scruff of the neck, giving him a swift kick in the backside by way of persuasion. Then, dragging his gasping catch back to the parapet, Chelkar threw him into the trench and leapt down on top of him just as the first of the screaming shells began its final deathdive shriek. A shriek that reached its crescendo in a sudden cacophony of explosions that set the ground shaking.

Now, thought Chelkar, hugging the straggler to him at the floor of the trench, assuming the barrage does not fall short, we may just survive this. And, if we do, it will be my great pleasure to kick this stupid bastard in the arse again.

For long minutes the bombardment continued, close enough to send clods of frozen earth falling into the trench. An eternity of ragged heartbeats and racing pulses. Then, abruptly, the explosions stopped.

Within an instant, Chelkar was on his feet, scanning no-man's-land for orks. The barrage had blown away the last of the smoke and he saw the normally grey landscape was now painted with dark green blood and body parts. It made a pleasing contrast. Their luck had held and the artillery had seen off the attack.

'Sergeant, it's Corporal Grishen,' Davir said, stubby fingers fiddling at the comm-link in his ear as Chelkar realised he had lost his own comm-link somewhere in no-man's-land. 'Lookouts report the ork survivors have returned to their lines. Also, we have received orders from Sector Command as to the disposition of the new troops – they are to be attached to our company. And, sergeant? Grishen says according to Command we should find our new company commander among the reinforcements – a Lieutenant Lorannus.'

'Thank Grishen for the news, Davir,' said Chelkar. 'But tell him he may want to advise Sector Command our new company commander is probably lying dead with the majority of his men out there in no-man's-land.'

'Not at all, sergeant,' said a new voice from behind him. 'I assure you: your new company commander is still very much alive.'

Turning, Chelkar saw the straggler getting to his feet. Now he had the chance to see the man clearly, he saw that he wore a single gold bar insignia at his collar. Lieutenant's bars.

It looked like kicking him in the arse again was out of the question.

ONE BIG LINE, sergeant,' the lieutenant said, jabbing an unbending finger into the map before him. 'That is the best way to defend our position. One big line, and we will break the orks like waves against the rocks.'

Two days had passed, and Chelkar stood with Grishen and Lieutenant Lorannus in the command dugout, around a map of the company's defences. Two days, and now the unveiling of Lorannus's grand design had forced Chelkar to a re-evaluation. His new lieutenant was not just a fool, he was a madman.

'Of course, a great deal of work is required,' Lorannus continued. 'But the failings of the present system – this array of trenches and foxholes in which our men hide like so many rats – should be self-evident. If we are to break the ork resolve, we need a show of strength. We must concentrate our forces in a single great trench running the length of the sector, protected by minefields and barbed wire.'

Perhaps the lieutenant was simple-minded. It was the only explanation Chelkar could think of which made any sense. Already, two days under Lorannus's command had been enough to turn Chelkar's initial dislike of the man into a deep loathing. Lorannus was a by-the-book soldier, a shrill martinet who, Chelkar was sure, would probably soil his uniform if he ever saw an ork. And that damned uniform, that was another thing again. Despite repeated urgings, Lorannus had refused to dispense with his sniper-bait uniform or even to wear a greatcoat to cover it.

'Well, sergeant? You have an opinion?'

'We don't use mines any more, sir. It only encouraged the orks to take prisoners and drive them across the minefields to clear them. Then, when they ran out of prisoners, they'd use gretchin instead. Either way, minefields don't work.'

'We will use punji sticks then, sergeant. Or pitfall traps. These are just details. There is a bigger picture here.'

'Yes, sir, there is. With your permission, lieutenant, I think it is time Corporal Grishen went to see if comms has received any new messages.'

Lorannus paused, looking at Chelkar's weather-beaten face with searching eyes. Then, with a nod, he indicated Grishen should go, waiting until the corporal was out of earshot before he spoke once more.

'All right then, sergeant. We are alone. What is it you have to say?'

'Permission to speak frankly, sir?' Chelkar asked. At Lorannus's gesture he continued, choosing his words carefully. 'With all due respect, sir, wouldn't it be wiser if you waited to acclimatise yourself fully to conditions here before making wholesale changes to our defences?'

'I believe I am "acclimatised" as you put it, sergeant,' Lorannus said, looking Chelkar squarely in the eye now. 'And it is my intention these changes should be made without further delay. Should I take it you find some fault in my plans?'

'Yes, sir. Our firing trenches and foxholes are spread out for a reason, same as they are in every other sector of the city. We do it that way to catch the orks in multiple fields of fire and cut them down before they can get close. At the same time, because there isn't any one single strong point, if a trench is about to be overrun the men in it can pull back without fear of the whole line collapsing.'

'Are you telling me it is deliberate policy to give ground to the enemy?'

'We don't give them anything, lieutenant. We lend it to them just long enough for the men in the other trenches to shoot them down. Then we take it back.'

'No matter how you dress it up, sergeant, it is retreat. And retreat smacks of cowardice.'

'Call it what you want, lieutenant. This is Broucheroc, and war here is not like what they tell you about in the scholarium.'

'I am well acquainted with the realities of warfare, sergeant,' Lorannus said, his face flushed and his lips tight. 'My homeworld has a martial tradition that dates back centuries. And for generations my family has committed its sons to the service of the Emperor.'

'And you have personal experience of fighting orks, sir?'

'I do not see how that is relevant,' Lorannus said. A dangerous edge had entered his voice, but this was too important for Chelkar to back down.

'You talked about "a show of strength" and "breaking the ork resolve", lieutenant? Well, there's only one way I know to break an ork's resolve and that's to kill him. As for "a show of strength", take it from me: they're stronger than we are. The one thing you don't want is to end up going hand-to-hand with an ork. Let them shoot at you all day – chances are they'll miss. But go hand-to-hand and you'll end up being fed your own liver. That's what this is all about, lieutenant. Put our men in "one big line", without multiple fields of fire and with nowhere to retreat to, and you're giving the orks the chance to get close by sheer weight of numbers. And, if you do that, you might as well give them the keys to the city right now.'

'You sound as though you are frightened of the orks, sergeant,' Lorannus said, his expression dark.

'Yes I am, lieutenant. I've always made it a policy to be terrified of anything that outnumbers me five-hundred-to-one.'

For a moment, struggling visibly to control his temper, Lorannus was silent. But Chelkar knew it was only the lull before the storm. Any second now, Lorannus would either dress him down or tell him to shut up and follow orders. Worse, he might even summon Grishen back and order Chelkar to be put under arrest for insubordination. Whatever the result, the lieutenant would have his way. Their defences would be relocated to one big line and, within a day at most, everyone in this sector would be dead. All because Command had decided to shackle them with a madman. But, no matter the folly of his plans, in the end Lorannus was the officer and Chelkar the sergeant. The lieutenant could send the whole company skipping naked towards the orks and no one would stop him. Unless...

'Sergeant! Lieutenant! You must come quickly! There's something going on over in the ork lines!'

It was Grishen, his voice over the comm-link shrill to the point of panic. An unlikely guardian angel, but for now Chelkar would take whatever he could get.

'It seems we are needed elsewhere, sergeant,' Lorannus said, placing his pillbox hat on his head and adjusting the strap under his chin. 'We shall have to postpone this matter until later. But understand: this does not end here.'

'As you say, sir,' Chelkar replied, picking up his shot-gun and shucking a shell into the breech. 'This is not over.'

Lorannus turned away, moving towards the dugout exit with Chelkar two steps behind him. Then, stepping outside, Chelkar saw something which only confirmed his doubts as to the lieutenant's sanity. Incredibly, instead of running or crouching, Lorannus went march-ing across the open ground towards the trenches as though it were a parade ground. Bad enough to be wearing that sniper-bait uniform, thought Chelkar. But the fool doesn't even have the sense to run or keep his head down.

Not that the thought of some gretchin sniper blowing the lieutenant's fool head off caused him any great con-cern. But there was always the danger the damned gretch would miss and hit someone else...

'You HEAR IT?' Grishen's voice was a dry whisper. 'That noise from the ork lines. Engines.'

The sound could be heard clearly now, drifting across no-man's-land from behind the barricades on the ork side. A growing cacophony of revving motors, grinding gears and rumbling exhausts. The sound of engines. And engines meant only one thing. Armour.

'I don't understand,' Lorannus said, staring towards the sound in utter confusion. 'Intelligence reports stated categorically that the orks had exhausted their last reserves of fuel.'

'Could be they found an old promethium cache somewhere,' Chelkar said. 'Either way, it doesn't matter. The reports were wrong, lieutenant. And, from the sounds of those engines, we don't have much time to get ready.'

'Yes,' Lorannus said, 'you are right of course, sergeant. We need to make preparations.' Looking into the lieutenant's eyes, Chelkar realised the man had no idea how to proceed. Confronted with an unforeseen situation, Lorannus was floundering.

'Artillery, lieutenant,' Chelkar prompted.

'Of course,' Lorannus said, his imperious facade abruptly restored as though somewhere a distant general had flicked a switch. 'Artillery fire. Grishen, contact Battery Command and tell them I want an immediate carpet bombardment of the area directly in front of the ork lines.'

Then, as Grishen hurried towards the comms-dugout, the lieutenant turned towards Chelkar once more.

'I'm sure, like me, you believe in leading from the front, sergeant. I suggest you take up position on the east of the line, while I take the west. It would be a tragedy, after all, if either of us were to wander inadvertently into the other's "field of fire".'

Without a word, Chelkar turned and ran crouching towards the forward firing trench on his side of the defences. Inside, Davir and Bulaven were already preparing for the assault; the big man was checking the pump pressure of the heavy flamer before him, while Davir flicked the safety off his lasgun and sighted in on no-man's-land.

'I am pleased to announce we are open for business, sergeant,' Davir said, glancing over his shoulder as Chelkar jumped into the trench. 'Just in time, too. From the sounds of it, we have a busy day ahead of us.'

'Yes we have, Davir. But for now I want you both to put the camo-cover back on the flamer and keep your heads down.'

'No offence, sergeant,' Davir said as, beside him, Bulaven stared dumbly at Chelkar, 'but I have found orks rarely drop dead of their own accord. You have to shoot them first.'

'Perhaps in your close study of the orks you have also noticed they rarely do much in the way of reconnaissance before an assault,' Chelkar replied. 'If we don't shoot at them, they are likely to think this trench is empty. And, if they do, they will concentrate their attack here. Then, once they get close enough, we will spring a surprise.'

'Not much of a surprise, sergeant,' Davir said, his tigerish smile revealing a mouthful of stained and crooked teeth. 'Three men with only a shotgun, lasgun and heavy flamer between them. Still, if the orks get too close, we can always try having Bulaven fart them to death.'

Overhead, the air began to scream with the sound of shells. Grishen had called in the barrage; shrapnel and explosives were turning the area in front of the ork lines into a quagmire. But it would take more than that to stop the orks from coming. The best the bombardment could do was thin out their numbers.

'Confirmation from all lookouts,' Grishen said, 'the orks are coming!'

No one with eyes or ears could miss them. From the ork lines the engine noises reached a crescendo, momentarily drowning out even the artillery barrage as dozens of ork vehicles smashed through their own barricades and sped into no-man's-land. A motley, mechanised army of scratch-built vehicles and buggies gunned their engines forward to come roaring across the frozen mud. In seconds they were past the limits of the bombardment, leaving a third of their number burning behind them. A third already gone, but it mattered not at all. The other two-thirds just kept on coming.

'All troops, upon my command,' Lorannus said, calm and even over the comm-link. 'Fire!'

A fusillade of missiles, lasbeams and mortar rounds hurtled into no-man's-land. Some found their marks, and more vehicles exploded. But many beams glanced off armour, missiles failed, mortar rounds fell short. The motorised horde kept coming.

With grim satisfaction, Chelkar saw the bulk of them were headed his way.

'Wait,' he told the others. 'I want them close.'

The death toll mounted as the other Guardsmen continued to fire. But the remaining orks kept coming in a mad dash to be first to the slaughter. One hundred metres. Eighty. Fifty. Twenty five metres now and closing. Twenty...

'Now,' said Chelkar.

Before the sound of the order was gone Bulaven was on his feet. Moving with a speed that belied his size, he pulled the camo-cover away, his finger already on the trigger of the flamer. He fired, and an oncoming tracked vehicle suddenly disappeared in an expanding cone of fire. It exploded, but Bulaven was already onto another target. And another, and another. One by one, speeding vehicles became fiery deathtraps for their crews, screaming orks leaping overboard as around them their comrades crashed and burned. And still Bulaven kept working the flamer, a bright finger of fire turning vehicle after vehicle into an inferno. And all the time, beside him, Chelkar and Davir worked the triggers of their own guns like madman, trying to make up for lack of numbers with sheer volume of fire. Before long, all Chelkar could see in front of the trench was a rising curtain of flame, all he could hear was the screams of orks, all he could smell was the stench of burning flesh.

He kept on firing.

'Reloading!' Bulaven yelled, as the flamer suddenly sputtered and died, his fat hands already working to attach the fuel-line to a new canister. With a machine-like efficiency born of long practice, Chelkar and Davir sent half a dozen frag grenades into the flames to buy Bulaven the seconds he needed.

But then, they were machines: machines made for the killing of orks.

The flamer sputtered once more, then spat fire again, sending more orks screaming to their gods. And, even through the haze of battle, Chelkar could see his plan was working. Having concentrated their attack here, the orks had become log-jammed. Already, their assault elsewhere in the sector was faltering and Guardsmen from other trenches were able to add their fire to back up Chelkar and Davir. It was the oldest tactic in Broucheroc: offer the orks an open door then slam it shut in their faces. The oldest tactic, and yet it worked every time.

Then, just as Chelkar began to think he might have survived yet another battle, he heard a message over the comm-link that made him think perhaps the orks were not so gullible after all.

'Lieutenant!' Grishen's voice crackled through the static. 'Lookouts report more orks advancing towards us on foot through no-man's-land. Sweet Emperor – their armour was only the first wave!'

For a moment there was only silence over the comm-link, then Chelkar heard Lorannus give an order of stark, staring madness.

'All troops: fix bayonets and advance into no-man's-land! You hear me? Forward, for the Emperor!'

In the trench, no one moved. Chelkar, Davir and Bulaven stood, staring at each other in disbelief. Turning to look at the other trenches, Chelkar could see they were not alone. Out of the whole company, only one man had left the safety of his trench. One man, who now charged forward single-handedly towards the army of orks hidden somewhere in the smoke. The only man who had followed the order was the man who had given it.

Lieutenant Lorannus.

Alone, while the troops he commanded stood watching him with total incomprehension, Lorannus leapt out of his trench and charged into no-man's-land with bullets flying all around him. Coming to a burning tracked vehicle, he vaulted on to its hull, pushing a dead gretchin out of the way, then grabbed the vehicle's twin stubbers and turned them screaming on a horde of approaching orks. One man, compelled by some unknown inner daemon to an act of suicidal madness.

It was the bravest thing Chelkar had ever seen.

'What are you waiting for?' Chelkar heard himself yell over the comm-link. 'Are you going to leave him to fight the orks on his own? That's your company commander out there! Charge!'

Before he even knew what he was doing, Chelkar was on his feet with Davir and Bulaven beside him. Together, they charged into no-man's-land with guns blazing, every other man in the company close behind them. A hundred men, inspired to the same madness as their commander, charging screaming to certain death.

Then, for the second time in a day, Chelkar saw something incredible.

The orks broke and ran.

Barely believing they were still alive, Chelkar and the others halted, looking at the backs of the retreating orks in dumb disbelief. Then, there came the sound of a single voice, soon joined by another, and another, until every man in the company – Chelkar included – was cheering Lieutenant Lorannus's name. And, from his vantage point above them on the burning hull of the ork vehicle, Lorannus smiled and raised his laspistol above his head in a salute of triumph.

Then the bullet struck.

Somewhere out in no-man's-land a gretchin sniper found his spiteful mark, the impact pitching Lorannus forward off the vehicle as a fist-sized spray of red gore erupted from the right side of his chest. Chelkar was by his side in seconds, his hands desperately trying to stem the flow of blood from the lieutenant's chest as he screamed for a medic.

'Tell them…' Lorannus gasped, blood bubbling from his mouth with every ragged breath. 'Tell them… it wasn't true. My family… we were loyal… tell them…'

'You will tell them yourself, lieutenant,' Chelkar said, not realising he was shouting. 'And you can show them the medal you're going to get for this. And not posthumously, lieutenant. You hear me? This is no more than a scratch – in a couple of weeks you'll be saluting when they pin that medal on you! Do you hear me, lieutenant?'

But his only answer came with a bloody-lipped and enigmatic smile.

Lorannus was already dead.

HE HAD EXPECTED questions, or another beating, but having finished his story Chelkar found himself left in silence as the commissar's attention returned to his data-slate once more. Minutes passed, the only sound in the room the quiet whirring of the vox-recorder and the scratching of a stylus as the commissar began to write something on the screen of the data-slate. Or perhaps it was hours: Chelkar could not be sure. He could only sit there, wondering. Surely, there must be more to it than this? If the commissar only wanted to ask him about Lorannus's heroism, why put him through this torment? Why the arrest? The beating? Why bring him here at all?

Then, Valk switched off the vox-recorder, the sudden click sounding like a gunshot after so long a silence.

'You may go, sergeant,' the commissar said. Then, seeing Chelkar staring blankly at him, he continued. 'Having read your most recent battle-report, I was understandably concerned to see you had recommended a traitor for posthumous commendation. But having heard your account first-hand, I can see you had no sinister motive. It was simply a regrettable lack of judgement. I am satisfied you were an innocent in this affair. As I said, sergeant, you may go.'

In shock, Chelkar stood and turned to leave, still half-expecting the guards to drag him back into the chair at any moment. Then, as he reached the door, he could not help but give one last look at the commissar sitting at his desk.

'Is there something else, sergeant?'

'Forgive my asking, commissar. But when you said "a traitor", did you mean Lieutenant Lorannus?'

'Yes. Some months ago a member of the lieutenant's family – a distant cousin, I believe – was denounced as a traitor to the Imperium. Of course, as is usual in these cases, his relatives were also purged. All except your lieutenant. Apparently some administrative oversight led to the order for his execution being delayed long enough for him to seek refuge among troops bound for this planet. No doubt he hoped to spread heresy and dissent here, but on this occasion it would seem the orks have actually done us a service. If nothing else, they have saved us a bullet...'

THEY HAD GIVEN him his clothes back. And his weapons. But all the same, as he limped alone back to the front lines, Chelkar felt little sense of triumph. Even cheating the gallows seemed no great victory. This was Broucheroc. At best he had lived to die another day.

Still, he had received better than Lieutenant Lorannus. It seemed strange, how he had gone so quickly from loathing the man to respecting him. And now, now they said the lieutenant was a traitor? Chelkar was too tired to think about it. Perhaps he would consider it tomorrow.

He smelled a familiar stench on the wind and Chelkar realised he was approaching the corpse-pyres once more. For a moment he contemplated going the long way round, but his body ached and it would have added another two kilometres to his journey. Besides, the pyres seemed to have burned down now, most of them little more than smouldering piles of ash. Of course new pyres were already being built; in Broucheroc, corpses were never in short supply. But for now, the smoke and stink had lessened.

It was then, as he made his way past a newly-constructed mound of unburned corpses, that Chelkar caught a glimpse of something. A flash of gold and blue amidst a mountain of green flesh. In a split second it was gone as a masked Guardsman put a torch to the pyre, the whole mound disappearing in a scarlet haze of fire. But Chelkar did not need to see it twice. He knew what it was already: a golden epaulette on the shoulder of the ridiculous powder-blue uniform of Lieutenant Lorannus. Consigned to the flames with its owner, no doubt at the order of Commissar Valk. It did not matter that the lieutenant had given his life defending this city. Broucheroc was sacred soil. There could be no final resting place here for a man condemned as traitor. No hero's burial for him.

Only a red reward.

MENSHAD KORUM

CS Goto

Behind our consciousness lies a profound abyss, about which we riddle and dance through the paths of our kind. The Aspects of Khaine are sprinkled around the rim like garrisons of our sanity. The exarchs are the champions of our souls, keeping the darkness at bay. Beware the Menshad Korum, the hunter who stalks himself. Although trapped in the Path of the Warrior, this exarch owes his soul to no Aspect and knows not who he is. None is closer to Khaine than the Lost Warrior, none closer to the abyss in our souls.

On the Transfiguration of Exarchs
– Seer Calmainoc, Ulthwé craftworld

THE RICOCHET CAUGHT him in the back of his head. Surprise flickered over his face as the cacophony of battle was arrested by the shock. There was a sudden silence. Arbariar discarded her shuriken pistol and drew the crackling chainsword into both hands, holding it vertically at her right shoulder in the death-stance of the Striking Scorpions. Vlalmerch fell forward onto his knees, his eyes wide in disbelief and his mouth working silently. A trickle of blood snaked its way round his neck, hissing with toxicity. His fusion gun clattered onto the shimmering wraithbone deck as it dropped lifelessly from his hand. The exarch lifted his gaze into Arbariar's face as he collapsed to the ground at her feet, motionless.

That Soul is Mine. The voice oozed into Arbariar's mind, riddling her thoughts and curdling her intent. She paused, unsure.

Take the stone, and let's get out of here, came the voiceless words of Bureea. Arbariar could feel the urgency in her daughter's thoughts and she snapped out of her nauseous reverie, stooping quickly. Rolling Vlalmerch over onto his back, she pushed her delicate fingers under his armour, where they quested and danced.

They are coming.

I know. Arbariar worked quickly, teetering on the edge of composure like a feather falling onto a blade. She could hear the footfalls of Vlalmerch's Kinsmen, the Bloodguard of the House of Saeemrar. She could feel them getting closer, chipping away at the fabric of time in their burning haste. There was an electric panic in the air that made her fingers fumble and twist: where did he keep his stone... where is it?

It is Mine.

They will kill us. This will be the end of us all. Hurry. We must leave... now.

'ABH AHG VAKARUM!' Quereshir shouted the opening mantra as he raced down the corridor. He held a flamer in both hands, pumping it from side to side as he ran. The Kinsmen flooded out in his wake, like a blast of flame from an afterburner. Their golden helmets spiked into the air in front of them, splintering off a heartbeat of time and sending them roaring into the fractional future.

Quereshir was fastest, driven by fear and drawn by the silence that had suddenly befallen his father's thoughts. He was already through the great doors of Saeemrar's sanctum before their flaming, molten substance had fully withdrawn into the cold wraithbone walls.

The Kinsmen arrived only moments later, but Quereshir was already in a deathhaze, spinning in exquisite splendour, sending gyring flames into the hearts of each shadow that swam and flickered around the room. Using the momentum of his spin, he kicked into the air and spiralled over the prostrate corpse of his father, bathing the Kinsmen in fire before landing, kneeling next to his father's head. The flamer died in his hands and the Kinsmen each dropped to one knee, flames still licking at the fiery orange of their armour.

We come too late. Quereshir's thoughts were uneven, as though he were stifling each one, fearing that they were weapons. Lifting his fingers gently from the exposed skin on the front of his father's neck, he looked up at his Kinsmen. Lord Vlalmerch, Menshad Korum Exarch and chieftain of the Saeemrar Wild Riders was dead. The Kinsmen bowed their heads, transforming the scene into a sea of oranging golds. It was as though they were themselves the flames of this great House.

Quereshir glanced round the chamber. The shadows had returned, but nothing could have survived his cleansing. There were no traces of intruders, not even the psychic echo of their dark intent. The Kinsmen were forcing down their shame and anger, glaring into the dizzying sheen of the polished wraithbone at their feet. Finally, Lureeal, oldest of the Bloodguard lifted his head. *Who is responsible for this?*

Horror gripped Quereshir as he carefully removed his father's blood-red breastplate. *I do not know but, by Khaine, they will pay for it with their souls.*

'You're sure?'

'Quite sure. This shape is little known and difficult to master. No other squadrons use it.'

Quereshir toyed with the microscopic disc under the closeseer, flipping and turning it so that light glinted from each of its venomous edges. Even he could see that the workmanship was truly breathtaking – the shuriken had been rendered into a tiny scorpion, its tail wrapped round into its chelicerae claws, leaving the pedipalps pincing outwards, forming a perfect barbed circle. He had found the tiniest of shards wedged into one of the pillars in his father's chamber and, sure enough, its exact inverse was missing from the sting of this micro-arachnid.

'A shuriken pistol would have to be fired at very close range even to scratch a wraithbone pillar,' advised the wraithsmith.

Quereshir considered the ageing eldar in front of him. 'Are you suggesting that the ricochet was a deliberate tactic?'

'That would be my deduction, yes.'

Even without the wraithsmith's insight into the unique shape of the projectile, Quereshir would have recognised the assailant's tactical signature. Only the Striking Scorpion Aspect Warriors were adept enough at close quarter combat to bounce a shuriken off a pillar into the back of their adversary's head. But the Aspect temples had little time for the volatile politics of the Wild Rider clans. Only the Scorpionida Wild Riders of Saim-Hann, whose chieftain had mastered the Aspect Arts of the Striking Scorpions long years before during her time on the Path of the Warrior, stung their projectiles with mandiblaster psychotoxins.

He was taken in combat then, not shot in the back? Lureeal's question bolted into Quereshir's mind, forceful and relieved simultaneously. Quereshir turned to face the staunch Kinsman.

'Yes, my old friend, but there is more to this than a chieftain's honour-duel. We must speak privately.' The son of Vlalmerch had control of his rage now; his torrential emotions were focused into a fine stream of calculation. 'Follow me.'

The two clansmen bowed slightly to the wraithsmith, who nodded a gentle response, and took their leave. They walked soundlessly from the workshop, sharing neither words nor thoughts.

Quereshir could feel Lureeal's fierce resolve as it flooded the space around them, giving the two eldar extra gravity as they walked, slowing them almost to the loping pace of the mon-keigh. But Quereshir was distracted by his own private thoughts and even the power emanating from the Bloodguard captain could give him no reassurance, although he knew that the old eldar would sacrifice his very soul to avenge this evil.

As the flaming doors of the Saeemrar sanctum melded together behind them, the two clan-brothers folded themselves onto the reds and golds of the cushions that covered the council chamber. 'They took his waystone,' said Quereshir levelly. Lureeal nodded slowly, with repulsed understanding. They sat in silence for seven heartbeats, bringing themselves into synchronisation, intertwining their souls. They closed their eyes and called to the other Kinsmen.

Blood Runs,

Anger Rises,
Death Wakes,
War Calls!

SOMEWHERE IN THE lashes of the Eye of Terror, Lelith Hesperax flicked open her eyes with a slow smile, the serrated perfection of her teeth glinting lightlessly. The intricate blackness of the seer-amplification chamber wove itself back into reality around her, ripples of sha'iel dissipating and morphing into the calligraphic runes that settled into the pearlescent darkness of the walls. The chamber was never fully in a single reality, and the runes continued to slip, mingle and twine like snakes of oil, hungry to be released into the warp once again.

The wych queen rose from her meditation without a sound, her movements clothed in shadow and sickly grace. Echoing her motion, an imperceptible doorway fizzled into existence from the curving wall behind her. Light streamed in, silhouetting a tall, slim figure who knelt in wait. Lelith revolved to face the inquiries of her underling, but Yhuki knew better than to verbalise her questions before the great wych had already offered the answers.

The Soul has been Taken. It has Begun.

The subtle yet emphatic force of Lelith's thoughts made Yhuki reel. *Very good*, was all that she could manage in response, as Lelith glided through the space that separated the two wyches. *Not Good, just Inevitable, as though common to all the Myriad Futures.*

Lelith swept passed her servant, her long hair caressing Yhuki's naked shoulders and fanning into a wake behind her. Yhuki fought to resist the need to touch the queen's legs as they slid through the eddying air at her side. She knew that to do so would send her soul screaming into the abyss of sha'iel, where it would be consumed by daemons or perhaps by Slaanesh himself. She had heard the whispered rumours of the queen's pact with the Satin Throne.

But might it be worth it? Yhuki could not tell whether those were her own thoughts, and she left her hands clasped in front of her, right fist enveloped by left palm, in the traditional deference of the Hesperax Retinue of the dark eldar. *Very Good,* came the thoughts again, *for there is a Fine Line between the Path of Damnation and the Road to Hell.*

THE GOLD AND red armour of the exarch lay ceremoniously upon the altar, its arms pulled across its chest. The image was pregnant with echoes of the Fire Dragon Aspect, from which Vlalmerch had fled as a Lost Warrior, the Menshad Korum. During his time as an Aspect Warrior for the Dragons, Vlalmerch had embraced his fate as the perpetual warrior, trapped into the glorious path of Khaine, the Bloody-Handed God. But, bursting with the pride of his clan, his soul had not been at peace in the Temple of Fire and the exarch had fled the discipline of the flame, returning to his clan as the greatest warrior the House of Saeemrar had ever known. Many eldar in this proud house had walked the Path of the Warrior for various periods in their lives, but Vlalmerch was the first to return to the clan as an exarch. He was their natural leader, inspiring awe, fear, and respect in equal measures. And with him came the flaming signature of the Aspect that he left behind – the Saeemrar gloried in his fire.

'The Path of the Exarch is lonely and savage, but it brings greatness to our kin and might to our flames. It is the Unparalleled Path, striking with fear and awe at our very souls.' As she spoke, the clan's seer surveyed the assembled Saeemrar, each kneeling, fierce with injured pride. It was an inspiring vision, with hundreds of blood-red helmets bowed in honour, filling the glistening temple with visions of fire. At the very front of the congregation were the dazzling golds of the Kinsmen – the clan's Wild Riders and the chieftain's Bloodguard. Swirling in the air around them and seeping up the three steps towards the altar was the flow of shame and the passion for vengeance that these chosen few exuded. *We were not there.* The air was thick and syrupy, sick with muttered promises of death. And there, amidst the gyring soup of intense emotion, sending eddies and ripples into the psychic field that swamped them all, knelt Quereshir, resplendent in his golden battle-armour, blood red burning on his shoulder guards and in his eyes.

The seer considered Quereshir closely, reaching out with her thoughts and attempting to divine his intent. Never before had Ehliji seen such a maelstrom of emotion erupt from the bereaved. She could see that the son of Vlalmerch was struggling to maintain his composure, battling against his hateful anger, hammering his gaze into the gleaming floor of the temple as though fearing that it might annihilate anything else it touched.

'Because of the horror buried deep in the soul of the exarch, the seers of Saim-Hann have never permitted them access to the infinity circuit of our craftworld, wherein swim the souls of our ancestors, held from the grasp of He-Who-Must-Not-Be-Named. Precarious enough is the existence of the eldar. Instead, the fearsome power and ineffable wisdom etched into the exarch's waystone is added to those who were once the exarch before him. The armour of the exarch is justly exalted, for it bears within it the ageless might of eldar past; its breast is studded with the colours of their waystones. It contains its own infinity circuit, a spirit pool, a haven for the soul of Vlalmerch. Now, for the first time in our long history, the passing of an exarch is also the passing of our Saeemrar chieftain; our clan should be enshrined with him in the spirit pool of this armour, granting us immortality and honour immeasurable.'

A wave of imagery flooded into the minds of the congregation, erupting from the prone armour of the exarch like a psychic volcano. Flickering pictures flashed across their eyes, depicting the innumerable manifestations of this Menshad Korum exarch over the millennia. At first there was Vlalmerch towering over the sprawling figure of a Hesperax wych, and then the images whirred into the ancient past. The Fire Dragons watched their exarch lead them from their home world, as it became overwhelmed by the insanity of the Fall, forging a new future for the Saim-Hann aboard this immense craft-world. And then, in the dimness of a half-forgotten past, they watched the moment at which the first aspect warrior was transfigured into the exarch that would always infuse this armour, as he vanquished the necron lord Ardoth and his retinue of Pariahs. The soul of each great warrior, enwrapped in their waystones to hide them from the thirsty quest of Slaanesh, lay embedded in the ancient armour. The exarch was battle incarnate.

Ehliji could sense the pride swelling in the hearts of the clansmen and she muttered a silent prayer that it would overcome the anger in Quereshir. The sons of Saim-Hann were moved more easily by honour and pride than were any of the other eldar whom Ehliji had served. It had been amongst the first of the craftworlds to escape after the Fall, and it carried the legacy of that desperate flight in its very soul. But the son of the exarch showed no signs of movement, his gaze was held by something hidden deep within the wraithbone deck, as though he could see plans emerging out of its profound darkness. Ehliji looked directly at him, hoping to prize him out of his deathly trance, but he was as closed to her as he would have been to a mon-keigh. *You are not alone. You must listen. There are things more important than the individual's loss. The eldar must be above such things. The future is splintered and unclear. We cannot afford needless bloodshed.*

Tell that to the Scorpionidas! Quereshir's retort thundered into Ehliji's mind, staggering her. She pushed out her left hand to steady herself against the altar as the blast threatened to throw her from her feet. Lureeal stole a glance up from his reverence, unable to ignore the immense exchange of energy that seered through unseen dimensions above his head. He caught a glimpse of horror on the seer's face before composure retook her and the ceremony continued.

'Lord Vlalmerch burned brightest of his generation, honouring his family and our clan as he took the tremendous burden of this armour. He left us and walked the Path of the Warrior for three hundred years, becoming master of the aspect arts of the Fire Dragons. We all gloried in his great victories,' Ehliji's tone softened, 'but none more so than he. As the time for his transition to another of our great ways drew near, he lost himself, never to leave the warrior way, and we were saved for another generation. But he did leave the Fire Dragons – Vlalmerch grasped the hand of the Bloody-Handed God, bringing him into the heart of our house, and we lived our lives around his horror. There is no sacrifice greater or more terrifying than that made by our chieftain.'

'Who will wear the armour now?'

Hundreds of faces lifted their eyes from the ground, searching for the origin of that voice. The Kinsmen were on their feet, standing before the altar. Lureeal, the eldest and most venerated captain of the Bloodguard, who had once journeyed the Path of the Warrior for five hundred years, stood forward of the group, his armour shimmering with immaculate honour. 'Without our chieftain we are dishonoured. But without the exarch we are weak – we have grown dependent on his strength. Another must be found.' Murmurs of affirmation rippled through the congregation. *Lureeal is right. He should take the armour.*

'The armour of an exarch cannot be conferred according to the whims of a Wild Rider clan, but only by a seer of an aspect temple. In any case, none of you are on the Path. There is no one here who is ready. None of you are yet lost to yourselves.'

'Seer Ehliji, I am prepared,' answered Lureeal, meeting the seer's gaze so that she might see the fire in his eyes.

'There is no preparation, Captain Lureeal. There is no will. There is only the future, and this is not your path. Your offer does you great credit, but this is not a matter for a warrior to choose – such is the way of damnation. The exarch simply is, although he may not yet know it.'

Lureeal bowed his head, acknowledging the seer's wisdom.

I will take my father's armour!

Ehliji gasped as the thought struck her.

'I will take my father's armour,' came Quereshir's voice, gentle, firm and quiet.

The clansmen of the Saeemrar searched for this new voice with their eyes as the Kinsmen parted to reveal Quereshir still kneeling at the altar, his attention still caught in the depths of his thoughts, gazing into the wraithbone.

You must not. You are not on the path. You are not yet lost. Your future holds many paths and possibilities. You must not will yourself onto this path, or you will be as lost to us as you will be to yourself. It is not a question of choice.

'I am lost without him. His death has fixed my path. It is set. The armour is mine.' Rising to his feet, Quereshir climbed the steps to the altar, where he turned to address the congregation.

Ehliji stepped back, drawing in her breath, keeping a space between them, fighting to conceal her horror.

'My warrior brothers, Lord Vlalmerch was indeed the greatest of us and the most terrible. There was never one more deserving of this armour than he. Countless enemies have cowered before his flames. Entire planets were rent asunder and starships rendered to dust if they dared to oppose him. Behind him, the Saeemrar Wild Riders of Saim-Hann have bathed in the flames of glory and destruction.

'Kinsmen – my father's Bloodguard – there are none who know better than you the single-minded passion and art with which he flowed into battle, scything into combat on his ruby jetbike, dispensing melta and death to our enemies.

'Yet, my friends, it is true that the soul of Lord Vlalmerch cannot blend into the honour and glory of our craftworld's ancient infinity circuit. However, neither will it swim in the infinities of this armour's spirit pool. His waystone will not adorn the breast of the next exarch. For he is lost to us, as he was lost to himself.

'Our lord did not die in a chieftain's honour battle, as befits the traditions of Saim-Hann's Wild Riders. He was assassinated in his chamber within these temple walls, and his waystone stolen. I have taken the counsel of the wraithsmiths and of my soul, and I know that our chieftain was killed by another eldar of Saim-Hann.'

Quereshir paused to let the significance of this accusation hit home. Feuds between the Wild Rider squadrons were not unknown – the eldar of other craftworlds found the Saim-Hann barbaric because of them – but this was the first time that one had involved an exarch, for whom such games served no purpose. In general, the aspect temples kept out of such political machinations, although eldar new to the Path of the Warrior would sometimes indulge in petty rivalries or honour matches. These were calculated as tests of skill, as rites of passage on the road to mastery of the aspect arts. Such tests always remained behind the closed doors of the temple. But the Menshad Korum was not part of any temple.

Deaths were extremely rare, both within aspect temples and in the conflicts between Wild Rider clans; behind these apparently lethal competitions lay the unspoken unity of Saim-Hann and the profoundly protective angst of the eldar race itself, which balances on the edge of extinction. The squadrons from the Saeemrar and the Scorpionidas had been rivals for millennia, but they were also the closest of allies whenever the craftworld of Saim-Hann went to war. Together they had crushed the vile wyches of Hesperax and driven their remnants into the Eye of Terror. That had been Vlalmerch's finest hour, but it was more than a century ago.

'I am all that is left of Lord Vlalmerch. With my body, I will imbed his memory within the psychoplastic of the exarch's armour. His glories will live on through me and, at the time of my passing, through my own waystone. We may have lost his soul, but his memory will never die. He was our chieftain, and we should decide the fate of his armour – the Fire Dragons have no claim to him.'

A great cheer arose from the Wild Riders in the sanctum of the Saeemrar, 'SAEEMRAR!', sending thunder stampeding through the corridors and passages that led from the great flaming gates. The sea of reds and golds pulsated with life, as though unified by a single organic purpose, the pride of the warriors whipped into a frenzy of proportions unique to the eldar race. The cheer went up again, 'SAEEMRAR!', this time accompanied by jets of flame from the Kinsmen, who showered the congregation with hungry light. The conflagration throbbed with fire and with the rhythmic chanting of the Menshad Korum exarch's new name: 'SAEEMRAR!'

'And now,' cried the voice of Quereshir over the tumultuous din, 'the Saeemrar exarch must prepare for craftwar!' With voices as one, the Wild Rider host began their chant to Khaine, the Bloody-Handed God.

'Blood Runs,
'Anger Rises,
'Death Wakes,
'War Calls!'

'WE MUST TAKE the waystone to the core.' Arbariar held Vlalmerch's soul in her hand, tightly gripped into a fist. She could feel its icy pulse repelling her fingers, as if disgusted by her touch. An intense wave of pity flooded into her as she considered what her great rival had denied himself, and she tightened her fist around him. The fool.

'There will be resistance. Not only the Saeemrar, but the whole of Saim-Hann will seek to prevent this.' As always, Bureea was right. It did not take the gifts of a seer to realise the peril of the Scorpionidas. They had murdered an exarch of their own craftworld, and now they sought to cast his soul into the infinity circuit, where his dark and deathly pollution might condemn the spirit pool to centuries of despair and bloody misdirection. The war-cries of an exarch, any exarch, fixated on death, amplified by the teeming millions of souls in the ancient circuit, risked flaring a beacon for the minions of the Satin Throne. The hint of such an awesome prize might even lure Slaanesh himself.

It was not for nothing that the Council of Seers had prevented the assimilation of the exarchs for millennia. The infinity circuit must be kept pure, for it was the last haven of a dying race, the only hope for the eldar's future. As each of the craftworlds navigated the distant stretches of the galaxy, they collected the souls of their dead into their hearts, keeping them from the clutches of the unspeakable daemons at their heels. Stealth and movement were vital to survival. The peripatetic craft-worlds never came together for very long, fearing that the immense concentrations of eldar souls would lure Slaanesh out of sha'iel to consume them. The craft-worlds could not risk anything that might endanger their spirit pools.

Arbariar looked into her daughter's eyes, momentary uncertainty flickering in her gaze.

Bureea saw her mother's hesitation, 'Yes, this deed is greater than us, greater even than Saim-Hann. Our action sends myriad new futures lancing into possibility, each one more glorious than the present, sickening pathways of our weak craftworld. We will bring the volcanic wrath of the Saeemrar upon us and suffer agonies of shame, but in the dimness of future realities they will sing of our virtue and truth. We will be exalted in our suffering.'

The seer's words soothed Arbariar's anxiety as she knelt before the Striking Scorpions altar, buried deep within the sanctum of the Scorpionidas. Arbariar had walked the Aspect Path of the Striking Scorpions for many long years before finally transcending the Path of the Warrior and returning to her clan. A fragment of her soul remained in that embattled past, and she devoted part of each day to the rites of the Striking Scorpions, just as other eldar might continue to practise sculpture or poetry even after having left the Path of the Artist. The altar was a reminder of an unforgettable past.

Intricate, artful red webs wove their way through the deep green of the steps beneath her, aspiring toward the altar where they congealed into a crescendo of arachnids, spilling over the magnificent scorpion throne, swamping its blood red form with the seductive threads of their genus. The patterns seemed to swim and float over the wraithbone, dancing and luring the eyes as though enchanted by some dark power. Arbariar had lost herself in this hypnotic web aeons ago, trapped by its apparent eternities. Now she contemplated its depth for a long moment everyday.

Climbing into the throne of the Scorpionidas chieftain, Arbariar turned to face her daughter. 'Lord Vlalmerch was once my honoured battle-brother, until, at the point of our powerblades, the Hesperax separated us, drawing us into her darkness, seducing us at the moment of our victory. That was long ago, but the darkness has grown powerful in Saim-Hann, and now is the time to act. The darkness draws us into war, and we will riddle it with shimmering flecks of death.'

Bureea bowed deeply to her mother, closed her eyes, and called for the Scorpionidas to assemble in the great hall of their sanctum. In the wraithbone of the craftworld infrastructure, she could feel the pounding of warriors responding to her voiceless call.

LELITH HESPERAX RECLINED into her throne, sending delicate jets of blood spraying into Yhuki's face. Bones in the throne creaked gently under her weight and the flesh shifted in desperate need to bring comfort. Lelith closed her eyes and pushed her arms above her head, stretching her tall, gracefully curving body, lying full length as the thronelings rushed to form a bed, aching for a touch of her skin. Yhuki knelt at her queen's feet, biting down on her own tongue with her filed and sharpened teeth. A trickle of blood seeped out from the corner of her mouth, and she cast her tongue around her lips lasciviously.

All is proceeding as you have foreseen it, my queen.

Of course.

The eldar are preparing for craftwar. There will be many souls to harvest. Should we prepare to depart?

No. The Time for Harvest has not yet Come – we are still sowing. Patience.

You do not inspire patience in me, thought Yhuki involuntarily, her tongue still poised with its tip on her upper lip.

Then do not be Patient. Yhuki shivered with shame and desire, searching her mind for the origins of that familiar voice. Her thoughts turned in on themselves, clouding her vision as she searched for herself, trying to steady her soul before it was lost. But it was too late. She could only watch in detached, horrified anticipation as her hand slid across the base of the throne and her fingers crawled onto the skin of Lelith's exquisite calf, picking their way between the complex straps of black psychoplastic that snaked their way up the queen's legs. Lelith let out a breath of pleasure and reached down to Yhuki, drawing her face up along her body, balancing her chin atop a single impossibly fine fingernail. Yhuki could feel a piercing pain where Lelith's nail touched her neck, but she was enraptured.

Look down. The thought appeared directly in the core of Yhuki's mind, and she obeyed without question or hesitation. She let her eyes caress the breathless contours of the queen's form as they extended their gaze down to her delicately barbed feet. There, lying across the base of the throne, blood gushing from an egregious wound on its neck, was her own decapitated body. Horror sprang from the depths of her soul, but she had no breath to scream. Her eyes widened in terror as she cast her gaze back into the infinite and irresistible darkness of the queen's face for the last time.

Lelith slowly withdrew her finger from within the sinewy mess of Yhuki's neck, and the last spark of light vanished from the eyes of her devoted servant. This soul she would offer to the Satin Throne, its twisted and unrestrained hedonism would please the dark lord of pleasure and fulfil the continuing terms of their ancient compact. *There is a Fine Line between the Path of Damnation and the Road to Hell*, repeated Lelith. Yhuki had just crossed it.

Lying back into her bloody throne, Lelith Hesperax lamented the weakness of her kind – so easily moved to emotion, so easily led astray and lost from their paths. Even the mon-keigh, a prey species, showed greater balance. A little over a century had passed since her mighty starship had been driven from the expanses of open space by the Wild Riders of Saim-Hann. It had been an epic battle, with the reds, greens and golds of the Saim-Hann dashing themselves against the immovable darkness of her wyches; jetbikes, vypers and riders screaming into insanity before they could even engage with the Forces of Strife. Her Reaver jetcycles, clothed in the blackness of space, had whipped Saim-Hann into a frenzy of death, as the craftworld's great guns gyrated and spun ineffectively, loosing volleys of death into their own warriors.

Then the tide turned; two squadrons had banded together to face the black mass of wyches and dark riders, and between them they had driven Lelith back into her own ship. They pursued her on their jetbikes, weaving through the corridors and passages of her flagship releasing bolts of melta and sprays of fire, showering shuriken and scything bladed slaughter as they flew. Hundreds of wyches had fallen. The souls of thousands of dark eldar warriors were lost into the sha'iel, as Slaanesh and his daemons gorged themselves. The Reavers were annihilated by the combined power of the Saeemrar and the Scorpionidas Wild Riders.

Lelith breathed a sickly and pungent laugh as she recalled the two chieftains who had towered over her on her own battle bridge, their bloody blades focussed on her neck as she lay defeated on the floor, prostrate in ghastly submission. *How Pathetic are the Eldar*, she hissed into soundless dimensions. She had been defeated. The chieftains could have finished her with a single sting or burn. But one had turned to rejoin the fight in the ghostly labyrinth of her ship, lost in its single-minded pursuit of combat, leaving the other the honour of her soul. Lelith had squirmed and contorted her form, writhing on the shimmering command deck. The remaining chieftain had hesitated, something stirring deep within its sharply focussed and unbalanced soul. Lelith beckoned to its thoughts, seducing it with dances of blackness and promises of an infinity of battle and death. She had filled the warrior's soul with her darkness and watched the waystone on its colourful breastplate blink into a glistening black.

For a century, Lelith had waited patiently for the moment to come, relishing the inevitable determinism of her vision as though it were battle itself. Just as they had united to confront her, so she would divide them to confront each other. Craftwar would bring her thousands of souls; enough to placate the Satin Throne for centuries.

THE COLD PLATES felt uncomfortable against his skin, as though they had been specifically designed to cause irritation – a kind of ritual penance for the violence encased in their powerful forms. Quereshir rolled his shoulders, trying to adjust the fit of the gleaming psycho-plastic, but the armour seemed to resist his every movement.

The sanctum was fiercely hot, with flames dancing up the walls, defining a perimeter around the sacred space in the heart of the House of Saeemrar. Quereshir had attended his father here many times before. Now

Lureeal attended him. Kneeling in deference at the feet of his new lord, Lureeal held up the magnificent golden helmet of the exarch's armour, the final piece in the intricate jigsaw. Reflections of flames flickered and sparkled off the perfectly smooth, curving surface.

Quereshir nodded his acknowledgement to the veteran captain and lifted the helmet from his hands, fitting it neatly over his own head and sealing it into the shoulders of the armour with a slight pressure. Immediately the suit began to shift and move. It twitched and thrashed, forcing Quereshir into impossible contortions, his flailing limbs smashing Lureeal from his delicate deference and sending him rolling across the floor into the flames against the wall.

The armour was sealing itself against the world, and Quereshir could feel the air being forced out of the pockets in the interior. It was shrinking, clinging to his body, wrapping itself around his face and suffocating him. All the time it forced him into random, energetic movements until he was gasping for breaths that he could not take. He tried to call out to Lureeal, but could make no sound. He reached out with his mind, but found his thoughts could not penetrate the psychoplastics that enveloped him. He was utterly alone and completely imprisoned, dying desperately.

Lureeal watched in horror as Vlalmerch's son threw himself around the sanctum, smashing himself against the walls and the shimmering wraithbone pillars. He had been with Vlalmerch when he had first donned the armour of the exarch, and it had not been like this. The suit had just hissed into place – a perfect fit.

Quereshir could hear voices whispering in his mind and could feel the icy tendrils of the psycho-plastic reaching through his skin, piercing his suffocation with bright moments of pain. The whispering grew louder and the voices multiplied. He tried to shake his head, wanting to empty the voices from his ears, but he could not move. There was chanting: *Saeemrar, Saeemrar, Saeemrar*. And there were questions spinning around his head, stirring his mind into a nauseating vortex: *What do you want? Who will you be? What do you want? Who will you be?*

In a flash it was over. The destructive, erratic movements flowed into a graceful dance – an elegant and faultless training form from the repertoire of the most advanced Aspect Warriors. The armour hissed finally into perfect fit, clinging to every fraction of Quereshir's skin. The whispering voices in his mind continued, but they had retreated into the background and Quereshir found his own thoughts once again.

Lureeal looked on in relief and then stooped into a deep bow.

The exarch spoke. 'I am the Menshad Korum.'

QUERESHIR AND HIS Kinsmen folded themselves into the wall on either side of the emerald, crystalline shield-doors of the House of the Scorpionidas. The great gates danced with the blood-red veins of webbing that marked the arachnid clan. The awesome reputation of the Scorpionidas for close quarter combat had been hard won through blood and toil, so the Saeemrar deployed stealth and surprise as their first weapons.

The exarch raised his clenched fist above his head, indicating that his squad should hold its formation. The Bloodguard held fast, neither breathing nor thinking, permitting no trace of their presence to escape. They were motionless against the deepening greens of the house walls, the dirty reds of their armour hazing incredibly into camouflage. A vague sting flooded out through the gates, and the Saeemrar feared that they had been discovered already. But it was no psychotoxin, merely the seer-wave of Bureea searching for danger. It passed in an instant, sweeping along the access corridor with wisps of psychic tendrils questing for prey.

Quereshir opened his fist again, and Lureeal started to set the melta-bombs, fusing each into the fabric of the gates using the intense fire of his flamer at close range.

Set.

On three, captain.

Understood.

'One.'

The seer-wave at the end of the corridor visibly spun on its axis and came storming back towards the gates, seeking the voice.

'Two.'

The cloud started to darken as it drew closer, charging itself with venom, sprinkling tiny shards of psychoconductive crystal as it flew. Behind the gates, in the great hall of the Scorpionidas, the Saeemrar could hear barricades being thrown precisely into place amidst the muffled barking of orders.

'Three!'

The melta-charges exploded sending a superheated backblast of fire jetting along the corridor away from the gates. The mighty gates buckled under the prodigious blast, arching back into the temple before being ripped apart. Molten emerald sprayed out into the interior, sending the defenders diving for cover behind their hastily erected barricades.

Outside, the venom of the seer-wave was beginning to bite, its crystals wedging themselves into the armour of Saeemrar warriors before being triggered by a tremendous psychic blast from somewhere in the inner sanctum of the temple. Tiny strafes of pain erupted in their flesh as a dozen clansmen dropped to the ground, their limbs spontaneously ripped from their bodies as they struggled to rid their minds of the invading toxins.

Quereshir was inside the breach an instant after the melta had blown. For a moment the scene was motionless and he paused in disappointment, scanning the hall for the promise of battle. The magnificent visage of the golden exarch standing unflinchingly amidst the rain of debris, cast into glittering relief by the fire from the flamers of his Bloodguard as they sought to cleanse the hall from the outside, was chillingly beautiful. Then, from behind him, came the searing whine of a shuriken, shattering the aesthetic of the moment, and the mêlée began.

The exarch ducked into a roll, flipping forward as the shuriken zipped over his head. He stayed in his crouch searching for the gunner, as the ricochet bounced twice between pillars before its energy was spent. Quereshir released three fusion bolts from his gun, and the sniper behind the entrance was lifted off his feet into a staccato flight before crumpling to the ground in ashes.

Lureeal hoisted the red and gold banner of the Saeemrar, its serpentine dragon fluttering at the tip of his firepike as he led the charge into the great hall to support the exarch. 'SAEEMRAR!'

Quereshir realised too late that the hall was a death-trap. As the Saeemrar flooded the chamber with melta and flame, creating a ring of death around the perimeter of the circular hall with the exarch resplendent at the centre, a hail of shuriken ripped through the burning air and tore into the rapidly diminishing squadron. Those shuriken that missed their mark ricocheted back from the pillars that punctuated the hall or from the giant curving walls, focussing the venomous projectiles back into the killing zone in the centre. The Scorpionidas themselves were tucked in behind their barricades, impervious to all but the most direct strike from a fusion gun.

In an instant, the hall was a dizzying mist of shuriken, as the Scorpionidas released thousands of the monomolecular projectiles each second. The Saeemrar were being ripped to pieces by the lacerations of the air itself, their flames obscuring their assailants rather than damaging them. With each passing moment a dozen or more warriors collapsed to the deck, their limbs, heads and abdomens serrated beyond hope, riddled with death.

This is not the end! Quereshir could feel the will of the ancient exarch reaching through the psycho-plastic of his armour, mocking his indecision, but he did not know what to do. Meanwhile, Lureeal stood with his back to Quereshir, projecting the intense melta-beam of his firepike directly into the barricade that blocked their advance into the inner sanctum. He stood his ground, daring the shuriken to sting him, knowing that his destiny would not end in this hall.

Kill them. Kill them all! The voice inside Quereshir's mind continued to taunt him, driving him insane with anger. Get out of my head!

This is your head. There is no escape from your path now. There is only escape from this hall. Kill them all. You are the Lost One.

Quereshir watched his mighty Bloodguard fall, following him with unquestioning loyalty to their deaths, fighting their brothers at his word. *Khaine forgive me!* The exarch launched himself into the air, fusion gun firing continuously as he leapt above the killing zone, like a fountain of fire erupting from the epicentre of battle. At the apex of his leap, he spun rapidly, extending his arms as stabilisers, like a gyroscope, hovering for a moment on sheer energy. His eyes dilated slightly, triggering the release of the melta-bombs that were fixed into constellations along the armour of his arms. They flew outwards, curving under the centrifugal forces of his spin, scattering themselves around the perimeter of the great hall.

The exarch landed lightly into a crouch in the centre of the chamber as his Kinsmen continued to blaze all around him. He rose to his feet and his melta-bombs exploded, incinerating huge chunks of wall and pillar, running cracks snaking into the ceiling, which collapsed, crushing those few Scorpionidas who had survived the blasts. The last ricochets of shuriken vanished, and the hall was cast into silence.

'Area secure,' reported Lureeal with laconic whit.

We will crush them like the insects they are! whispered the Menshad Korum, sending terrible chills into the souls of the remaining Saeemrar clansmen.

THEY ARE AT *the gates.*

I know.

You must leave. The exarch is with them.

Gather the Riders, we must get to the core before Quereshir finds us.

The explosion that breached the gates sent shivers through Bureea as she detonated the psychoconductive crystals embedded in the Saeemrar warriors and simultaneously called for the Scorpionida Rider Host to assemble in the sanctum. There Arbariar lay in her jet-bike, waiting for her wing to fall in. Twelve riders came running in through the blast-shields of the sanctum an instant before they were automatically sealed, following the breach of the great hall. Their jetbikes were already in formation, poised ready for an instant strike at any time, and the riders slid into them as though into a second skin. Indeed, the deep green deflector armour, laced with trickles of blood-red webbing echoed the armour of the Scorpionida Warriors. The bikes sported red-black scorpion's tails at the rear, which encased a shuriken cannon, and two matching pedipalp pincers protruded from the front, which housed the venomous powerblades of jetbike scythes.

The engines fired up, temporarily obliterating the cacophonous chaos of battle in the outer chamber of the temple. *We must get this soul to the core.*

In unison the Riders responded, *Understood.*

Arbariar turned her face to Bureea, though her elegant features were hidden behind the startling red of her helmet, *Hide.* Then, with a twitch of her right wrist, the engine roared into life and the jetbike parallaxed into a stream of greens and reds, searing through the escape tunnel that ran from the back of the sanctum and bursting out into the jungles of the life-dome of Saim-Hann, her Wild Riders in close pursuit.

Bureea felt the fatal silence fall in the great hall, and she climbed up the steps in front of the scorpion altar to face the enemy when they came through the blast-shields. The emerald doors to the sanctum began to glow with orange heat, radiating out from the centre where the melta-beam must have been concentrated on the other side. With a sudden roar and a deafening sonic blast, a golden figure burst through the molten ruins, tucked into a ball as though fired from a cannon. The Menshad Korum exarch rolled to his feet at the base of the stairs to the altar, and his Saeemrar Bloodguard climbed through the ruins of the blast-shields to fan out behind him.

Where is She? Where is She?

The question echoed powerfully in Bureea's mind, but she could not identify its psychic source. She considered Quereshir closely.

Again you come too late, son of Vlalmerch. Bureea held her ground in the face of the towering might of the exarch. She was a wych-seer of the Scorpionidas and would give nothing to this weak and deluded mind.

Where is She? The question returned, more powerful, more emphatic, and Bureea pushed her head into her hands in a vain attempt to shut out the voice.

Where is She? The question repeated itself over and over, beating against the inside of her skull, obliterating her own thoughts and yet compelling her to answer. In an instant, Quereshir knew Arbariar's plan, and he summoned his Wild Riders who lay in wait outside the temple.

Bureea slumped to her knees in front of the altar, her eyes bulging in their sockets under the pressure in her head, aghast at the single-minded power of the exarch before her. Was that really his psychic voice? Sharing her last moment of horror with her one-time ally, she asked, *Did you ever see your father's waystone? Do you know why he hid it beneath that armour you wear?*

By the time the Saeemrar Wild Riders arrived, Bureea was dead, and he who was once Quereshir slid easily into his jetcycle at the head of the squadron. The Saeemrar Riders shimmered in their bloodstained bikes, golden fins projecting on each side, bristling with fusion barrels. On the nose of every machine, enlivened by icons of twisting flames, protruded a rapier-like fire-lance.

'They are heading for the core,' hissed the voice of Quereshir through the bike's comm-channel. 'They seek to cast the soul of Vlalmerch into the infinity circuit and bring doom to Saim-Hann. Our ancient House shall not be implicated in this black treachery, this compact with the unspeakable ones.'

For Vengeance and Glory! 'For vengeance and glory!' cried the exarch as he kicked his jetcycle into gear and it rocketed forward into the escape tunnel. 'For the Saeemrar and Saim-Hann!' called Lureeal, as he powered after his lord.

* * *

ARBARIAR FLASHED THROUGH the jungle, the blurred greens of her bike blending incisively into the foliage. She wove urgently through the trees, scything down those that she could not avoid. Following in her jet-stream came the Scorpionida Riders, each willing themselves to greater and greater speeds, conscious of the plans that were unfolding amongst the leaves around them.

Second wing, fall back and provide cover.

Understood.

Six riders broke away from the pack, peeling off to the right in a delicate chain formation, curving back to retrace the vapour trails of the leading riders. They slowed to subsonic speeds as their seer-screens flickered into life, indicating twelve hostiles approaching hyper-sonically. The six Scorpionida Riders fanned out to form an offensive pincer, with the flanks twenty metres in advance of the centre.

'Accelerate to attack speed.'

'Understood.'

The Scorpionida Riders lay flat onto their bikes as they accelerated through the trees, heading directly for the advancing Saeemrar, who showed no sign of slowing.

'There, on the horizon.'

'Affirmative. Targets acquired.'

As one, the Scorpionida squadron banked slightly to their left, widening their formation to outflank the larger numbers of Saeemrar Riders who roared through the space that separated them. Scorpionidas and Saeem-rar opened fire simultaneously, shuriken cannons and fusion bolters filling the rapidly diminishing space with horrifying noise and superheated shards of death. Two of the Saeemrar machines abruptly fell behind the attacking line before accelerating off into flanking arcs to each side. Two more coughed and plumed smoke into the air, losing their stabilisers in a hail of shuriken, spinning over and over before drilling into trees in javelins of fire.

Then the space was closed and the Wild Riders flashed past each other, weaving through a frenzy of lances and scythes. Four Saeemrar Riders slowed into a turn to continue the joust whilst the rest powered on after Arbariar, joined belatedly by the two flankers who had fled the fight. Three golden helmets rolled on the jungle floor, sliced from their bodies by the pincer scythes of the Scorpionida wing. Impaled on the lances of two of the turning Saeemrar, the surviving Scorpionidas could see two of their comrades, hanging limply. Balls of flame in the undergrowth indicating the fate of their bikes.

Lureeal released a blinding flash of fire from his lance, incinerating the eldar slumped over the nose of his machine, and gouging great chunks out of the attacking line of Scorpionidas. He kicked his bike into gear and charged back into the fray, fusion barrels glowing with discharge and his lance blazing a path before him. The two green bikes in the centre of the Scorpionida formation pulled up in flames before exploding in mid-air, sending burning shrapnel scattering into the foliage, igniting fires in the undergrowth wherever it landed.

The two remaining Scorpionida Riders had closed into proximal range, sliding their bikes sideways into the stampeding line of Saeemrar, twisting their pincer scythes and wrenching the firelances free from two of the blood-red machines, causing the bikes to destabilise and strafe with internal explosions.

Lureeal banked his machine sharply as he overshot the combat zone, and then accelerated back into the mangled mess of explosions and twisted chassis. He arrived with fusion flaring from his golden fins, catching the fuel cells of a Scorpionida bike which was struggling to free itself from the contorted remains of its prey. The bike bucked and exploded, obliterating a Saeemrar Rider who was blazing in from the rear.

Lureeal drew his powerblade as his guns overheated and launched himself from his bike onto the back of the remaining Scorpionida, sending his own jetcycle spiralling uncontrolled into a tree. Lureeal lifted his blade and plunged it vertically down through the back of the Wild Rider who lay beneath him, fighting desperately to keep control of his machine. The blade passed straight through the treacherous eldar, rupturing a clutch of fuel lines in the bike below, and the machine was transfigured into a sudden fireball. Lureeal, captain of the Saeemrar Bloodguard, grinned with the perfection of his end as the flames consumed him.

LELITH'S TEETH SHONE brilliantly in the intense darkness of her seer-chamber. Her lips were a breath apart, as she carelessly toyed around the point of an extended incisor with her tongue. The images cycling through her mind pleased her, and she was enjoying the delicate pleasure of picking between the various victories that were unfolding into her future. The seeds planted a century before were blossoming perfectly into barbed and poisonous fruits – she could taste their bitter delights in her own acidic saliva. The craftwar of Saim-Hann was underway.

A gentle breeze breathed into the chamber, swirling the cool air into a vapour that curdled around the wych queen like a cloak of mist. Lelith shrugged her sculpted shoulders, as though shaking free of an unwanted hand, sending her hair into cascades of shimmering blackness. The mist swirled into an eddy in the centre of the chamber, dragging its rejected tendrils across Lelith's skin, leaving tiny, reluctant silver trails drawn over her back.

The runes that swam over the iridescent walls of the chamber began to glow with a red so deep that it was almost imperceptible in real space. Waves of sha'iel pulsed through the calligraphy, rippling the colours and shapes between multiple realms of existence.

Lelith shivered slightly, disliking the moisture that was seeping into the atmosphere of her chamber from an infinitely fertile world. She narrowed her eyes, waiting for the messenger to take its chosen form, squinting her disdain into the shapeless mist that intruded in her space. The languorous fog offended her with its lack of urgency. The liberties it took with her skin would have damned any other being to exquisite heights of pain and suffering. But there was no threat that she could extend to this visitor, and that angered her even more.

Eventually, a shape began to form in the spiralling mist. It was hardly visible in the darkness of the seer-chamber, just the suggestion of vapour in the air. Lelith recognised the vague face at once. She had been expecting him. The under-determined figure in the mist suggested a staggering beauty, and even Lelith felt a smile fight for a brief moment on her face. In the air around the manifestation, a gorgeous scent started to disseminate into the chamber. Lelith noted it without any outward signs of recognition, allowing the rich stench of blood to flood in between her lips, leaving the tantalizing taste of death on her tongue. The cool of her seer-chamber was ruined by fecund moisture and, despite herself, Lelith loved it.

I have come to thank you, Lelith, for the morsel you sent to me.

Lelith watched in fascination as the figure's mouth formed the soundless words that eased into her mind with velvety smoothness. This thing was disgustingly impressive.

We have a bargain, she replied. *There is no place for gratitude here.*

Yes, we have a bargain, and morsels were not part of it, Lelith. I grow weary of waiting.

Lelith twitched at duplicity of the languid wretch, wrenching herself out of the nauseating reverie that had threatened to overcome her. *Be gone, messenger! I am aware of our terms. My ways are more subtle than yours. My plan is underway and there will be thousands of souls ripe for our harvest soon.*

THE BURNING WRECKAGE of two more Scorpionida Riders blurred past Quereshir, falling behind in plumes of smoke and flame. They tumbled into the oncoming rush of his wingmen, destroying the last of his squadron in an immense collision. The exarch's fusion guns fired continuously, sending molten volleys into the trails of the fleeing traitors. Bursting out of the jungle and into the wraithbone edifice of the craftworld itself, he wove through the narrow infrastructural corridors of Saim-Hann with consummate skill, anticipating the ventilation tubes or sudden corners before they appeared – as though guided by some external force. Not even Arbariar could match his skill. Despite the years she had spent mastering the Aspect Arts of the Striking Scorpions, she was no match for an exarch. He was gaining on her, drawing more speed from his hate and his desperate need not to be too late again. At last his bolts tore into the engine of the final Scorpionida Rider, sending it spiralling into the immovable wraithbone wall.

Now it is only us!

The two riders flashed through the labyrinth of tunnels that perforated the craftworld of Saim-Hann, heading deeper and deeper into its skeletal structure. Despite himself, Quereshir was impressed by the skill of his prey; he grinned in anticipation of the battle to come, clicking his fusion guns from automatic to manual.

This is not what you think. Quereshir squinted his eyes to shut out the thoughts of Arbariar, squeezing off a thread of light from his firelance to silence the voice in flame. The Scorpionida chieftain bobbed smoothly over the lancefire as it scored the underside of her bike, sending pulses of heat through the machine's chassis. *Your father will be safe in our spirit pool, it is his only hope. He would bring doom to you, exarch.*

There is No Hope, only Fate. A distant thought echoed into both of their minds.

Arbariar flicked on her guidance-seer and inhaled sharply when she saw how close she was; perhaps ten seconds separated her from the core. She moved her feet into the firing stirrups of the shuriken cannon and turned it through 180 degrees, facing back toward the hunter at her heels. Clicking the mechanism to automatic, she could hear the plasti-crystal generator whine into life, and the magnetic repulsor began to rattle off thousands of arbitrary shards into her wake.

The exarch watched the Scorpion's sting revolve to face him, jetting out showers of tiny shurikens, filling Arbariar's slipstream with a dark venomous cloud. He angled his jetcycle up to the ceiling of the passage, skimming over the lining of the fog and scraping all of the paint off the belly of his machine. From his new vantage point he rapidly squeezed off two fusion bolts, which flashed down into the coolant chambers on the Scorpionida's bike, pushing it towards the ground and disabling its thrusters.

Arbariar wrestled with the controls, but her bike was shaking violently. It ploughed into the wraithbone deck with a shrill scrape, sending sparks flying through the passage way. The machine skidded and tumbled along the corridor, but Arbariar leapt clear before it crashed into the apex of a vicious twist in the tunnel, rolling to her feet into readiness.

Quereshir dipped the nose of his bike and spun the rear through 180 degrees, sliding into a stationary hover as he overshot the wreckage on the deck beneath him.

With only a fraction of hesitation, he clicked the fusion guns back onto automatic and fired up the lance, everything searing through the air toward his downed foe. Then he kicked the bike into motion and charged down at her.

Arbariar danced beautifully between the droplets in this rain of death, spinning and flipping her way through an invisible, safe path in the torrent. As Quereshir drew near, she powered up her Scorpion's Claw, releasing a tirade of shuriken from the cannon that ran from the gauntlet along her arm, and then forced the cleaving powerfist up into the weakened underbelly of Quereshir's machine. The jetcycle spluttered and then erupted, oozing flames through the passage and sending the exarch clattering to the ground.

Quereshir landed heavily, but was quickly on his feet, bathing in the flames that licked at his golden armour. Immediately he was charging at the Scorpionida chieftain, fusion pistol flaring and power sword circling with a lethal flourish. Arbariar dropped to one knee, perfectly placing a single shuriken into the left arm of the frenzied exarch.

Quereshir winced with the impact, and seethed in anger as the psychotoxins forced him to release his grip on the fusion gun. But then he was on her, his blade piercing her chest as she staggered to her feet. The mandiblasters in her helmet spat impotently as the exarch lifted her off her feet, draped over the blade of his sword.

'Give me my father's soul!'

That Soul is Mine. Arbariar had been nauseated by those voiceless words before, and they made her hesitate. *Quereshir, wait…*

With both hands, she clasped the blade that punctured her body, trying to relieve some of the weight that was slowly cutting her in two. 'You must not blend his soul into the spirit pool of the Menshad Korum,' she whispered, blood beginning to trickle from the corner of her mouth. 'It is too close to the abyss already. He will bring ruin to your Kin and darkness to our people. It is the worst of all possible futures. He will reap war on Saim-Hann. In craftwar only the unspeakable ones can win.'

Quereshir could not believe his ears, 'You dare to insult the honour of the Saeemrar! You who would commit us all to ages of war and destruction by casting the waystone into the core?'

'Perhaps, but that future is uncertain, and is a less bloody path in the end. We can protect him. Let the core cleanse his soul and intertwine him with the good. It is his only hope. Do it for him. For us there is only calculated risk.'

There is no Hope, only the Inevitable. The distant voice echoed into their minds again.

Quereshir could contain his fury no longer, and he ripped his blade from the body of Arbariar, splitting her in two and flicking her own pulsing emerald waystone from her breast. He stooped down to her body, watching the last remnants of her life blink silently out of her eyes. There, tightly gripped in the lifeless Scorpion Claw, was his father's soul, shimmering and utterly black.

The son of Vlalmerch stared wordlessly into the palm of his vanquished foe, and something deep within him stirred in revulsion, but it came too late. From somewhere outside, a voice oozed into his mind, *That Soul is Mine, it was Pledged to Me Long Ago.*

Quereshir could feel the voice seducing him, fragments of it already riddled the psycho-plastics of his armour, compelling his body. *The Path of the Exarch is Lonely and Savage, Precarious. You are the Menshad Korum.*

The son of Vlalmerch reached down for his father's waystone. Resigned, desperate and horrified, he pushed it into the breast-plate of his ancient armour, already studded with the souls of all of those who had worn it before. He could feel the icy chill spread out over the spirit pool, and he could sense the other souls reeling in anguish as the darkness descended upon them. Horror flooded into his blood as the spirit swam through his body, already irrevocably synthesised with the ancient armour. His own soul twisted in revulsion and withdrew into itself, petrified with shame and terror. It could do nothing as Quereshir's mind fell into the abyss and his intent became filled with darkness.

Far away, in the lashes of the Eye of Terror, he who was once Quereshir felt the motion of a giant starship entering the webways.

Sow the seeds, reap the harvest. Darkness comes for you.

Picking Arbariar's emerald waystone from the floor, the Lost Warrior turned to harvest more fruits before the arrival of his queen.

XENOCIDE

Simon Jowett

Prologue

AGRA – 'THE EMPEROR'S *Garden'. Imperial Cartographic Designation: Samax IV. Alpha-class agricultural world. 1.75% Terran mass. Single continental landmass. Climate: temperate. Soil profile: high yield. Exploitable ores, minerals, etc: low-yield.*

Surveyed M35,332. Conquered M35,375. Lost M40,666.

– Extract from 'A Concordance of Pre-Heresy Cartographic Data Spools' Vol. XXV. Librarium Collegium Astropathica.
M41,572

'FATHER! COME QUICK!'

Brael Corfe was in the livestock shed when he heard his son's shout of excitement. Moloch, the young buck Brael was hoping would replace Magog, the ageing sire that presided over the farm's herd of milk-heifers, had gone lame. Brael had moved him into the shed and was treating the traces of green-white hoof rot that he had found on one of the animal's front feet.

The mould was a common enough pest. If it was noticed soon enough and treated with a well-known medicament composed from various local roots and herbs, it was soon eradicated. If left to develop, however, it would invade the core of the animal's hoof, reducing it to an evil smelling mush and leaving the farmer no choice but to destroy the animal.

'Father! Mother! The sky's on fire!' Bron was jumping up and down in the yard. Brael dipped his hands in the water trough by the shed door and wiped them dry on a scrap of cloth as he walked across the yard towards Bron. The yard was a squared-off half-circle, centred on the well from which Corfe men and women had been drawing water for generations, and bounded to the east and west by the long, low structures of the livestock shed and the hay barn.

Across the northern edge of the semi-circle, its door facing south, stood the farmhouse. The shed and barn had wooden roofs, the farmhouse roof was thatched. Warm, yellow light from an animal-fat lantern burned in the window of the kitchen, its shutters were open as were all the others on this gentle summer night. Bron had been born beneath the farmhouse's broad low thatch, as had Brael, his father and his father before. Men of the Corfe clan had lived and died hereabouts for countless generations; Brael fully expected that he and Bron would do the same.

Bron was jumping about in the middle of the yard. Had it been daytime, he would have been able to look out across the flat, fertile grassland upon which Brael and his cousins grazed their herds. On a clear summer's day, it was possible to see as far as the Southern Hills, three days' ride from Brael's farm. Ownership of land meant little when there was so much of it. Ownership of stock and crops was much more important and, for better than three days' ride in every direction, the name attached to the livestock and crops was Corfe. Hardly a day went by without Brael looking forward to teaching Bron what it meant to be a Corfe and to work the land.

Brael saw Vika emerge from the house, also wiping her hands. Bron got his excitable nature from his mother, Brael was sure. He loved to listen to her stories of heroes from the distant past, of men who could fly like birds and shoot fire from their eyes. Some of the stories were thrilling, even Brael would admit that.

Unlike his wife, however, Brael didn't believe them to be true.

'Can you see them?' Bron asked, pointing up into the night sky. 'You can see them, can't you?'

Brael reached his son and followed the boy's gaze skyward. Lines of light were drawing themselves across the night, arcing north along long curved trajectories.

'Falling stars, Bron,' Brael told his son. He ruffled the boy's fine, fair hair. He got that from his mother, too; Brael's hair, like his father's, was thick and dark. 'You've seen falling stars before. That's all they are.'

'I've never seen this many before,' Bron replied. He looked up at Brael, and then at his mother, who had joined them and was also watching the starfall.

'Is it the star gods?' Bron asked. 'Are they coming?'

'Bron...' Brael began.

'We live in hope, Bron,' Vika replied. 'We have faith in the Varks.'

'Vika, they're just falling stars,' Brael said. 'Nothing more.'

'The *Dogma* says there'll be signs and wonders, doesn't it?' Bron looked to Vika for confirmation. The only book in the house was Vika's copy of *The Dogma of the Holy Varks*. Vika used it to teach Bron to read; he was the first Corfe that was able to do much more than make his mark. Vika smiled down at him and looked as if she were about to say something.

'Your Aunt Brella used to believe in signs and won-ders,' Brael cut in. Vika rolled her eyes. She had heard this story before. 'Once she claimed to have seen a buck walk backwards and say her name. She said that this meant your mother would have a girl child and that she would be unlucky. You were born eight months later.'

'But she didn't know I was pregnant,' added Vika.

Brael couldn't find an answer to that. Brella had already been ancient when he was born and had a rep-utation for knowing things she shouldn't have known. By the time Brael had brought Vika home, Brella seemed impossibly old, clinging onto life by her iron will and the preservative effect of the grain liquor that was her preferred tipple. The drink was held to be responsible for some of the wilder inaccuracies in her presentiments.

But somehow she had known of Vika's pregnancy before Vika had mentioned it to anyone but Brael.

'Does this mean we're going to visit the temple again?' Bron asked. Vika had wanted him blessed by the priests of the Varks, in their temple in the southern city of Mallax. It was called the Iron Town, thanks to the foundries and workshops that fouled the air with their smoke and noise. 'I'm old enough to remember it, now.'

'We'll go again one day,' Brael replied, remembering the clattering iron caravan journey south – ten days and nine nights. 'When you're older and I've taught you how to run this place.' He massaged his neck. An ache was beginning to blossom at the back of his head. He recognised it as the start of the throbbing pain that had, on occasion, confined him to a darkened room for the best part of a day.

Brella had a phrase for it. 'Wisdom trying to fight its way out,' she'd say, then fix Brael with a significant look. Brael would smile, kiss the old woman, and offer to refill her glass.

'Headache?' Vika asked. Brael nodded. 'I know just the thing to make it go away.' She paused and smiled. 'And if that doesn't work, I'll just have to send you to bed with a cold cloth over your eyes,' she added. She took Brael's arm and turned back to the farmhouse.

'Can I watch the sky a bit longer?' Bron asked.

'Why not?' Brael replied, smiling at his wife. 'They're only shooting stars, after all.'

Vika thumped him playfully on the chest.

'Don't stay out here too long,' she told Bron. 'I'll expect you to be in bed before moonrise.'

'I will,' Bron replied. 'You go and look after Dad's headache.' There was such a knowing tone in his voice that Brael and Vika stared at each other, both struggling not to laugh, as they walked to the kitchen door.

BRAEL DIDN'T REMEMBER falling asleep. He woke to find a shaft of silver light cutting through a gap in the bedroom shutters. The moon must have risen while he slept. Judging by the intensity and angle of the moonlight, it was close to its zenith. Dawn was still some way off.

Brael couldn't remember what he had been dreaming, or why it should have woken him. He eased up into a sitting position, careful not to disturb Vika. Blinking and absently rubbing the back of his neck, he looked down at her, still asleep beside him, fair hair fanned out around her head. He felt a familiar tightness in his chest. He had felt that same tightness the first time he laid eyes on her.

Brael's father had been still years from the grave when Brael accompanied his elder cousin Ralk on an iron caravan to the annual market at Giant's Pass, at the foot of the North Hills. The gentle, rising country marked the border between the wide rich grasslands and the ragged hill country that grew wilder and steeper with every day's travel north. The ancient, smoke-belching engines that travelled the iron roads, all of which had their terminus in Mallax, were of no use in the north country. Here the people moved their flocks from peak to peak in search of pasture and wintered in valleys where the snow would pile as high as the roofs of their stone-walled cabins.

'Northern women are like the bleaters they tend,' Ralk had warned Brael with a smile. 'Always ready to wander off and never know when to quieten down.' Brael laughed; he knew how Ralk's wife, Jenna, would react if she heard her husband. Women raised among the wide, grassy plains of Brael's homeland were more than capable of using a sharp tongue or flying kitchen bowl to make their opinions known, and Jenna's aim was legendary.

Brael stayed in the north after Ralk returned with the rest of the caravan to the grasslands. He endured the biting winds and unremitting cold of the hilltops and the well-meant ridicule of Vika's kinfolk; they were sure he'd be dead before Vika deigned to return his attentions. Luckily for his frozen, aching limbs they were wrong.

Vika's independent mind and adventurous spirit both attracted and puzzled Brael. Even by the standards of the hill clans, her family were particularly well travelled. Brael was surprised to learn that they had travelled as far south as Mallax, primarily to visit the Temple of the Holy Varks, home of an obscure sect, hardly known beyond the city walls. Brael had considered this no more than a curiosity of her family history until she fell pregnant with Bron. One night, as they lay together, she had told him that after the birth she wanted to take their child south to be blessed at the temple.

Brael had been unsure. All he had heard of Mallax were travellers' tales of a smoke-clogged, soot-blackened scab of a place. Once the men of Mallax worked in shafts and galleries beneath the ground, tearing rock from the earth, then transforming it through ancient processes into the knives and ploughshares used by farmers everywhere, and the swords and lances with which the city barons armed their militias.

But that had been long ago. Men no longer ventured beneath the earth. Instead, the men of Mallax spent their time repairing what their forefathers had made: the tools and the machines, including the engines that pulled the iron caravans. Meanwhile, the stones of their city grew ever blacker from the dirt spewed into the air by the chimneys of the city's workshops.

He had been about to forbid the journey when he caught sight of something in her eyes, in the set of her jaw. She would go without him, and take their new babe with her. Some men in his family would have called him a fool, but the moment he realised that, he also remembered why he loved her.

Six months after Bron's birth, he arranged for his nephew Rebak to look after the farm while he and his new family travelled south.

Mallax was everything he had heard it to be and more. The noise was worse than deafening, it was an assault: the hammering of metal on metal; the cries of foremen and workers; the rushing, artificial inhalations and explosive, hissing exhalations of engines like those that pulled the caravans, only much, much bigger. There was a reek of burning metal always in the air and grit crunching between your teeth. When Brael looked skyward, past the forest of smoke stacks that seemed to jostle for space above the tallest of the city's rooftops, it was as if he were looking through a grey veil, a gauze of smoke and grit and the combined excrescence of too many souls packed too closely together.

Brael was not a bumpkin. He had visited Vinara, the city-state that claimed administrative control over the region in which his family farmed and to which they paid regular tithes of produce. He had also made one trip to Primax, the greatest of the city-states. Both were large, bustling, curtain-walled cities, home to powerful families and their militias and the temples of deities associated with the seasons and the fertility of crops, beasts and men. They were every bit as crowded as Mallax and probably not much cleaner. But the smells of Vinara and Primax were those that he recognised – animals, crops and dirt – and they didn't seem to cling to your skin like a thin film of oily fat.

Vinara belonged to its landscape; its stepped streets mirrored the vine-planted terraces that surrounded it. Primax seemed to share the grandeur of the vast prairies of productive farmland at whose centre it sat. Mallax, by contrast, was a dark, cacophonous imposition on the land.

During their journey, Vika had explained to Brael the Dogma of the Varks.

'It is a beacon,' she had told him, shouting over the constant clattering of the caravan's iron wheels. 'It is by its invisible light that the gods will find their way back to us.'

The gods had been born among the stars, Vika explained. They had travelled together in peace and joy until, becoming tired, they had set down on this world and rested here for centuries. During this time, they gave birth to the first true inhabitants of this world, the ancestors of everyone now living on the world they named Agra, which meant 'farm' in the star gods' holy tongue. But, just as paradise seemed complete, they were called away to confront a vast, unknowable danger that threatened to destroy all that was good and pure.

So that their children should not feel abandoned, the gods gave them the Varks. Some stories claimed that every child of the gods had a Varks of their own, through which the gods spoke, promising their anxious children that one day, when the danger had been defeated, they would return.

But they didn't return. The Varks fell silent. Generations passed and the children of the gods changed, forgetting their heritage and the knowledge their parents had given them. The huge, glittering machines with which they once tended the open grasslands and even took to the air like birds fell out of use, then fell apart as the knowledge required to maintain them was lost.

The last remaining Varks was housed in the temple in Mallax and only in Mallax did people struggle to preserve the knowledge of the gods and to maintain what few examples remained of their wonders. Without their efforts, the iron caravans would have long ago ceased to run and the only means of transport that remained would have been of the four-legged variety.

Though he said nothing about it, Brael was amazed that his wife could believe such nonsense. While there may once have been machines as miraculous as those in the stories – it was not unusual for unfamiliar objects, battered and rusted by unguessable ages underground, to be unearthed during the digging of a sewer ditch – they had been made by men and abandoned by those same men, probably for very good reasons of their own. As far as Brael was concerned, the land was the land, men were men and beasts were beasts.

Brael remembered the dark and relative quiet of the Temple of the Holy Varks, separated from the rest of the city by its high precinct wall. There was a low hum that seemed to pervade the space, but it was not unpleasant.

Hooded priests moved to and fro, their footsteps scuffing on the flagstoned floor.

He hadn't known what to expect, but this wasn't it. It looked pretty much like every temple he had ever seen.

'Only the priests stand before the Varks,' Vika had explained. 'They take our prayers to it and bring its blessings back.'

One of the priests had noticed them. He padded over to greet them and threw back his cowl.

BRAEL OPENED HIS eyes with a jolt of surprise. He had dozed, only to jerk awake again when his head lolled forward. The memories of meeting Vika, having Bron and travelling south had raced through his mind in a matter of heartbeats. And, judging by the familiar tightness at the base of his skull, the headache he had gone to bed with was about to pay a return visit.

Easing himself out of bed he padded from the bedroom to the kitchen, where moonlight shone brightly in through the unshuttered windows. His mouth was dry and gummy, so he decided to wind up a bucket from the well, take a sip and then splash the chill water over the back of his head. He glanced out through the kitchen window. There was something in the yard. A body.

Bron had not gone to bed as his mother had asked. He had lain on the packed earth and counted the shooting stars, eventually falling asleep where he lay.

Brael smiled down at his son, then went outside and gathered him gently into his arms. Before turning back to the house, he spared a glance skywards. The light of the moon had all but obliterated the stars he knew to be there and there was no trace of the falling stars that had so entranced his son.

A sickly yellow blotch blossomed behind his eyes and his stomach lurched. Vika's ministrations had merely delayed the inevitable. By the time he reached the kitchen door his head was pounding. After slipping Bron into his bed he returned to lay beside his wife, pustules of gaudy colour swimming behind his closed eyelids until morning.

Part One

From the collation of survivors' reports and the analysis of the few pieces of documentary evidence thus far unearthed and translated from this planet's debased form of pre-Heresy Imperial Gothic, the invasion of Samax IV appears to have proceeded exactly as one would have expected. The invaders were technologically superior. The indigenous population were limited in their technology, but enjoyed a vast numerical superiority.

At first the invaders' advance was swift, seizing control of the most northerly quarter of the planet's single continent. Very few reports of the attacks appear to have reached the rest of the population. Transcriptorum Servitors record only one reference to a rumour concerning 'storms in the north' and 'fires among the mountains.'

Over the next year (approx. 1.25 Terran solar cycles) the invaders moved south. Again their initial gains were swift, but news of their advance travelled quickly through the more populous central regions. Evidence has been found of some *disbelief in early reports of the invaders' progress from the mountains. Gorna Haldek, a diarist and civil functionary in the court of Luydos, self-styled High Baron of Caspera, describes early reports as: 'the stuff of a child's nightmares, no more.' Caspera was shortly to fall beneath the invaders' advance.*

The few survivors of Caspera's hastily assembled defence force – little more than the city baron's standing militia augmented by every able-bodied inhabitant of the region – were forced to retreat and to swell the ranks of the forces being assembled by the as-yet untouched city-states. This process of catastrophic loss followed by the retreat and regrouping of the remaining forces was to continue down the length of the continent.

These larger forces would succeed in slowing the invaders' advance, albeit briefly. Some units of the defenders were equipped with ancient slug-throwers (Cross ref. 665/1468-archeotech designations: flintlock; wheel-lock; musket) and the wreckage of primitive artillery pieces has been unearthed along the invaders' route south. There appear to have been rare instances of the defenders learning to use weapons captured from the invaders. However, the defenders' main weapon was their numbers and their willingness to fight to the death.

When this was set against the technological superiority of the invaders, and combined with the invaders' inhuman predilection for bloodshed, the eventual outcome could never have been in doubt.

The inhabitants of Samax IV were doomed.

> *– Extract: 'Inquisitorial communiqué 747923486/aleph/Samax IV' Author: Inquisitor Selene Infantus. M41,793*

WIPING THE SWEAT from his eyes as he ran, Brael wondered for what might have been the ten thousandth time if this was the day he was going to die.

Ahead of him, Fellick stumbled and almost dropped the long musket he was carrying as the toe of his ragged boot clipped a piece of the debris that littered the streets. Even before the attack, the town – Grellax, Brael remembered someone telling him – had looked like it had been sacked and abandoned.

Grellax had been a well-established market town, set among a landscape of rolling hills. The farmer that Brael had once been, a year and what felt like a hundred lifetimes ago, couldn't help but note that the grass on the hills he had marched over to reach Grellax, in column with the rest of the army – an amalgamation of regiments from Primax, Mundax, Caspera and Terrax – was richer than that of his flatter homeland to the north. The animals raised on this feed would have produced rich milk and dense, wholesome meat.

Grellax had grown prosperous enough to spill beyond its ancient and crumbling walls. Those buildings outside the walls were now ablaze and the walls themselves were shattered, the stone blown to dust by engines of destruction that had no place in this world.

The buildings of Grellax's older quarters were built stoutly of stone quarried some way off, their roofs made of red tile, another indication of the wealth that had resided here. Brael and Fellick were running along one of the broad avenues that ran through the centre of the town, in what must have been a district of shops and taverns, an area dedicated to giving the Grellaxians something to do with their money.

However, since the three ragged armies had rendezvoused outside the town, with the intention of re-provisioning and moving on in a single, combined column, Grellax's inhabitants had been quick to pile what belongings they could into what transport they could find and attach themselves to the rear of the

column. It moved out two days after the last army –
Brael's as it turned out – had arrived.

Brael had been lucky so far – luckier than any normal
man had a right to be, according to some – but he
knew it couldn't last. He and his men were assigned to
join the rearguard.

As he drew level with Fellick, Brael reached out –
with his left hand, the one that had been shorn of its
first two fingers in a skirmish during the withdrawal
through the Cornos Forest, the dense woodland that
marked the border between the baronets of Caspera
and Vinara – and slapped the broad-backed Primaxian
on the shoulder.

'Keep moving!' Brael shouted.

'I wasn't planning on doing anything else!' Fellick
replied without taking his eyes from the street ahead.

The street was lined with shops no one would patro-
nise again, taverns in which tankards would never
again be raised. Their doors hung open, some off their
hinges, as if their owners had torn them away in their
haste to be gone from their homes. And, given what he
had seen in the year since the lights fell from the sky,
Brael could understand why.

A guttural roar came from the end of the street
behind them. Automatically, both men accelerated
their pace.

'Too soon!' Fellick hissed through clenched teeth.
The market square towards which they were running
was still half a street-length away.

Brael heard a second inhuman shout, followed by a
harsh metallic clatter. 'Cover!' he shouted as he
swerved suddenly to the left, slamming into Fellick and
propelling him towards a tavern's hanging door.

An appalling cacophony erupted from the end of the
street: a coughing roar from the many-headed animal
that was devouring the world. As Fellick crashed into

the tavern's main room, Brael knew what was coming next.

Thunderous impacts chewed a line in the dirt behind the men, throwing up a shower of fragments of the street's cobbled surface and the hard-packed dirt beneath. In the heartbeat before he crossed the tavern's threshold, Brael risked a glance along the street.

Two of them came towards him at a run, firing from the hip, bandoliers jangling about their impossibly broad and deep torsos as they came. They looked like statues come alive, statues carved from dark green boulders cast upon the shore from the furthest depths of the ocean. Tusks like those of the sea-cows that migrated every year from the frozen northern sea jutted from their lower jaws and, even at this distance and in so brief a glance, Brael would swear that he could see the malevolence burning redly in their deep-set eyes.

Another burst from the engine-driven rifles they carried so casually, when it would take a strong man most of his strength even to lift one, tore the doorway to shreds moments after Brael had disappeared inside.

The tavern had been ransacked during the evacuation. Pitchers, flagons and jars had been smashed, tables and chairs overturned. A trapdoor behind the bar stood open, and the rich scent of spilt ale rose from the cellar beneath. The landlord clearly had decided that his stock would provide no refreshment to the invaders.

Fellick preceded Brael through the bar room, moving parallel to the street as quickly as possible. The thunder of the greenskins' engine-rifles continued to batter their senses and flying splinters slashed and bit at their faces as the rifle shells chewed through the lathe and plaster of the tavern's frontage. The projectiles burst into the bar and slammed out through the rear wall, their momentum barely impeded by the building's substance. Supporting uprights and crossbeams were sliced through like saplings cut down by a single axe-stroke. With a chorus of explosive groans, the bar began to collapse in on itself in the wake of the fleeing men.

Ahead of them was the end wall. To Brael's relief a door stood in its centre. 'Hope it's not a broom cupboard!' Fellick shouted above the skull-shredding shriek of the greenskins' weapons. Two more running strides and he hit the door, left shoulder lowered to take the force of the impact.

The door exploded outwards, spilling Fellick and Brael into a narrow cross-street. A left turn would take them away from the street down which they had been running and along which they knew the invaders were advancing, still spraying the tavern with gunfire and reducing it to little more than kindling. As what remained of the tavern roof fell into the bar with a splintering crash, expelling a cloud of dust and debris out through the end door, Brael and Fellick turned right.

The two men sprinted from the mouth of the cross-street and across the entire width of the main street before jagging back and forth, anxious to present as difficult a pair of targets as possible to the greenskins, who had ceased firing when the tavern roof fell in. Catching the scent of fermented products, they were about to begin picking through the debris when the humans reappeared.

Brael and Fellick raced down the street, their paths crossing and re-crossing, past more abandoned shops, an apothecary's and a butcher/surgeon's. It was important that the greenskins didn't lose sight of them for long. Despite the hazards of the debris-strewn street, Brael risked another glance back. Their pursuers had spotted them; already they were bringing their engine-rifles to bear. And behind them, Brael saw three more hulking figures were making their way down from the far end of the street.

Come one, come all, Brael called to them in his mind as he ran. Ahead, the street opened into the market square. *We'll see our land soaked in your blood before we let it go.*

GRELLAX BELONGED TO the invaders from the moment their war-party appeared on the horizon. Though little more than a vanguard for the army that was advancing inexorably southwards, burning, looting and pillaging as it came, the sight of the creatures, the roar of their war engines, louder and more terrible than the largest iron caravan, and the reek of oil and smoke that soon reached the town walls caused more than one of Grellax's defenders to foul themselves in fear. Brael knew how they felt.

THE FIRST TIME Brael had seen the invaders he had been part of one militia company among many on the flank of the Casperan Combined Companies. He had managed to maintain his self-control until after the battle. The Casperan barons, tutored since childhood in romantic fantasies of war, chose to meet the invaders on a broad plain edged by a low sierra to the west and a wide, fast-flowing river to the east. Stories of war machines that gouted smoke and fired thunder were discounted as the ravings of the mad.

When the greenskin army came into view, the barons had expected them to stop, perhaps to parley before the battle, as the heroic code demanded. The last thing they expected the invaders to do was to speed up, closing the gap between the armies faster than a gallop, their roaring, wheeled machines pluming black smoke and their engine-driven rifles barking death.

Brael, along with most of his company, broke and ran before the invaders reached their lines. They left twenty men lying dead on the field, holes punched in their bodies by the greenskins' weapons, fired from impossible distances. His company only stopped running when they had reached the cover of the woods that hugged the riverbank. Then his self-control deserted him and he vomited uncontrollably into the bright, clear water.

Brael learnt a valuable lesson that day – a year ago, by the time he arrived at Grellax: do not engage the invaders in a pitched battle on open ground. If only the barons had learnt the same lesson.

THE SMALLER WAR engines attacked Grellax first, racing in on two or three fat wheels, trailing clouds of smoke and oil. Machine-rifles chattered and coughed from fixed mounts on the engines' bodywork or from separate gunners' stations behind the rider or in sidecars. A few of the attackers tossed explosive charges at the old town walls, hastily patched up in anticipation of the attack and manned mainly by Grellaxians who were too old or too stupid to leave, bolstered by a smattering of more experienced fighters. The shells from the invaders weapons did enough damage, punching through ancient stonework and shredding the bodies sheltering behind it; the explosives tore holes in the fortifications large enough to drive bull-carts through, two abreast.

The foot soldiers ran forward as the war engines retreated, some of them spraying the walls with gunfire from the machine-rifles they carried, which were not very much smaller or lighter than those that were mounted on the two and three-wheelers. The defenders could only reply with a handful of blackpowder muskets, whose lead balls ricocheted from the plates of metal hung on the attackers' monstrous green bodies. The pair of aged cannon which had stood in the town's main square for generations did more damage, until first one then the other exploded, either due to a fault line in the aged muzzle cracking under the sudden strain or because of inexpert packing by the terrified crew. No one knew or cared. By that point, most of the defenders had fled the walls to begin the ugly process of fighting through the streets, doing their best to delay the inevitable. Grellax would fall. It was just a matter of time.

Brael and Fellick raced across the market square, one of several dotted around Grellax, lined by the houses of the more prosperous merchants. At each corner of the three avenues that led into the square were shops and teahouses, that had once sold pastries and other delicacies. Now the grand front doors hung open, scraps of finery dangled from open windows and littered the square – luxuries dropped and forgotten in the hurry to be gone.

'Five!' Brael shouted, apparently to no one, to the open doors and the empty houses. 'Wait till they're clear of the street!'

Brael ducked behind an upturned farm cart next to the ornate fountain in the centre of the square. Already crouching behind the cart and below the lip of the fountain were several of his men. Two of them – Costes and Perror – had been in the first unit of scratch militia Brael had joined, when the caravans of refugees from the north had begun arriving, adding credence to what had been considered 'only stories.' He knew that Perror in particular was responsible for some of the stories that had begun to circulate about him, but he meant no harm and no one could argue that he wasn't a good man in a fight.

Costes handed Brael a loaded rifle, the pouches containing the musket balls and what remained of his ration of blackpowder. Brael had not wanted to risk the loss of his rifle, should the greenskins have brought him down before he and Fellick had drawn them to the square. Fellick, however, had not let his rifle out of his sight since the war began and had become superstitiously possessive of the weapon. He was convinced that the one sure way to guarantee that the greenskins would have his head would be for him not to take his rifle with him, despite its weight and unwieldy length.

Fellick angled his run towards one of the buildings that edged the square. Brael made a wager with himself that it would turn out to be another tavern. Until the invaders came, Fellick once told him, his life had consisted of two things: beer and butchery. He had worked in the slaughterhouses that supplied meat to the noble houses of Primax. These houses had supplied many of the generals and field commanders of the armies whose retreat Brael's men had been assigned to defend and about whose competence and courage Fellick had strong, uncomplimentary opinions.

As Fellick disappeared through the building's front door, a muzzle appeared above the stone window ledge next to it.

'They're here!' Perror hissed.

Brael peered around the side of the cart. The first pair of their pursuers had come to a stop a few paces inside the square. Warily, they scanned the apparently deserted area, sweeping their machine-rifles in slow arcs. Brael offered a silent prayer to gods he had long ceased to believe in that the greenskins would not notice the rifle barrel pointing at them from across the square.

'Come on, where are the others?' Brael shot a look at Berek, the skinny Casperan who was crouching between Perror and Costes. 'You said there were five,' Berek whispered, struck by Brael's gaze. Costes punched his shoulder and, when Berek turned to protest, placed a finger against his lips.

Perror, who was peering through the gap between the overturned cart and the lip of the fountain, pointed in the direction of the greenskins, then splayed his hand, palm outwards. Five.

'Fuses!' Brael shouted after a glance around the cart confirmed Perror's report. Before pulling his head back behind the cart, he saw the muzzles of five machine-rifles swing in his direction.

The cart disintegrated under the fusillade. Brael was already on his feet, running behind Perror, Costes and the others, hoping to draw the greenskins' fire past them as he ran for the far corner of the square. To the invaders he looked like merely another fleeing human.

Once the arc of fire had passed over their heads, decapitating the ornate stone fountain in the process, Brael's men brought their weapons to bear over the lip of the fountain bowl and let fly. Two of the musket balls panged harmlessly off the greenskins' armour. A third hit one of the invaders just beneath its drooping dog-like ear.

Releasing the trigger of its machine-rifle, the creature swatted at the stinging impact of the musket ball. Seeing on its fingers the ichor that began to run from the wound more and more freely, it bellowed its outrage and adjusted the direction of its fire.

The men were on the move before the greenskin's renewed cannonade smashed chunks from the fountain's stonework and then raced across the cobbles after them.

'Split up!' Perror yelled, then turned sharply away from the others, who also made sudden turns to the left or right. Berek seemed to trip, then make an ungainly jump to his right before landing heavily on the cobbles, his back an exploded ruin.

Musket fire was coming from windows and doors around three of the four sides of the square. The green-skins returned fire, hammering lumps of masonry from the buildings. Though it was probably due to the way the tusks jutted from their lower jaw, lifting the corners of their thick upper lips, Brael thought that they seemed to be almost smiling, enjoying his men's futile attempts to harm them.

Brael took a shot from his new position at the corner of what had once been a shop selling sweet breads and pastries, then ducked back to reload. His fingers dug into the small leather pouch that contained the musket balls. Selecting one, he unconsciously noted that only two remained. In his blackpowder pouch there was enough left for three shots at most.

'Fuses!' he shouted as he reloaded, tapping the ball down and priming the pan with as few grains of the precious powder as he could get away with. Most of the unit's powder reserve had gone towards the charges Kobar had assembled and set in the buildings on the far side of the square.

'Kobar, answer me!' he shouted again. The former quarryman from the north should have retired to cover by now and the twisted fuses should be burning towards the charges. 'The fuses! Did you set the—'

A cannonade of muffled explosions echoed across the square. Compared to the raw, hateful cacophony of the greenskins' machine-rifles, they sounded pathetic. Then came a growing rumble, the grinding of masonry in motion.

Brael risked a look around the corner. The buildings to either side of the street down which he and Fellick had led the invaders were falling, sliding down to earth and throwing out stray chunks of their substance as they fell. All but one of the greenskins was already lost in the plume of dust and debris. There was no time to lose.

'Go!' he bellowed, racing from cover. He left his rifle where he had sheltered and, as he ran, he unhooked the oversized meat cleaver that hung at his belt – a green-skin trophy of the retreat from Erewell. Without having to check, he knew that the rest of the men had also broken cover and were closing on the lone greenskin.

Confused by the sudden acceleration of events, the creature took four or five long heartbeats to realise that he was under direct frontal attack and to decide upon a response. At last it pressed its weapon's trigger.

Jarran flew backwards, her body virtually bisected by the burst of gunfire. Those nearest to her hit the dirt. One of them at least still held a rifle. Its ball pinged uselessly off the beast's breastplate, but it held its attention for long enough for the others to close in.

The greenskin was looking to its left as Brael closed from the right. He was close enough to see the corded muscles of its neck shift; it was about to turn its head towards him. He cocked his right arm back so far that the heavy cleaver threatened to overbalance him. Then, without slowing his pace, he brought it forward.

With a sound like an axe head biting into wood, the cleaver slotted through the gap between the beast's shoulder plate and its bucket-like helmet and bit into the neck. There was no chance of him extracting the blade quickly enough for a second strike, so Brael sprang back, almost stumbling on one of the lumps of masonry that were still falling in the vicinity of the booby-trapped buildings.

Brael heard a shout. Tylor, who had been with them since Erewell, was charging at the stricken greenskin, pike lowered, the weapon's heavy metal tip aimed at the creature's throat.

The pike-head struck sparks from the rim of the beast's breastplate before slamming into its throat. Bitter experience had taught the Agrans that the invaders' skin was as thick and tough as well-tanned leather. To get through it, you needed to strike with the kind of commitment that did not allow for a second chance.

The head of Tylor's pike came to a stop when it struck the massive column of bone and gristle that supported the shovel-jawed head. The greenskin fell where it had stood, bellowing its pain and trying to stem the tidal rush of ichor that issued from the wound.

Still wary of any last reflex-traces of life in the invader's body, Brael stepped around the out-thrown hand that still grasped the oversized machine-rifle, wrenched free the cleaver and hung it back on his belt. Though blood was still singing in his ears from the explosions and the frontal assault on the greenskin, the sounds of other conflicts reached him.

The dust had all but settled from the explosions. Two of the greenskins were nowhere to be seen; buried, Brael assumed, beneath the rubble. That was more luck than they could have expected. Of the remaining two, one had been felled in much the same manner as the corpse that lay at Brael's feet. Fellick, appropriately, was leading the butchery of the still-twitching beast.

The last of the greenskins still had plenty of life in it, despite the fact that it was pinned to the ruined wall of a nearby building by two pikes, the head of one jammed into its shoulder, the second through what in a human body would be the lower ribs. While three of Brael's men and a boy that Brael didn't recognise applied their weight to the pike staves in order keep the creature pinned, it continued to rage and bellow, make sweeping grabs for its tormentors and then reach out for the machine-rifle it must have dropped when the pike-heads struck home.

Something began to nag at Brael's mind as he bent to examine the corpse at his feet. It might have been there for a while, but the noise and confusion of battle had muffled it.

There. Brael spotted a stubby pistol lodged in one of the wide belts that hung about the creature's tree-thick waist. It took both hands to cock the hammer action. Brael held it like a sawn-off scattergun as he quickly approached the trapped and raging beast.

The greenskin was beginning to weaken due to blood-loss and pain, but it was still a long way from being dead. Seeing Brael's approach, Fellick and several of the others began shouting, drawing the beast's attention off to its left. Brael stepped up from its right and pressed the gun to its skull, just behind one ear. Without waiting to see how the creature would react, he braced himself against the recoil and pulled the heavy trigger.

'TIME TO GO,' Brael told Fellick. Most of the men were stripping the green corpses of what little was light enough to be useful: knives as large and long as short swords, hacking weapons like the cleaver Brael wore at his belt, the odd piece of armour or a thick and wide belt made from the skin of an animal that had never walked on Agra.

Costes and Perror had decided to take one of the machine-rifles with them, along with as many belts of shells as the rest of the unit could carry. They had selected the lightest of the weapons and were busily distributing the ammunition belts to the other men.

'You all right?' Fellick asked. He had seen the slightly nauseous expression on Brael's face before. Brael nodded.

'Time to go,' he repeated. The nagging something that had been scratching at the edges of his mind had grown louder, more insistent. As he returned Fellick's concerned gaze, a bilious yellow blob exploded behind his eyes, growing to fill half his vision before it faded.

'Get them moving,' he added, waving Fellick away. Fellick nodded then moved off, shouting for the men to prepare to move.

'I can hear something!' It was the boy – young man really, perhaps seventeen summers old. Brael thought of Bron and immediately regretted it.

The boy was standing beside one of the piles of heavy rubble. He pointed. 'I can hear something,' he repeated. 'Something's moving.'

'What are we supposed to do when they won't even die when you drop a building on them?' Kobar asked. Several of the men laughed.

'More blackpowder next time, Kobar!' called Tylor, prompting more laughter.

'Leave it, boy,' Fellick called. 'We'll be gone by the time they crawl out from under that lot.'

'You're leaving?' the young man seemed incredulous. 'But... but you're here to protect us!'

His words got the loudest laugh of all.

'Sorry kid,' said Costes. 'We were left here to die as slowly as possible so that the rest of the army can get as far away as possible.'

'And now we're leaving, right?' Fellick directed his last word at Brael who, head swimming, managed an unsteady nod.

'Quickly,' he said. 'Very quickly.'

They left the square at a run, most of them jangling with looted ammunition belts, Costes and Perror already swearing about the weight of the machine-rifle they carried between them.

A high-pitched whine peeled through the air, growing in volume, but descending in tone.

In the market square, a slab of masonry shifted. It slid down the side of the pile of other such debris, revealing a green-skinned hand, fingers thick as a baby's arm, and a massively corded forearm, covered in crudely drawn tattoos. A choking sound issued from within the pile; the sound of a creature dying from crushing internal injuries. Those appalling wounds did nothing to dampen the creature's burning, instinctual rage, its over-whelming desire to kill.

From within its ready-made tomb, the creature heard the sound of the incoming ordnance and knew its waaagh was over.

The ground bucked under the men's running feet. Slates fell from the surrounding buildings, shattering on the cobbles over which they ran. The young man, whose name was Vikor Lodz, glanced back as he ran. All he saw was a vast rolling cloud of dust racing along the street towards him.

When the dust cloud overtook them, the men ran on, coughing and spitting as they went. Leaving it behind, they kept up the pace, running over ground that continued to shake from the sound of other impacts. A bombardment had started.

'I thought they'd at least spend some time looting before they pulped the place,' said Tylor. They had finally come to a halt in another square, smaller than the last. The streets in this part of town were narrow, as were the buildings, which seemed to lean across the street towards each other.

At the square's centre stood a votive shrine to a minor harvest deity. Vikor Lodz realised with a start that he was only a few streets from his family home, though his family – just his mother and sister, really – had joined the caravan of wagons that left with the soldiers.

'They probably worked out that they can come back here and loot any time they like,' muttered Tombek, a massively built Vinaran with a melancholic streak. 'It's not as if anyone's going to try to stop them.'

'I thought that was what you – I mean we – were supposed to do,' Vikor blurted out. 'I thought we were going to stop them.'

The absurdity of his words struck him the moment they were out of his mouth. This time, however, the others did not laugh. That only made him feel even worse.

'I'm afraid we're done here, kid,' Brael said. 'All we can do now is stay alive long enough to kill some more of them.'

'We going out the south gate, following the army?' asked Costes. The combined column of the armies and the caravan of refugees had gathered there before moving off. Brael shook his head, as much to clear it of the nagging ache as in answer to Costes's question.

'Even a blind man could follow that trail. You've seen how fast those two-wheeled wagons move. They'd run us down before dusk. I got a look at a map during the briefing for the rearguard. A river cuts through the land on the other side of the hills to the south. The army is heading for a shallow ford that'll allow them to get the wagons across. They've been gone a day and a half, which means they're not far from it by now. There was another crossing point marked on the map, off to the south-east. It looks deeper and wider, but we haven't got to get wagons and horses across it.

'But we still have to get out of here through the south gate, so let's get moving.'

The rest of the men nodded.

Vikor raised his hand. 'You – we – don't have to go out through the south gate,' he said. 'We can go through the stockyards. It would be much quicker and we'd already be heading south-east.'

Brael regarded him for a heartbeat, head cocked as if he was waiting to hear someone whisper to him from his shoulder. Then he nodded.

'All right, young man, lead on.'

As he led the strangers through the stockyards, whose wide gates the retreating army had neglected to secure, past open-sided butchers stalls and over the open blood-sewers that criss-crossed the flagstoned floor,

Vikor thought about his mother and sister, huddled aboard one of the wagons that would be jouncing along in the army's rutted wake. His heart sank at the thought of the invaders' smoke-belching machines catching the civilian wagons at the rear of the column.

'C'mon, kid.' Kobar, who was walking alongside him, looted ammunition jangling across his chest, a pike propped over his shoulder, slapped Vikor on the back. 'Whatever it is you're worrying about, don't bother. What really happens is always going to be worse.'

NAVIGATING BY THE angle and direction of the sun's path across the sky, Brael's men marched south-east at a brisk pace. Their course took them through a gulley in the rolling hill-country, what might have once been a tributary to the river towards which they were heading, but which had dried up generations ago. The land rose on either side of them and the sound of the bombardment, which had hammered at their backs as they left doomed Grellax behind them, gradually faded away.

The gulley curved around the foot of a low hill, taking Brael's men out of direct sight of Grellax. Before he lost sight of the town, Vikor looked back. Plumes of smoke rose over the houses, lit from within by licks of flame, and over the shattered town walls. The wind shifted and he thought he caught the scent of burning wood and something else: the tang of oil.

He remembered his outburst in front of the strangers with whom he now marched and felt a rush of embarrassment. Grellax was dead long before he had realised it. All the greenskins were doing was cremating its corpse.

Then Fellick called to him to keep up and he hurried after his new comrades.

Dusk fell and they marched along the gulley into the night. The moon was on the wane when the sound of fast-running water reached them. They made camp amongst a stand of trees a short way from the steeply-sloping, reed-strewn riverbank and Brael dispatched men to scout the bank in either direction. Only when the scouts had returned with reports that the bank was deserted in both directions and, as far as they could tell, on the far side of the river as well, did Brael allow a small fire. Someone produced a small, battered can and a handful of tea leaves. Someone else had liberated a few scraps of meat from a butcher's stall in the stock-yards.

The combined smells of tea and cooking meat drifted on the air as Vikor told his story: after seeing off his mother and sister – his only family after his father had succumbed to a wasting illness a year and a half ago – in the caravan that followed the army away from Grel-lax, he had been given a pike and was assigned to a reserve platoon. They were to reinforce areas of the wall defences as it became necessary. He and a few of the others were on their way to do just that when something exploded nearby, throwing everything – even his memory, it seemed – into confusion. He remembered blood and screaming and the blank, vacant expression on the face of an old friend as he lay slumped against a wall, one side of his chest a mess of seeping meat and exposed bone. He remembered little after that until he found himself in the market square, where Kobar had been directing the positioning of the booby traps.

'And we were out playing bait,' said Fellick. 'Brael's idea, of course.'

'Sounded like suicide to me,' said Massau. Vikor had noticed that the slender man with what had once been a carefully-clipped moustache drooping over his upper lip did not share the others' sense of closeness.

'Brael's no fool,' Costes replied. 'He was probably safest of all of us.'

'What do you mean?' Vikor asked.

'Bumpkins' superstitions!' Massau scoffed before anyone else could answer. The others shot him looks that ranged from pity to contempt.

'You weren't with us at Erewell,' Perror said. 'There were twenty of us just before things got really bad. Ten of us didn't listen to Brael.'

'Coincidence!' Massau blustered.

'And why aren't we still in the square back there, picking over the greenskins as the bombardment came in on top of us?' Costes asked. 'You may not have had much use for things you can't record in your guild's ledgers, but you're not in Primax now, you–'

'I agree with Massau.' Heads turned sharply. Brael was standing over them. He had been listening, unseen, from a short way off. 'We make our own luck by keeping our eyes and ears open for things that might kill us...' He surveyed his men, their faces painted by the firelight.

'And then make sure we kill them first.' The men laughed and nodded. Brael noticed that Massau had missed the point; the Primaxian wore a self-satisfied expression, sure that Brael had proven his argument for him. All Brael cared about was making sure that his men aimed their hatred at the greenskins, not at each other.

He moved away from the fire. Looking up through the trees, he saw that the sky was almost cloudless, the stars as bright as gems. It reminded him of a similar night, a year ago. But he forced himself to think ahead to the route they should take to catch the rest of the army.

It would be so easy to think of Vika and Bron, to imagine how their lives had been since he set them upon an iron caravan's open wagon and waved to them as they pulled away. It would be so easy to imagine how it would feel when he saw them again, among the crowds of people who will have gathered behind Mallax's high walls by the time Brael and his men arrive.

If only he had not woken, less than a month after their departure, gripped by the sure and certain knowledge that they were dead.

DAWN HAD BEGUN to tint the sky when the remains of the fire were kicked over and the men moved down to the riverbank. The water rose to mid-chest and ran quickly and forcefully over slick, rounded rocks. Vikor found the noise of its passage oddly soothing – a reminder of the natural world, after the overwhelming noise of the greenskins' infernal machines. Invisible among the treetops, birds began to sing their greeting to the new day.

They moved carefully across the river, holding their powder pouches overhead as they felt their way around the largest of the riverbed rocks with their toes. Brael was first across, half-sliding down the steep bank into the icy water, pushing through the stiff reeds and then fighting to hold his balance against the strong current, all the while feeling his way with the toe of his boot as the water rose to chest height before the riverbed at last began to rise towards the gentler, less reed-clogged opposite bank.

On the far side, Brael secured a line around the nearest tree and threw it back to Kobar, who was waiting waist-deep in the water. He and the rest of the men used the line to help maintain their balance against the force of the river. With his mutilated hand, Brael would have been unable to take much advantage of it.

The land rose gently ahead of them as they marched away from the river, covered with tough, low-growing shrubs and the occasional moss-encrusted boulder – whether they had rolled down from the hilltops in ages past, or else were left there by ancient floodwaters, Brael couldn't guess.

Again steering by the sun, Brael tried to keep them moving along a south-westerly route that would bring them back in line with the army's southerly course. That was assuming he had remembered the map correctly – he had only seen it for a moment; the minor baron who had given the briefing didn't expect any of the men he was addressing to survive.

Gradually, the roar of the river faded behind them and for a while they marched in silence. The grassy land undulated softly beneath them and maintained a gentle upward gradient. Only the muted noises of the equipment they carried marked the time.

The sun was approaching its noon-point when a new sound reached them: a low rumble. At first, Vikor took it to be distant thunder, though the storm season was still two or three months away. The looks on the faces of his companions made him think again.

'Distek! Kleeve!' Brael beckoned and broke into a run. Distek, a farmer like Brael, and Kleeve, a trader in tanned hides, slipped the ammunition belts they were carrying from their shoulders and ran after Brael, quickly disappearing through a stand of trees that marked the crest of the long rise they had spent the morning climbing.

Those left behind didn't slacken their pace. As they marched, they began to check their own and each other's equipment; those who had rifles loaded and primed their weapons. Costes and Perror began to debate how best to set up the machine-rifle.

The sun had passed the noon-point by the time Distek reappeared, a look of urgency on his face. He beckoned them on then turned and ran back the way he had come. The rest of Brael's men ran up the still-rising land after him. The sound that Vikor had taken to be thunder had long since resolved itself into the sound of explosions punctuated by the ratcheting cough of engine-driven rifles and the deeper growl of two-wheeled war machines.

They passed through the line of trees and were surprised by the suddenness with which the land dropped away, scooping down into a shallow vale dotted by stands of trees. A taller hill rose from the far side of the valley, its top disappearing into the blue distance. Brael and Kleeve were standing at the edge of the drop, staring down at the carnage.

The dead lay along the length and breadth of the valley: a few greenskins, many more Agrans. Trees and shrubs were burning, the ground appeared to have been scorched by the passage of the engines that had rolled over it, slaughtering as they went. A phalanx of two-wheeled machines had run the length of the column from the rear, firing indiscriminately, first at the packed wagons, then the foot soldiers. Wagon drivers had whipped their horses into a gallop, making for the valley sides. The war machines had driven them down, pumping round after round through the wagon's bodywork and the screaming refugees within. The corpses lay with the ruined wagons across the length and breadth of the valley floor.

The small number of mounted fighters had wheeled their horses to face the oncoming greenskins, with predictable results: the torn and shattered bodies of men and their mounts lay among the other corpses of militiamen who had tried to fend off the sudden attack.

Brael remembered the first lesson he had learned: do not engage the invaders in a pitched battle on open ground.

He counted four men still on horseback. A rider whose purple helmet plume identified him as belonging to the Primaxian hussars weaved between two

overturned and shattered wagons, jinking his horse
right and left to avoid the greenskins' fire, until he was
finally able to outflank one of the two-wheeled monstrosities and skewer its rider with his cavalry lance. The
greenskin was hurled from its saddle and the machine
careered away, the gunner seated in the sidecar frantically lunging for the handlebars.

A burst of gunfire from another of the wheeled attack
vehicles cut short the hussar's moment of victory. Both
he and his mount were punched to the ground, gaping
holes torn in their bodies by the high-calibre shells.

Seeing this, the three remaining horsemen wheeled
their horses about and made for the far end of the valley at a gallop, disappearing into the drifts of smoke
that wandered across the vale from the pyres of shattered wagons and scorched corpses.

Gunning their engines, the greenskins roared after the
horsemen, their wheeled war wagons eating up the distance at an impossible rate, their riders howling with
barbaric glee, until they too disappeared into the smoky
distance.

'They must have expected us to run,' muttered Brael.
Fellick had come to stand beside him. All of his men
watched in silence, momentarily rooted to the spot.
'They must have sent scouts around Grellax while the
main force came through the town.'

'But how did they find the column so quickly?' Fellick
asked. 'I know they left a hell of a trail but any scouting
party would still have to cover a lot of ground to–'

A broad shadow passed overhead. Everyone ducked
involuntarily. Tylor was the first to look skywards.

'Gods of harvest and home!' he breathed. 'It's not
possible. It's... it's unholy!'

The flying machine swooped gracefully away from
them, its path taking it out over the battlefield. It
appeared to be little more than a child's kite,

constructed on a much larger scale: a framework of struts and vanes, roughly lashed together, covered by a sheet of fabric that somehow caught the wind and held the whole thing aloft. And, hanging face-down in a harness beneath the wings: a greenskin.

'Now I know we're doomed!' said Tombek.

'I can't believe it's taken you this long to work that out,' replied Kleeve.

It was as if the sight of the impossible machine – somehow more impossible than the engine-driven chariots, the machine-rifle and the mere existence of the greenskinned invaders from the heavens – unlocked something in Vikor. His last memory of his mother, being held aboard a wagon by his sister, Freytha, and a woman he didn't recognise, flashed before him. Lowering his pike he charged down the incline, into the valley.

'Little idiot's determined to get himself killed,' declared Massau.

'He'll have family down there, somewhere,' Brael replied. He turned to his men. 'Whatever happens, we'll need transport out of here.' He jabbed a finger at Kleeve and Tombek, who nodded then headed off down the slope. 'The rest of us are going to see if we can't take some survivors with us.'

'Corfe,' Massau stuttered. 'You can't seriously mean–'

'It's coming back!' Tylor interrupted the guildsman. Those still gathered around Brael followed his pointing arm. The flying machine had climbed, then wheeled round to retrace its path overhead.

'It's letting its friends on the ground know we're up here,' Fellick commented. 'Maybe we should get moving.'

'That's exactly what I–' Massau began.

'The greenskin riding it can't be wearing much armour,' Brael said, almost to himself. 'You wouldn't want to make that machine weigh any more than it already does.'

As he spoke, Brael unslung his rifle from his shoulder. Almost unconsciously, those among his men who also had rifles did likewise. Eight of them, they aimed high.

The greenskin aboard the flying machine must have realised what they were planning. Working a set of pulleys, whose cable-ends hung before him from the glider's frame, he began to alter course. It was, however, too late. The muskets fired in unison, several punching tiny holes through the fabric of the wings, several more hitting the pilot in the face and chest.

Brael's men watched as the flying machine pitched away, rapidly lost altitude and slammed into the ground halfway down the incline and some way off to the left. A couple cheered, but Brael was already reloading and moving down the slope.

'Think you can cover us?' he shouted back to Costes and Perror, who were lashing together a pair of pikes to serve as a stand for the machine-rifle's barrel. Kobar was the last of the men to deposit at their feet the ammunition belts they had carried away from Grellax, then follow Brael into the valley.

SMOKE FROM BURNING wagons moved in drifts along the valley floor. Vikor had recovered some of his senses and now used the wrecked wagons for cover as he moved across the battlefield.

'Freytha!' he called for his sister, knowing that she would not have left their mother. All he heard in reply was the sound of the invaders' seemingly-inexhaustible weapons and the roar of their war engines.

A shadow, taller than a man, loomed out of the smoke. Vikor recoiled instinctively and brought up his pike as the riderless horse, bleeding from several wounds, galloped across his path. He heard musket fire away to his right and wondered if Brael and his men had followed him onto the battlefield. The smoke seemed to be getting thicker and a tang like cooking porker drifted on the air.

I'm already dead, he told himself. I'm already dead and this is where the damned spend eternity.

'THAT WAY! HURRY!' Fellick roared at the small group of militiamen and civilians he had found huddled in the lea of an overturned wagon. He jabbed a finger towards the wagon that Kleeve and Tombek had succeeded in righting. Kleeve, something of a rider in more peaceful times, was soothing the horses that had been unable to free themselves from the harness when the wagon overturned.

Dropping to his haunches behind the wagon, Fellick grabbed one of the soldiers by the collar and shouted in his face: 'Weapons! Powder! Do you have any weapons or powder?'

The militiaman – the unicorn on his shoulder crest marked him as a member of the Mundax Reserve – stared blankly at Fellick for a moment, then managed to shake his head.

'Powder wagon took a direct hit,' he stammered. 'Lost everything. Nothing left. No shot. No powder.'

'Then take this.' Fellick unhooked an old butcher's knife from his belt. 'We're heading for the wagon over there. See it?' Again he jabbed a finger towards the wagon. Tylor and Lollack had arrived. They had a couple of survivors with them. The militiaman nodded and took the butcher's knife.

'Th-thanks,' he mumbled.

'It's okay,' Fellick replied. 'Now follow me and bring your friends.'

BRAEL THREW HIMSELF to the ground as the war machine roared past, firing blindly into the smoke. Whatever strategy the greenskins may have had appeared to have been abandoned; they continued to ride over the battlefield, shooting at shadows, because they enjoyed it.

'Massau, you all right?' Brael shouted, craning round to look for the guildsman, but finding no sign of him. Brael cursed. Massau was an effete fool, but he was a good shot and Brael was loath to lose his marksmanship.

The roar of the war machine had faded, so Brael climbed cautiously to his feet. He carried the long rifle balanced loosely in his crippled hand, the looted greenskin cleaver in his right. The stubby pistol with which he had dispatched the greenskin in Grellax pressed against his back where he had holstered it through his belt. He moved silently, senses alert for any kind of movement nearby.

The shot came from the right: a sharp report, a flash and the buzz of a projectile as it narrowly missed his ear. Brael ducked, moved quickly away to one side, then back at an angle that brought him up behind the sniper's position.

She was perhaps sixteen summers old, huddled with the corpse of an older woman. She swung the empty pistol round to face Brael as soon as he emerged from the drifting smoke.

'It's empty,' he told her, then had to knock it from her hand as she rose at him, attempting to use the pistol as a club.

'My skin's not green,' he said, hastily hooking the cleaver onto his belt and then grabbing her wrist as she made to claw at his eyes with her nails. 'And I don't have time to waste. We have transport – or we should have – and we are getting away from here.'

The girl stared at Brael for a heartbeat then uttered a single word – 'Mother' – before wrenching herself free from his grasp and dropping back beside the dead woman. 'I promised I wouldn't leave her,' she explained when Brael crouched before her.

'She wouldn't want this,' Brael replied. 'I have a son and, if I was dead, I'd want him to go on living. The last thing I would ever wish for would be to be the cause of my son's death.' Swallowing hard and remembering the faces of his wife and son as the iron caravan pulled away, Brael held out his free hand.

FELLICK HAD LOADED the refugees aboard the wagon. The militiamen had recovered themselves and were standing with the others around the wagon while Kleeve continued to talk to the horses calmly.

'How much longer?' asked Tylor. The smoke was thinning as the wagons burned themselves out. It was becoming ever more likely that they would be spotted.

'Soon,' Fellick replied. He didn't like the way he was expected to assume command in Brael's absence. 'We give them a chance to get back to us.'

'There's Massau!' Kobar pointed to where the guildsman had emerged from the drifting smoke. Massau ran towards them, shouting. 'Get moving! I lost Brael then heard gunfire.' Massau shouted as he reached the wagon. 'Surely we can't risk waiting any longer,' he continued between gulps of air.

Tombek snatched Massau's rifle from him and checked the firing pan. 'This hasn't been fired,' he announced.

'I couldn't, I told you,' Massau began to splutter. 'They fired first. I couldn't risk lifting my head to aim.'

'You said you only heard gunfire,' Tombek persisted, stubbornly.

'There!' shouted Distek. Two figures were running towards them through the last wisps of a drifting curtain of smoke.

'And there!' Lollak – a reticent former tanner from Terrax, far to the west – pointed away at an angle, where a lone figure was also running towards them. The smoke was clearing fast and they could make out who it was: Vikor.

'Kleeve, get the horses ready to go,' Fellick ordered. Kleeve climbed aboard the wagon and readied the reins. 'Come on, Vikor, lad, move!'

VIKOR HAD NO idea how he had found his way back through the smoke. He only knew one thing: he had failed to find his mother and sister. His mind swam with images of them, lost somewhere on the battle-field, calling his name and receiving no reply.

Then why was he running towards the wagon that his new comrades had been able to make ready? Shouldn't he turn back, continue his search? To do that, he realised, would mean going to his death. And he wanted to live.

The cheerful one – Fellick – was beckoning to him, urging him on. Then, between one step and the next, death took him, tossed him aside in broken, bloody pieces and roared away to claim his friends.

THE BURST OF gunfire punched Vikor off his feet and through the air. By the time he hit the ground he was already dead. The war machine roared out of the smoke behind him. Its fat front wheel rolled over Vikor's pelvis, snapping bones like old twigs and grinding them into the dirt as its rider steered towards the wagon.

'Gods, Kleeve, get moving!' Fellick shouted. 'Every-one aboard!'

Flicking the reins, Kleeve urged the horses on. The animals, hearing the scream of the approaching engine, needed no encouragement; they took fright and bolted up the slope, hauling the bucking and jouncing wagon after them.

BRAEL PUSHED THE girl to the ground the moment Vikor was hit. Shielding her body with his, he watched the young Grellaxian fall and his men and the wagon head for the rise. He saw Fellick look towards him from the wagon, clinging to the jolting boards and wearing a helpless expression. They had been through a lot together, seen things neither would have believed possible. This, it seemed, was where it ended.

TOMBEK GRABBED MASSAU'S rifle and fired at the oncoming greenskin. The shot went wide and Tombek was almost thrown from the wagon as a wheel hit a sudden dip.

Kleeve worked the reins frantically, desperate to urge a little more speed from the horses, whose flanks were already slick with sweat, their lips pulled back and flecked with foam.

The war machine roared closer with every heartbeat. Its rider fired a short volley – a ranging shot which chewed up the ground to the right of the wagon, spraying its passengers with dirt. Everyone on board the wagon ducked, then stayed crouched low, expecting the next burst to be the last they heard. But the next burst of alien gunfire chewed a single line of impacts that ended at the war machine and its rider. Several shells punched through the machine itself; one exploded the fat rear wheel, causing the machine to fish-tail wildly. The rider struggled to regain control of his ride. Then a second burst slammed him from the saddle.

The riderless machine veered off, bleeding oil from its punctured innards and tearing a furrow in the dirt with its collapsed rear wheel. As the wagon continued up the slope, its passengers watched as the greenskin staggered to its feet, still able to move despite the ugly impact wound it had received high on its chest. It howled after the fleeing humans and unslung a wide-barrelled rifle from across its back.

A third burst of gunfire from the top of the slope hit the beast, throwing it backwards off its feet, this time rendering its misshapen skull into raw meat and bone. Splayed out with its feet facing the retreating wagon, its corpse continued to twitch as if some instinct remained after life had gone, knowing that its quarry was getting away.

Kleeve barely succeeded in reining in the panicked horses and brought the wagon to a stop a few strides from where Costes and Perror were celebrating, shouting to be heard over the ringing in their ears, their faces and hands coated with smuts ejected from the machine-rifle. The weapon sat propped against the lashed-together pike staves, smoke drifting from its barrel and the reek of hot oil tainted the air.

Brael hauled the girl to her feet and ran with her up the slope. They reached the wagon as the machine-rifle was being loaded aboard.

'Good to see you,' Fellick said.

'You too,' Brael replied. He surveyed the number of people gathered around and sitting in the wagon. Too many for them all to ride in the wagon without killing the horses in less than a day. As before they would only be able to move as quickly as the slowest of them could march.

'Who's your friend?' Fellick asked.

Brael looked at the girl. Tall and slim, she had the dark hair and olive complexion of the local population. Her eyes still held a trace of the wildness that had been in them when she tried to club Brael with the empty pistol. She had retrieved the ancient-looking weapon from where it had fallen before following Brael away from her dead mother and was holding it limply in one hand.

'I have no idea,' Brael said. 'What's your name, girl?'

'Freytha,' the girl replied. 'Freytha Lodz.'

'We're ready to move!' Kleeve called from his seat aboard the wagon. The women and children among the civilians Fellick had found had been loaded aboard the wagon, along with Perror and Costes, who had set up the machine-rifle to point to the rear. The men were grouped around the wagon, awaiting orders.

'We should get going,' Fellick said. 'The greenskins will be on our tail soon enough.'

Brael nodded. 'Head south,' he said. With the army gone – either lying dead in the valley, or scattered to the winds in small groups of battle-shocked survivors, there was only one place left for them to go: the iron city. Mallax.

Part Two

MALLAX WAS FOUNDED *on the few mineral and ore deposits that were ever found on this primarily agricultural world. Over the generations of decline which followed Agra's loss of contact with the Imperium (cross ref. 666/852-hist: Age of Apostasy) the Mallaxians continued to mine these deposits and, in their manufactoria, to work them into agricultural implements and weapons of war.*

As the ore deposits were exhausted, Mallax's manufactoria were turned to the repair and maintenance of those Imperial artefacts and machines that had survived the generations since contact was lost – though their origin and the existence of the Imperium was already slipping into the realm of myth and legend. Mallax became the workshop of the world.

The other city-states, such as Primax (the site, its city charter suggests, of the first human settlement on Agra), Terrax and Mundax, looked down upon Mallax, despite their reliance on its workshops for the maintenance of their agricultural machinery and the weapons with which they occasionally fought their petty wars. Contempt turned to envy, however, as the invaders rolled across Agra's verdant continent. Only one city had sufficient stockpiles of weaponry, ancient and patched though much of it was, to stand a hope of offering any real resistance.

– Extract: 'Inquisitorial communiqué 747923486/aleph/Samax IV' Author: Inquisitor Selene Infantus. M41,793

AN ANCIENT LANTERN held in his damaged hand, the stubby greenskin pistol in the other, Brael moved as swiftly as he dared along the tunnel beneath the city. Though the tunnel floor had been worn smooth by the passage of countless feet in ages past, the roof was of uneven height; the threat of dashing out one's own brains on an unexpected overhang was very real.

The lantern gave off a thin yellow light and the scent of animal fat. Its glow illuminated a few paces of the tunnel ahead, but neither Brael nor the men who had followed him down the shaft into the darkness beneath Mallax needed to see too far along the tunnel to guide them towards their destination. The shouts, screams and loud guttural roars, punctuated by the occasional gunshot were enough.

It had been almost three weeks since Brael and his men arrived at Mallax. They made their way warily through the deserted districts outside the city's tall curtain wall and identified themselves to the sentries – although Brael was sure that they had been tracking them for some time before making their presence known. After a short debriefing, they were assigned to a defensive station atop the wall and a reserve station below the battlements where they were to spend their off-duty hours.

A week after they had reached Mallax, the vanguard of the invaders' army had topped the horizon. As more and more of the infernal machines roared into view, carrying with them the greenskined plague that had wiped the Agran people from the rest of their land, the harrying attacks began. Two- and three-wheeled war engines rushed through the outer districts, firing up at the defences, testing them. Brael was of the opinion that they weren't trying to breach the wall. They were just amusing themselves until all their forces were assembled. Then they would come, together, to erase the last Agran stronghold from planet.

Brael's unit had been the third to respond to the cries of 'Attack from within!' Runners had been sent from the first unit to discover the attack and descend to meet it. Appalled that the greenskins might have found a way under the curtain wall, Brael led his men down from their reserve station and east through the streets to the head of the mineshaft.

To their great chagrin, Brael ordered Costes and Perror to stay with the machine-rifle. There were those among the city's swollen ranks of defenders and refugees who were not above stealing such a weapon and selling or bartering it to another militia company.

'And besides,' Fellick added when Brael's orders didn't manage to quieten their protests, 'you finally seem to have worked out how to hit something with it. You wouldn't want to waste all that practice.'

At the mineshaft, a tower stood over the hole in the ground, with a wheelhouse huddled at its base. The area immediately surrounding the mine was clear of buildings, but was overlooked by warehouses that ringed the open space. The area itself was not completely featureless; it was dotted by ancient piles of slag and other debris brought up with the valuable black rock that Mallax's engineers used to refine and use as fuel for their machines. The slag heaps were so old, hardy weeds had sprouted and covered them with grey and green patches.

By the time Brael's men had made their way down from their reserve station to the head of the ancient, disused mine shaft, a second platoon had descended to reinforce the first. Neither had returned, nor sent out a man with word of their progress. Brael and his company were the third to descend into the darkness.

'The next gallery's clear.' Mab, their Mallaxian guide, appeared in the light from Brael's lantern. On the long ride down the shaft, huddled close in a metal cage hung from an ancient chain whose links were bigger than a man's fist, Brael had been surprised to learn that their guide didn't come from a mining family.

'I'm a historian,' she had told him, smiling at the absurdity of the notion. 'Mining ended in Mallax so long ago, we're the only people still interested in the mines. I've only been down a couple of times, but have made careful studies of the plans.'

'I'll do my best to feel reassured,' Fellick said with a smile that was swallowed by the utter blackness through which they fell.

BRAEL WAS SURPRISED by the size of the man-made cavern he stepped into. The uneven roof rose over them in a shallow dome almost two man-heights high and wide enough for twenty men to stand side-by-side. It was virtually featureless, just a vast cave drilled into the earth – the very idea set Brael's mind spinning. To be down here, away from the sunshine, the wind and the seasons seemed an awful way to live, no matter how impressive it was to think that men had once been able to do so.

Ancient timbers, thicker than a man, supported the roof and were themselves supported by a lattice of smaller timbers wedged diagonally between them. Several of Brael's men eyed them warily.

'If they've stayed up this long, I doubt we've got anything to worry about,' said Lollak.

'We should be worrying about what's down the next tunnel,' muttered Tombek, morosely.

'Oh, I'm worrying about that, too,' Distek replied as he gingerly placed a hand on one of the timbers as if to reassure himself of its stability.

Niches had been carved into the curving walls by the men who had dug out this gallery long ago. Presumably they had been to accommodate more lanterns of the kind Mab was carrying. Mab's lantern – more powerful than those handed out to Brael and his men – illuminated the entire space when she opened its shutter to the fullest.

'So men used to dig metal out of the ground here?' asked Kobar. He ran a hand over the rock, mentally comparing it to the raw salt deposits he used to blow out of the cliff faces in his homeland.

'Not here,' Mab replied. 'Further on. The next tunnel branches out towards the work faces. This was where they collected the unrefined metal that they had mined. They would load it into wheeled wagons and tow it back along the way we came, then up to the surface.'

'This is where all the tunnels come together?' asked Brael.

Mab nodded. She ran a hand over her close-cropped hair. Brael caught sight of the additional digit that grew out of the knuckle joint of her little finger. There was one on her other hand, too; Mab made no attempt to hide them. Brael had first seen them on the surface, in the daylight that seemed only a fantasy in the utter blackness of the mine – he had experienced the same sudden shiver he had felt years ago, in the Temple of the Holy Varks.

'Charges here, then,' Brael said to Kobar, who nodded and dipped a hand into the canvas bag that was slung across his chest. He withdrew the first of several cylindrical objects he had brought down from above: a kind of compact explosive, more powerful than twice the same amount of black powder. Mallax had preserved through the generations the secrets to its costly manufacture. Also in the bag was a coiled length of a fast-burning fuse, more reliable than the greased twists of cloth Kobar was used to.

'Charges?' Mab echoed Brael's word with concern.

'Here's where we'll stop them,' Brael replied. 'One way or another.'

IN A LOW-CEILINGED space beyond the gallery intersection, the remains of the first and second companies were gathered behind the bodies of their comrades, losing a desperate attempt to defend the main tunnel that led towards the surface. That they had succeeded in holding back the greenskins for so long was testament to their courage. Courage, however, would only last so long.

Brael's men emerged from a slit-narrow tunnel that had been practically invisible, appearing to be little more than a shadow, even in the powerful light of the greenskins' lanterns. Mab, refusing to return to the surface after guiding them along one of the tunnels that led from the intersection at which Kobar had been left to work on the charges, led them along the crevice. Historians believed it to have been constructed to provide ventilation to the furthest work faces, perhaps even a means of escape in the event of a cave-in.

Whatever the intentions of those who had created it, the tunnel allowed Brael's men to strike at the flank of the greenskins, driving a wedge through the centre of their force as the bulky invaders struggled to turn and meet the surprise attack in a co-ordinated manner.

They emerged into a scene painted in shadows and light. The long, low space had once been a work face from which Mallaxian miners tore unrefined metal from the rocks. Most of the light came from the invaders' torches, strapped to foreheads or breastplates, which appeared to use some power source other than animal fat to produce beams of powerful yellow brilliance. Brael had been all but blinded when the first of the creatures turned to meet his attack. Luckily Fellick, directly behind Brael and therefore shielded by his shadow, was able to thrust a pike – its shaft cut to half-length before the descent into the mines – into the animal's face.

One of the greenskins had fallen before the rest of them began to realise that they were under attack from another direction.

A shot from the heavy pistol Brael had taken from the dead greenskin in Grellax blew out the back of another's head. The recoil kicked up Brael's arm to his shoulder and the report in the confined space set his ears ringing. Cracking the barrel open along a hinge in its stock, he removed the smoking shell case and inserted another from his belt.

Brael and his men discovered shortly after their arrival that Mallax had become a marketplace for stolen greenskin weaponry. Along with tales of long, hard retreats from the invaders, many of those who had gathered behind Mallax's walls had brought with them all manner of alien artefacts: engine-driven swords, whose blades were made up of countless fast-moving teeth; machine-rifles like the one Costes and Perror had made their own; all manner and size of ammunition.

Brael stepped over the green corpse, snapping the pistol shut as he did so. His next target saw him coming and brought its rifle to bear.

Instinctively, Brael dropped to the floor the moment he saw the rifle barrel swinging in his direction. He shouted a warning to those behind him and, through the ringing in his ears, he heard answering shouts and cries of alarm.

Then the greenskin fired.

The ringing in Brael's ears suddenly became a high buzzing, then nothing. Silence settled round him like a blanket while sharp, hot fragments of rock scored his forehead and cheek, carved from the wall and ceiling by the wildly ricocheting shells.

To his right, a body hit the floor. By the light from the torch fixed to its breastplate, Brael was shocked to see that it was one of the invaders, half its face a smoke-edged crater. In the tunnels and galleries beneath the last human city, at least some of the greenskins' unholy weapons were as much of a threat to their users as their targets.

With no way of knowing if the fusillade had ceased, Brael lifted his head. The greenskin with the machine-rifle had released its trigger. Perhaps the expression on its shadow-splashed face was one of appalled surprise at what it had just done. Perhaps orders had been issued forbidding the use of machine-rifles until the surface was reached.

Brael pushed himself to his feet. A glance to one side located another corpse. A lantern lay a short way from it, the shutter wide. It was Mab, her face pale and upturned, eyes open, the rest of her dark with shadows and blood.

A beam of light stabbed across Brael's eyes. Raising his damaged hand to shade them, he aimed his pistol and fired directly into the light. He didn't hear the sound of his gun, but the light swung upwards, slashing its beam across the uneven ceiling and he moved away, not waiting to see how much damage his shot had caused.

His men were pressing towards the defenders at the end of the gallery. The greenskins had already adjusted to the new situation and were beginning to push back.

Distek fell, torso bisected by a machine-sword, the only engine-driven weapon it was safe to use in the confined space. Tylor, fighting at Fellick's back, took a crushing backhanded blow to the throat. While Fellick spun, short pike still in hand, to counter and return the attack, the young man from Erewell choked and died as his shattered, swollen larynx closed off his windpipe.

'Forward!' Brael shouted at the top of his lungs. He hoped that at least some of his men could hear him, even if he could not hear himself; his voice was a low, muffled thing confined within his skull. He could see that his men were faltering, their attack slowing as they lost the advantage of surprise. They had to drive on, to reach the small group of shattered-looking survivors from the first two companies, and then sweep them along the tunnel towards the gallery in which Kobar waited with his charges.

Without the time or even the space to reload his looted gun, Brael had re-holstered it in his belt at the small of his back and unhooked his greenskin cleaver. The press of bodies at the tunnel mouth had become so tight it was barely possible to swing the weapon. The sweat, anger and fear of the invaders mingled with that of the defenders. The body of every combatant was smeared with a mixture of Agran blood and the sickly ichor that ran beneath the greenskins' hide.

He kept shouting as he pushed and hacked, as he used the pommel end of the cleaver to put out a glowering red eye then reversed the weapon to slash it across the exposed vein that throbbed between the cords of the creature's neck. A second slash severed the fingers that the beast pressed against the spouting wound. And still he shouted, urging his men on and the defenders to hold out for one heartbeat longer, one–

With a start, Brael realised that he was staring into the exhausted, almost dead eyes of another human being. A man from one of the first two companies, his clothing hung in tatters and he was covered in the blood of two species.

Brael shouted instructions. The stranger nodded and turned away. At that moment, Brael was hit by the kind of certainty that he had become used to being accompanied by a drumming inside his head and a bilious display of lights before his eyes. Whether it was the utter confusion of the battle or his deafness, those accompanying sensations did not materialise. All Brael knew was that something awful was about to enter the gallery. Something that could spell the end for them all.

Still shouting, he grabbed the nearest of his men – Kleeve, as it turned out, wearing the same half-crazed expression Brael was sure was also on his own face – and all but threw him into the tunnel. Brael turned, grabbed another of the defenders – this time a man he didn't recognise – all the while shouting that despite the risks, they must get out of this gallery now.

Where possible, the defenders ducked away from the conflict, heading for the tunnel mouth – which was only two or three steps behind any of them, so close had the press become. Several were cut down by the greenskins, who were in turn forced to retreat by Brael and Fellick, each standing to one side of the tunnel, stabbing and slashing with cleaver and cut-down pike.

'Now!' yelled Brael and turned to run down the tunnel, slapping Fellick on the shoulder as he did so. And at that moment, the greenskins paused. Several cocked their heads as if they had heard something, though Brael could still hear nothing. That gave the last two living Agrans the chance to sprint down the tunnel, heedless of the uneven floor, stumbling and righting themselves as they ran.

Someone had left a lantern on the tunnel floor, without whose light to warn them, Brael and Fellick would have run at full speed into the rock wall as the tunnel made a sharp left turn. As they made the turn, the first shells impacted the wall that they would have hit, punching craters into the rock and filling the air with razor-sharp splinters.

Fellick stumbled, uttering a sharp cry that Brael was unable to hear. Catching his balance he continued to run, hand pressed to his side.

'REINFORCEMENTS!' FELLICK GASPED out after he and Brael had burst from the tunnel and all but fell into Kleeve's arms. Though unable to hear Fellick's voice, Brael saw that others were already working to staunch a wound in his side. Fellick winced, his back arching involuntarily, as Tombek eased a long sliver of rock from his back, just below the curve of his ribs.

'Damn greenskins sent reinforcements!' Fellick gasped out as his wound was bound in a length of filthy cloth torn from the remains of someone's shirt. 'Either they got impatient or always planned to send them, but they're on their way.'

'We'd have still been in the gallery when they arrived,' realised one of the survivors from the second company to enter the mine. 'If we hadn't moved *before* they arrived, they'd have cut us down like grass.' He was staring at Brael as he spoke.

'Coincidence,' said another from his company.

'I said that,' added Tombek, looking up from fastening the makeshift bandage around Fellick's torso. 'Once.'

'If they're on their way, then we haven't got time to chatter,' Kobar cut in. He was standing at the entrance to the tunnel that led to the metal cage and the shaft to the surface. With an almost inhuman detachment, Brael watched Kobar's mouth work frantically as he beckoned to the others and pointed at the tunnel. At his feet were bunched the ends of the fuses he had run the length of the gallery, leading to charges placed around the tunnel mouth and in natural nooks and crannies around the walls.

'Kobar's right!' Brael shouted unintentionally, causing everyone to start. 'Let's move. We have no time!'

Kleeve looped Fellick's arm over his shoulder and led the way along the tunnel, followed by those of the first two companies that had sustained wounds. There were only three or four, Brael noted. Greenskin weapons were not intended to wound, but to annihilate, on the scale of the individual or of cities, lands, perhaps whole worlds. Vika's stories of distant worlds and creatures that might bestride the gulfs between them seemed far less fanciful now.

Brael made sure he was the last to enter the tunnel. He paused as he passed Kobar, who crouched by the bunch of fuses, striking the tinderbox he had brought with him from his home in the shadow of a distant range of mountains.

'Go,' Kobar said, then waved along the tunnel. 'I'll be directly behind you.' The tinderbox caught and he lowered it gently to the fuse-ends, which began to fizz and burn away towards the charges.

Kobar rose and Brael turned to take a step along the tunnel. With a start he realised that he could see his own shadow, clearly defined by a light far stronger than an oil lantern's, stretching along the tunnel floor.

Alien gunfire erupted from the far side of the gallery. Though unable to hear it, Brael could feel the machine-rifles' drum-like concussions in his guts and bones. Ducking instinctively, he glanced behind him.

Kobar had been hit. A glancing blow, the shell had still managed to tear an appalling, ragged hole in his side. The impact had spun him round and deposited him against the slightly-curved wall of the tunnel, a stride or so from the opening to the gallery.

Brael turned and took a crouching step towards Kobar. Seeing him coming, Kobar held up a shaking hand, then jabbed a finger at something on the floor between them. At first Brael could see nothing, then he spotted it: the tinderbox. By the time he looked back up at Kobar, the former quarryman had slipped one of the cylindrical charges and a length of fuse from his canvas bag.

Another burst of gunfire almost forced Brael to his knees. Ducking flying splinters, he scooped up the tinderbox, then darted forward and handed it to Kobar. Kobar nodded his thanks through a rictus of pain, then nodded away along the tunnel. He had bitten off a tiny length of fuse and inserted it into the charge. The last Brael saw of him, before sprinting away along the tunnel, racing to get out of the powerful light of the greenskins' lanterns and into the sheltering dark, Kobar was striking his tinderbox alight for one last time.

BRAEL WAS RUNNING in darkness, head bowed to avoid any dangerous protrusions from the ceiling, when the sound wave of the explosion reached him. The dry, burnt scent of the explosive reached him on the air that was forced along the tunnel. Up ahead, Brael saw a pale, weak light: the rear of the survivors' column, heading for the up-shaft. He ran on.

It must have been Kobar's intention all along, Brael realised as he ran, to close the tunnel entrance, to make sure as many of the greenskins as possible were bottle-necked in the gallery, working to clear the fallen rock when the main charges blew.

'Where's Kobar?'

Brael had caught up with the others and Tombek had noticed that he was alone. Brael pointed at his ears and shook his head. Tombek pointed back down the tunnel and furrowed his brow to indicate a question.

Realising what Tombek wanted to know, Brael just shook his head.

At that moment, the tunnel floor shifted beneath their feet. Brael felt a rising pressure, rolling through his chest. Tombek and several of the others looked anxiously upwards as dust and small fragments of rock fell from the ceiling.

The main charges. Brael couldn't resist a smile at the thought of what was happening in the gallery they had just left: the weight of the earth, the weight of the city above them, pressing down upon the greenskins, crushing them beneath it. Brael wondered briefly whether a greenskin could feel fear as a man could, the absolute terror that comes with the knowledge that one's life is of no account in the events one is caught up in – the abject knowledge that your life is over. He hoped so.

The storm of dust and rock fragments rushed along the tunnel and enveloped them, extinguishing most of the lanterns. The survivors were forced to cough and gasp, to feel their way towards the shaft. Beneath their feet, above and around them, the earth continued to move, to creak and moan as if in protest at the acts that had been committed within its depths.

One of the first company wounded was dead by the time they reached the bottom of the shaft, where the lift cage was waiting for them. 'He stays down here,' Freytha told his three surviving companions.

Brael had been unable to prevent Freytha slipping aboard the cage moments before it had descended into the mine, but he had ordered her to remain at the bottom of the shaft, ready to tug on the cage's telegraph handle, which would give the signal to those above to raise the lift. Even if every human down here was dead, those above had to be told. 'The less weight we have on board, the faster we get to the surface.'

One of the dead man's comrades stepped forward menacingly, unwilling to be told to leave another friend below ground, equally unwilling to be ordered to do so by a girl. Lollak stepped between them.

'You know she's right,' he said quietly. 'Honour his memory by staying alive and killing more greenskins.'

Even though the dead weight was left at the bottom, propped against the shaft wall in a seated position, cold hands clasped in his lap in an attitude of prayer, the ride to the surface was agonisingly slow. The grinding rumble of falling rock faded and light seeped down from above. Instinctively, everyone in the cage lifted their faces, like plants seeking sunshine, anxious to be out of the dark.

A wave of tiredness rolled over Brael as the lift made its way to the surface, a reaction to the powerful sense of dread he had experienced just ahead of the arrival of the greenskins' reinforcements. As always when he felt this tired, he found himself thinking of his home, his bed and his family. And as always, he pushed those memories back down, as deep inside himself as possible.

'...an... ear... thing...'t?' Freytha touched his arm and, Brael assumed, was shouting her question. He frowned a question in reply and she repeated herself.

'A little!' Brael shouted, after working out what she was asking. He could hear some of the louder clanging and grinding from the cage superstructure and the chain as it drew them to the surface. Hopefully, this meant that his hearing would return to him.

The cage rose into soft light and a cold breeze. Time seemed to have stopped while they were underground but, above them, the day had come to a close. Dusk painted the sky a delicate rose and the early evening breeze dried the sweat on their skin as they stepped from the cage. An anxious crowd awaited them. Brael estimated there were at least two companies of men, armed and ready to descend, should the news from Freytha have been bad.

Beyond the armed men was a crowd of civilians – though no one in Mallax could really be counted as a civilian any more. Women, older men and the very young – some might have gathered around the pit head in the hope of seeing a loved one emerge alive. Others may have wanted to know if the greenskins had broken through and, therefore, how much longer they had left to live.

'You!' Tombek had spotted a familiar face in the crowd: Massau. The former guildsman had disappeared on some unspecified errand of his own, moments before the call to the mineshaft came. Now he hung around the edges of the crowd, perhaps hoping to discover to how many of his comrades he would have to explain his absence. Seeing Tombek lunging through the crowd towards him, Massau's face assumed an expression of almost comic alarm and he darted away.

'Tombek, leave him,' Brael called after the tall Vinarian and was relieved to discover that he could hear his own voice again, even though it sounded as if he was speaking from a distance. 'You need rest. And food. We all do.'

'And we need to mourn our dead,' added Kleeve, who was still supporting Fellick. Brael saw that the normally voluble Primaxian looked haggard, his face pale from the amount of blood that continued to seep through the rough dressing.

'First we take care of our living,' Brael countered, indicating Fellick. Tombek slipped Fellick's other arm over his shoulder and he and Kleeve went in search of the nearest physic station. The bonesetter would only be able to stitch the wound shut and dress it with a clean bandage. It would be up to Fellick's powerful constitution to get him back on his feet. When the final assault came, Brael feared he would have to meet it without his oldest comrade at his side.

From amongst the gathered militia companies, officers and men alike were firing questions at Brael and the others. How many greenskins were down there? Were they sure the rock fall blocked the tunnel? Brael answered those that he was able to work out from the fragments of speech he was able to hear. No one who was down there could doubt that Kobar's charges had brought down enough rock to completely block the greenskins' passage into the city via the mine. However, Brael realised as he answered the question, it also had cut off any hope of escape under the walls when Mallax fell.

AFTER STANDING IN line to collect food from one of the communal kitchens set up throughout the city, Brael returned to his company's reserve station on its wide walkway, halfway up the tall curtain wall. The station was occupied by a company of strangers, who informed him that his company – 'Both of them!' one of the strangers laughed – had been sent to take up position on the wall itself.

Costes and Perror, still dutifully guarding the machine-rifle, greeted Brael's arrival with twin looks of horror. Realising that they thought he was the only survivor, he quickly reassured them as far as he could, considering the losses their company had sustained. 'The others are getting food, some are looking for baths to wash off the greenskins' blood.' Brael looked down at the mess of drying blood and ichor that coated his clothing and wondered if he shouldn't do the same. 'I think Lollak said something about a sweet-faced young wound-dresser at the physic station under the foundries to the west.'

'Tylor, Distek, Kobar,' Perror muttered. 'After so long together.'

'And Fellick?' Costes asked.

'Time will tell,' was all Brael would say. He looked out through the firing hole in the barricade that had been built on top of the wall's ancient metal and stone battlements through which Costes and Perror had mounted the machine-rifle. It was summer and the long dusk was coming to an end. The sky was still streaked with pink, but the horizon was already dark – except where it was lit by the campfires of the enemy. The hulking shadows of their encampments lined the horizon from flank to flank. Flames gouted from the exhausts of their war machines as they made ready for what Brael was sure would soon come.

He imagined that they had been awaiting word from the infiltrators; had they broken through, some signal would have been given and the rest of the army would have roared towards the city. But the defeat of the probing mission through the mines would not stop them. Soon the greenskins would send their whole army against Mallax. He imagined that he saw them coming: a black, flame-belching line rushing towards the city from the horizon, through the abandoned districts outside the gates, to wrap itself around the city walls and begin the brutal, unstoppable process of battering their way in.

'Time will tell,' Brael repeated softly as he watched the smoke from the distant army blot out the last of the sky's colour. 'Time will tell.'

ACCORDING TO MOST *of the primary sources found in the vaults beneath the city's central librarium, Mallax was known not only for its manufactoria, its workshops and the pall of*

*dust and smoke which was said to hang perpetually over it, but
also for the effect which some of the ores that were mined by
its inhabitants and the processes by which the ores were refined
and worked (cross ref. 695/446-A. Mechanicus archive:
smelting and related processes; chemical cracking and com-
bining) had on future generations of the miners and refinery
workers.*

*Those most grossly afflicted rarely survived post-partum.
Most mutations, the sources report, were minor – a third eye-
lid, perhaps, or additional digits. However, without the
guiding hand of the Imperium to weed them out, Mallax's
population grew to exhibit greater variations from the blessed
human norm.*

*The Priesthood of the Varks, Agra's oldest religion, was one
such self-selecting variant group.*

*– Extract: 'Inquisitorial communiqué
747923486/aleph/Samax IV' Author: Inquisitor Selene
Infantus. M41,793*

MALLAX HAD ALWAYS been a restless city. At its height, the
mines, foundries and manufactoria worked day and
night. The warehouses that sat grouped around the iron
caravan termini were always receiving or dispatching
goods: foodstuffs, wines and luxury cloths came in; farm
machinery, parts for steam- or water-powered looms
went out. And to slake the workers' thirst and satisfy their
hunger, the streets were always busy with food vendors,
the taverns always open to welcome men at the end of
their shift.

Though Mallax's glory days were generations past, it
maintained much of its insomniac energy. Brael had
been awed by it the first time he had come here. It had
seemed unnatural, a ceaseless motion divorced from the
rhythm of the seasons. Though he never admitted it to
Vika, it unnerved him that men could create such a place.

Since the greenskins came, however, he had come to share Mallax's insomnia, even before he arrived at the city for the second time in his life. And though dusk had passed and night had fallen, he roamed the streets while the rest of his company – how had they become a 'company', Brael wondered, when once they were just a group of men thrown together within a brigade of scratch militia – dozed atop the battlements.

People streamed through the streets, some carrying messages between generals, each of whom had command of a section of the defences, others on the look-out for fresh weapons, powder or ammunition for their companies.

Brael knew that he would never find what he sought in the city's streets, but that didn't stop him looking.

VIKA HADN'T WANTED to leave Brael, but, head throbbing, he had insisted. Many of his clan had already sent their families south on the iron caravans that travelled the rails less and less frequently. The men and boys of fighting age had presented themselves at the gathering places in the market towns nearest to their farmsteads. The time it took Brael to persuade Vika to take Bron to Mallax meant that he was the last of the Corfe clan to leave the land.

Word had it that the next iron caravan to pass through Clovis Halt, the staging post closest to Brael's farm, would be the last. On a clear day, it was said, columns of smoke were visible, towering into the sky on the northern horizon. Brael made it clear to his beautiful, stubborn wife that he expected her to take their son to safety, to a city she revered. Something in her eyes told Brael that her faith in the Dogma of the Holy Varks was not as powerful or as comforting as once it had been.

'I need you to be safe,' he told her late into their last night together, camped along with ten or twenty others around the small collection of huts that made up Clovis Halt. 'I need to know that whatever happens, whatever I have to do if any of these stories are true, that, when it's over, I'll be able to go and find you and bring you home.'

Brael was as surprised by this speech as his wife. During the months since he loaded them aboard one of the caravan's iron wagons, he wondered if she only really decided to go after hearing that.

If that was the case, then no one could argue: he had killed his wife and child.

FOLLOWING THEIR ARRIVAL at Mallax, Brael's company was debriefed by a major from a Primaxian regiment who, Brael estimated, could be no older than the boy Vikor they had found and lost at Grellax. If boys had risen to become majors, it didn't bode well for the defence of Mallax. After debriefing, the wagon and horses they had taken from the battlefield outside Grellax were commandeered to join the pool of wagons being used to ferry men and arms through the city streets. Brael and his men were assigned a section of the wall to defend when the time came and a reserve post at which they would spend the hours when they were not on guard.

As soon as his men had settled, Brael went in search of the terminus at which Vika and Bron's caravan would have arrived. He remembered it from his last visit: its metal roof had been turned green by a lifetime's exposure to the rain and to the effluvia of the neighbouring manufactoria.

Beneath the vaulted cathedral roof the iron caravans sat silently. Refugees – mostly the elderly and the very young – had set up camps along the platforms. He moved among them, asking if anyone had worked on the caravans, if anyone could tell him what had become of the last caravan from the north.

An old man claimed to have travelled on the caravan that had been sent out to the site of a disaster – a 'derailing', he called it. The southbound caravan had somehow jumped from the tracks and twisted itself into a tangle of iron and blood.

'So many people dead,' the old man's reedy voice took on an almost priestly tone in the cathedral space of the terminus. 'Crushed and broken. Women. Children. So young.'

Brael described Vika and Bron to the old man – Vika's northern complexion and fair hair would have marked her apart from most of the caravan's passengers – but the old man could tell him no more. They could do nothing but salvage what parts they could from the engine and the wagons – Mallax was a city devoted to salvage, to maintaining the ancient machinery. The rails were beyond swift repair. The few survivors – wide-eyed, most of them, and trembling with shock – were loaded aboard the caravan along with the salvage and carried the rest of the way to Mallax.

AND SO BRAEL walked the city. He knew Vika and Bron had died on the caravan he had insisted that they take. He knew it with the same certainty he had known when to leave Grellax, that reinforcements were about to enter the mine gallery, and as he had known when and where to move to avoid countless dangers during the long hard year that had led him to Mallax. He felt it in his heart, just as he felt the itching of the fingers he no longer possessed – lost the last time he tried to ignore the wisdom, as old Aunt Brella would have it, that was forcing its way out of him.

Brael knew it, but the old man had not said for certain that he had seen their corpses.

And so he walked in the vain hope of seeing a face, a splash of fair hair in a crowd or hearing a voice inflected with a northern accent or a snatch of the boyish laughter that echoed in his mind during the moments he allowed himself to rest.

THE SOUND OF raised voices reached him as he walked through the narrow streets of the old town. Ironically, the old town was the most brightly lit part of the city, the only place where the oil-fired gas lanterns still worked. Brael was walking through pools of gentle yellow radiance when he heard the voices, then the sound of something breaking.

Cutting down a side-alley in the direction of the noise, Brael emerged in a street he was surprised to recognise: a thoroughfare that cut through the close-packed old town. It was lined with open-fronted shops that once sold fruit, meats and wines intended for tribute, sacrifice and libation in the pyramidal temple whose precinct dominated the square into which the thoroughfare opened. He had walked down this street once before, when Bron had been very young.

Brael jogged along the road and out into the open square. Yet more stalls that once had sold religious tokens, artefacts for the faithful to have blessed within the temple, then returned for installation in a household shrine. Brael caught a faint whiff of old straw and remembered that one of the stalls was a chaos of caged birds and young porkers and bleaters – the stallholder, claiming some minor dispensation from the temple elders, would bleed an animal and prepare it for offering to the priests within the precinct.

At the far side of the square lights burned atop the gateposts of the precinct, illuminating the angry crowd at the gates. The sound Brael had heard was that of the gates being forced inwards, one wrenched off its hinges by the weight of the crowd.

Brael jogged across the square, hands unconsciously checking the weapons at his belt. The last of the crowd, whose shouts had grown louder and more violent since they had achieved their initial aim of gaining entry to the precinct, had pushed through the gateway, leaving a robed figure slumped against the precinct wall.

'Are you badly hurt?' Brael asked the priest of the Holy Varks. His hood had been partly torn from his robe in the scuffle that erupted when he stepped out between the gates in an attempt to calm the crowd. At first, all Brael could see was the top of his shaven head as the priest raised a tentative hand to the middle of his face. Blood had already begun to drip from his nose and pool on the flagstones.

'I think my nose is broken,' the priest replied, his voice shaking slightly. Removing his hand from his face, he regarded the blood on his fingers, then looked up at the stranger who stood over him.

'They want the Varks,' the young priest said as he looked up, his single eye blinking away the last of the tears caused by the punch that broke his nose. Every member of the priesthood was the same, each had but a single eye set just above the bridge of the nose. 'They say we're to blame.'

Brael was surprised to experience a powerful sense that he had been here before, talking to this priest outside the temple. He half expected that, if he looked to his side, Vika would be standing there, six-month-old Bron in her arms. Of all the unusual forms the bodies of some Mallaxians took that shown by the priest of the Holy Varks was the one that shook Brael the most.

The priest was on his feet and running across the precinct in the wake of the mob, which had hit the doors of the Sanctum like a crashing wave. On its way to the Sanctum, the mob had vented some of its anger on the plinths atop which were set votive candles and bowls of scented water and had shattered the small shrines that lined the walls before which Brael remembered Vika kneeling while the priest took Bron before the Holy Varks, behind the Sanctum's tall wooden doors.

Brael followed in the priest's wake. He doubted that the priests still inside the Sanctum would be foolish enough to open the doors while members of the mob struck it with their fists, slammed against it with their shoulders and howled for the destruction of the holy thing within. None of them had ever seen the Varks – only initiated priests were ever allowed into the Sanctum – but, from their shouts and threats, it was clear that they blamed the Varks for the arrival of the green-skins.

Brael could see their point. The Varks, it was claimed, was a relic of the days after the star gods' departure, to be used by the children they left behind to speak with their parents, no matter how far away. Inside the Sanctum was the last of the devices somehow still capable of sending a message into the darkness beyond the sky, still calling out to the star gods, telling them that their children still awaited their return.

If even half of the dogma was true, if whatever was kept behind the Sanctum doors – which were beginning to bow under the weight of the mob's continued assault – had somehow been sending a message into the void all this time, then it may have acted like a beacon to draw the greenskins, who must be creatures from a void more terrible than the worst imaginings of man.

'Stop!' The priest had reached the crowd. 'This is blasphemy! Now, more than ever, the Varks is our only–'

A broad-shouldered man detached himself from the rear of the mob and hooked his fist into the side of the priest's head. From the fluidity of the motion, Brael guessed he could have been a prizefighter before the war.

The priest stumbled but didn't fall. Seeing this, the broad-shouldered ex-fighter cocked his fist for a second, and no doubt more damaging, attack.

'You!' Brael shouted as he jogged the last few paces between them. 'What's your company? Why aren't you at your post? If the greenskins come tonight, where will you say you were? In the temple, beating up a priest?'

The ex-fighter paused, then lowered his fist. Several others looked round from the mob.

'If the greenskins come tonight, it'll be their fault!' shouted one of them, jabbing an accusing finger at the priest. Most of the mob seemed to hear this and to shout their agreement.

'Why should you care?' shouted one of the mob. 'I'll bet your hand had all its fingers this time a year ago.'

'My wife was a believer,' Brael replied. He knew now that there was nothing he could do to stop them.

'Then she was a fool and you were a bigger one for having her!' declared the ex-fighter, before grabbing the priest by the front of his robe.

Without thinking, Brael stepped forward and punched the big man in the side of the head, where the bone beneath the skin was thin. A year of fighting the greenskins had given him an eye for an opponent's weak points and an understanding of the value of being the first to strike.

The big man let go of the priest and staggered to the side. Brael saw that his knees were no longer steady and he advanced on him, fists cocked.

The splintering crash of the door to the priests' quarters, set to one side of the precinct, caused all heads to turn away from Brael and the ex-fighter, who had dropped to one knee and was pressing a hand to his bruised temple. A splinter group of five or six from the main mob pushed its furious way inside. The sounds of furniture being overturned and smashed began to emerge from behind the shuttered windows.

'Come on, we should be in there!' shouted someone in the middle of the mob outside the Sanctum. Ignoring Brael, they turned as one and began reapplying their weight to the tall doors. Something must have been broken during their last assault. With the sound of ancient hinges giving way and an exhalation of sweet, incense-laden air, the doors swung inwards.

The mob rushed up the three low steps and through the doorway. The young priest, his nose still bleeding, ran after them. Brael looked down at the ex-fighter, then held out his hand. The big man regarded the hand for a heartbeat, then took it and eased himself to his feet.

'Might was well see what they've been keeping in there all this time,' Brael said. The sound of shouts, scuffles and breaking furniture came from the dim-lit space behind the open doors.

'You know, I don't think I give a damn any more,' the ex-fighter replied. 'Good luck when they come,' he added then turned and began to make his way out of the precinct.

'You too,' said Brael, then he turned and followed the mob into the Sanctum.

Apart from the heavy scent of incense and the less powerful illumination provided by oil lamps set in high brackets on the walls, the Sanctum looked very similar to the roofless precinct outside: more votive bowls atop plinths, a slightly larger trio of shrines set in a line across the middle of the space, and more priests braving the angry fists of the mob, desperate to save their treasures.

Ranged along the sidewalls were sets of shelves, each of them bearing a number of decorated and carved boxes. Members of the mob swept the boxes from the shelves – their lids popped open or splintered when they hit the floor, ejecting the objects they had held for generations: pieces of metal bearing strange designs; a hollow metal finger from the statue of a giant; scraps of cloth. Rubbish being treated as relics. Some of the intruders waved the relics in the faces of the priests, before stamping them to dust or hurling them through the air.

Brael moved through the space, ignoring the sounds of breaking bowls, shattering plinths and the shouts and cries of mob and priests alike. This is where that priest brought his son, while he and Vika waited in the precinct. Bron was here once.

But where was the so-called 'Holy Varks'? Did the priest just cool his heels in here for a while, then return to the precinct, hand Bron back to his mother and accept a handful of coins in tribute? Was the Varks a joke, a moneymaking scheme that had lasted down the ages?

The Sanctum building was four-sided, its roof stepped. The space within, however, was different, Brael noticed. From the outside, the four sides were of equal length. From within, he saw, the walls to the left and right were shorter – almost half the length they should have been.

A glance at the roof above him confirmed his suspicion: the rear wall met the stepped slope of the ceiling at a higher point than the front or sidewalls. The rear wall, upon which hung an ancient, ragged banner whose design appeared to be that of a two-headed bird, wings spread, concealed another space.

Brael stepped up to the rear wall and cautiously drew aside the hanging. Despite its obvious age the fabric felt soft beneath his fingers, as if it were the product of a finer loom than had ever weaved cloth on this world. Behind the hanging was a door, its upper half a decorative grille.

Brael's cleaver sheared away the old lock and, letting the banner swing back into place behind him, he stepped cautiously into the room beyond.

'In the star gods' name begone!' The priest that flew at him must have been older than Brella had been when she finally passed away. He flapped weak, liver-spotted hands at Brael, who brushed him away as carefully as possible. Old knees gave way and the priest slumped to the floor, keening in an almost child-like voice.

'Our only hope!' the old priest wailed. 'Our only hope!'

Another priest – this one about Brael's age – rushed to the old man's aid. Brael didn't notice. He was staring at the Varks.

The web of wires and metal supports almost filled the otherwise bare space, reaching from wall to wall and from floor to the ceiling, which was barely visible in the weak yellow light given out by the three of four oil lamps that sat in niches in the walls. A low hum and a vibration that Brael felt in his breast gave him the sense that something living might be sitting within the web, drawing life along the cables and wires, which seemed to pulse with an almost imperceptible beat.

The delicate sound of well-oiled wheels turning in the darkness above drew Brael's attention upwards. Weak yellow lamplight caught the moving edges of a complex arrangements of cogs and gears. Thick, brass rods, their lengths turning and shining a dull, golden colour in the lamplight, reached down from the shadows to complex, geared connections with thinner rods of the same substance. These thinner rods then reached out to linkages with the web of hair-thin wires amongst which the Varks seemed to crouch, like a patient, hungry spider. Somehow, Brael was sure, the rotating rods fed power to the humming wires, which in their turn fed the pulsing, throbbing machine that beat in the room like an ancient mechanical heart.

Brael pressed a thumb to his temple as the beat seemed to seep into his skull. Behind him, the younger priest eased the still-keening elder to his feet.

'The Varks is our only hope,' the old priest wailed. 'As it was in the beginning, as it has been throughout our generations of solitude, so it is now.'

Brael spared a glance in the priests' direction. Satisfied that they were unlikely to try to eject him a second time, he took a step deeper into the room. The vibration in his chest intensified slightly, as did the pressure in his head. Looking at the dizzying construction of metal and wire that crossed and re-crossed the room induced a sense of vertigo, which Brael countered by focussing on one hair-thin wire that ran taut just above his head. He reached up towards it.

'NO!' The young priest's voice carried enough genuine fear that Brael paused before his fingers brushed the wire. 'The balance is delicate. One unbidden vibration will cause another and another...'

'This is the Varks?' Brael asked. 'This child's puzzle? My wife believed... I was told that the Varks was a beacon.' Brael was surprised by a sudden rush of anger. Vika had been duped into believing this nonsense could somehow speak to the stars. He thought briefly of not waiting for the young priest to answer, of just grabbing a handful of the wires and tearing the fragile construction to pieces.

'It is a beacon,' the priest replied. 'Can't you feel it?' He placed a hand against his chest. 'It's not a beacon as you might imagine – a fire atop a hill or the sound of a horn. Its signal passes invisibly through flesh and stone. It reaches up past the sky and out towards the stars. The web that fills this room provides it sustenance and serves to augment the signal, send it further into the void. The Holy Varks sits at the centre – as it should. There.'

Talking about the Varks had calmed the young priest; even the old man had stopped wailing. Brael squinted through the yellow gloom in the direction in which the young man was pointing. Through the web of intersecting wires he saw it: a metal box, no larger than the baskets that fruit-pickers would wear on their backs at harvest-time. Its surface glowed dully in the light, showing irregular patches of what might have been its original colour or the discoloration of the ages. Above the plinth on which it sat, the wires came together, twisting around each other as they swooped down towards it, becoming a single, tightly-wound cable before plunging into a socket set into its top. A single red light pulsed beside the machined collar that reinforced the connection.

'That speaks to the stars?' Brael was incredulous. 'I don't know who's the more ridiculous: you one-eyed clowns or the idiots that blame you for bringing the greenskins down on us.'

Brael strode towards the door. His head had begun to pound and he wanted to be out of here, out of this room, away from the buzzing in his head and the humming in his chest, out of the temple, away from everything that had somehow achieved the impossible, everything that had made Vika look foolish in his eyes.

The door burst open when Brael was still several steps from it. The old priest turned and he let out a screech when he saw the intruders pushing through from the outer chamber.

'Our only hope!' he wailed again. One of the first through the door broke his jaw then slammed him aside. As he fell, one of his legs broke with the sound of a snapping branch.

'No!' The younger priest held up his hands in a doomed attempt to halt the tide that just broke over him. He was punched to the ground, where he was kicked and stamped on almost in passing by everyone else who pushed through the door.

The mere presence of so many people in the room at one time had already begun to affect the network of wires that supported the Varks. The pulsation had become more noticeable, wires began to give off notes of differing pitches as they rubbed against each other or against the thicker metal frame from which they hung. The vibration in Brael's chest had changed, too. It had become irregular, like the broken rhythm he had felt in the chests of farm animals before the moment of their death.

'This is the Varks?' a thin, bald man asked Brael, who by now had pushed his way through the crowd and was about to leave the room. Brael just nodded. Then he heard it: the high-pitched snap of a tightly stretched wire giving way.

'One unbidden vibration will cause another and another...' Brael recalled the younger priest's words as the room was filled with the sound of snapping wires and crashes as sections of the frame were hurled to the floor. The rioters were not going to wait and see if one snapped wire was all it took. The network of wires and cables had already begun to sag around them as they tore at its fabric. Cables and struts fell from the shadows that obscured the ceiling, hitting those below. This only intensified their anger, which had already been stoked up by the destruction of the relics in the outer chamber.

The older priest's voice rose above the cacophony of the Vark's destruction once more: a single, ululating note of despair. Something about the sound made Brael's stomach roll over. Brushing past the bald man, he ducked out of the room.

MOST OF THE priests had abandoned the outer chamber. Those that were left were tending to the more badly injured, then helping them to their feet and heading for the main doors. When they saw Brael walking quickly through the chamber, they hastily stepped aside, not wanting to provoke another attack.

Brael ignored them. His stomach hadn't stopped churning and the ache behind his eyes was getting worse. He wanted to be away from the temple before he threw up.

There was a large crowd in the temple precinct. Brael presumed they had been drawn here by news of the riot. They were not, he noticed looking towards the Sanctum doors, through which he had just stepped. They were looking up at the night sky. Some were pointing. Others were muttering. No one seemed very happy at what they saw.

When he looked up, Brael saw that he sky was on fire. Lights fell through the inky blackness, drawing short, burning trails behind them. With a shock that was like a punch in the chest, he was standing in his yard with his son again. In a moment, his wife would emerge from the farmhouse and they would stand together, watching the display. There was no war, no invasion. No one had died. There was just a nagging ache at the back of his skull.

'Gods of harvest and home, no more!' wailed one woman. The man beside her put an arm around her and drew her to him. Others took up her lament.

'This is your doing!' A priest cried hoarsely. Dragging his gaze from the falling lights, Brael saw that it was the young man with the broken nose he had met outside the precinct.

'You and your kind have defiled the temple, destroyed the Holy Varks and have brought more misery upon us all. Look!' He jabbed a shaking finger skywards. 'Our damnation is confirmed! Our only hope is gone!'

And not one voice was raised against him.

Part Three

THE KEYS TO *the defence of Mallax were threefold:*

Time. Mallax was able to organise its defences in the year it took for the invaders to reach it. The manner in which the more northerly cities fell was analysed through the interrogation of survivors, collated by the city's Librarium staff and incorporated into the defence plans.

Manpower. Mallax appears to have been the defenders' ultimate fallback option almost from the moment they raised the citizen militias to augment the small standing armies maintained by the city barons. During the first six months of the invasion, those moving to Mallax were refugees – the very young, the very old and women with families. In the latter half of the invasion, fighters retreating from shattered cities and towns or from battlefield routs made directly for Mallax. By the time the assault began, the city's population had increased by a factor of four.

Technology. Mallax's guardians had made an effort to preserve its heritage, albeit obscured by myth and preserved in

*fragmented and debased forms (cross-ref. 663/159 – A.
Mechanicus Archivum: manufactoria processes; ballistic
archaeotech). The weapons held in museum storage were
made ready for the attack that was sure to come. Treatises on
siege warfare were unearthed from vaults beneath the Librarium and their High Gothic script pored and puzzled over.*

*Further investigation has led to the conclusion that,
though these preparations had a positive effect on the defenders' morale, most were under no illusions as to how the final
battle would be fought: street-by-street; hand-to-hand; to the
death.*

*– Extract: 'Inquisitorial communiqué
747923486/aleph/Samax IV' Author: Inquisitor Selene
Infantus. M41,793*

THE FIRST WARNING was the sighting of black shadows
chasing across the sky, long wings held rigid, too big to
be birds. Then they dropped. Then the bombs fell. The
attack had begun.

The bombs beat an explosive tattoo in the city at
Brael's back. His company had moved up from their
reserve post and now occupied a short stretch of the
curving eastern wall. Piles of debris had augmented the
ancient stone and steel battlements – scrap from the
manufactories, lumps of masonry from buildings in the
outer districts that had been demolished for the purpose. Incongruously, what could only have been an old
bedstead jutted out from the detritus a short way west
of their position.

Beyond the skeletal shape of the bedstead could be
seen the tall gatehouse towers of the heavily defended
North Gate. Every other gate had been sealed. Only the
North Gate might one day be opened to allow the population of Mallax – which probably now counted as the
population of the whole of Agra – to leave the city.

Looking along the curve of the wall, packed with armed men and women, weapons ready, their faces set and determined, it might be possible to believe they had a chance. But, when Brael looked out over the inner lip of the battlements' walkway, he saw the plumes of dirt and smoke kicked up by each bomb's explosion, he saw buildings crumble and he heard the cries of those trapped beneath the falling stones. As he looked over the city, he saw a manufactory's roof disappear beneath the impact of another bomb. A cloud of industrial filth puffed out of the building's windows and enveloped the district in which it sat. People would be choking in the streets, blinded by the thick, sooty cloud. Some might die, their throats fatally clogged.

It was almost a relief to turn away from the cityscape and to return his gaze to the horizon and the smoke-belching war machines, ridden by the greenskinned abominations that were assembled there.

Brael had returned from the Temple of the Varks to find Costes and Perror scanning the lightening horizon through the fire slit. The rest of the men were checking their weapons by the light of several oil lamps.

The company had grown, Brael noticed as he moved amongst them. Men from the mines had chosen to join his company rather than return to their own. Brael didn't ask why, nor did he attempt to reason them out of their apparent willingness to believe in an old aunt's tale.

'Keep your heads down!' Brael shouted over the sound of the explosions, more for the benefit of the new arrivals than the men who had fought and survived with him, some for the better part of a year. 'Keep your nerve!'

'We brought one of those damned things down outside Grellax,' Kleeve shouted. 'Why not now?'

'They're too high!' Brael replied. At that moment a shadow passed over them. Brael glanced up. The black silhouette that wheeled against the dawn sky seemed as large as the flying machine they had brought down outside doomed Grellax, but it wheeled and swooped higher above them, which meant it must be larger, the wings broader and perhaps better armoured.

'Maybe if they come down towards us,' he added.

'To get a better view of the slaughter?' Kleeve asked, a wry smile on his face.

'They're retreating!' Tombek shouted. The drumbeat of the bombs had ceased, to be replaced by the sound of falling masonry, the cries for help, the ringing of fire bells and the shouts of those assigned to man the mobile pumps that now clattered through the streets.

'I'd heard about those things, but I never imagined they were real,' said one of the survivors from the mines, a Mundaxian named Karel. 'Don't think much of their aim even now. I doubt any of them managed to hit the walls.'

'I doubt they were trying,' muttered Tombek. 'They just want to tell us what we can expect when they're through the walls.'

Karel looked as if he was about to say something in reply, but a familiar whistling cut through the air above them.

'Artillery!' came the shout from further along the street-wide walkway that ran behind the battlements. Once again, heads dropped between shoulders, hands covered ears and prayers were offered up to gods few believed in any more.

Not like this, Brael asked silently. He thought of the shattered Varks and of Vika and Bron. I want more blood on my hands before I die. Greenskin blood.

The walls bucked as the first shell landed. A cheer went up; it had landed in the empty districts in front of the wall.

'Ranging,' Tombek muttered.

The second artillery shell sailed over the heads of the men atop the western battlements and landed in the streets behind them, causing more damage than all of the bombs dropped from the flying machines. A chapel that had been converted into a physic station was vaporised, along with its immediate neighbours. Those buildings that escaped utter destruction were left shattered and teetering on the edge of a broad, deep crater.

The cheering on the walls ceased.

'Here it comes,' muttered Tombek.

The artillery fire came down upon the walls of Mallax like a hard rain, scouring away the metal and stone detritus that had been hauled up from the city streets to augment the ancient battlements. The men and women who sheltered behind, praying for a chance to strike back against the attackers, were reduced to tatters of skin and fragments of bone. Some panicked, broke cover and ran, only to be cut down by swarms of shrapnel from a hit further along the wall. The walls shook beneath the defenders' feet, as if a giant as tall as the sky was stamping down upon them.

Karel half rose from where he crouched against the battlements. Lollak, crouching beside him, put a restraining hand on his arm.

'I don't want to just sit here and wait to die!' the Mundaxian shouted over the bombardment. Lollak shook his head and pointed to where Brael crouched, back to the wall, beside the firing slit and the machine-rifle.

'We move when he says it's time!' Lollak shouted. 'He'll know when. Don't ask me how.'

They didn't need to do more than they were already doing, Brael thought as he sheltered in the lea of the battlements. So long as their ammunition lasted, they could pound Mallax to scrap and rubble from a distance that made them untouchable by the few ancient war machines that had been rescued from the city museum and pressed back into service on the wall: a handful of cannon; a complex-looking construction of wood and iron that hurled rocks by means of some kind of slingshot action; a pair of huge crossbows, able to fire bolts the size of small trees. The wall shuddered again, like an old man with the ague, as Brael wondered how many of the museum pieces had survived the bombardment so far.

The invaders could destroy Mallax from the horizon, but they would not. It wasn't their way. Something in their nature demanded that they tear apart whatever they found with their bare hands. Their appalling engine-driven weapons were just machines by which to accomplish this – to prepare their victims, to transport the greenskins to the battle at unnatural speed and to enable them to stand at the heart of the destruction. Their capacity and their enthusiasm for bloodshed was breathtaking, as unthinking as the fury of a storm and every bit as unstoppable.

They would come, Brael knew. Sooner or later, they would come.

THE DESTRUCTION OF *the North Gate, along with much of the gatehouse and neighbouring defences, appears to have acted as a signal for the ground assault to begin, though the city wall had already been breached at several other points by this time. Motorised units – objects of terror and awe even among those that had fought against them in the past – led the assaults at the North Gate and the other breaches. Bomber-variant gliders (cross ref. 775/xeno-tech – engine-driven catapult launching mechanism) re-joined the attack; one might assume they did so in order to sow confusion within the city ahead of the ground troops, though sheer bloodlust would be an equally credible moti-vation for this xeno-type (cross ref 114/xenology – Orkoid species).*

Despite the city's preparations, its destruction could now be measured in hours.

– Extract: 'Inquisitorial communiqué 747923486/aleph/Samax IV' Author: Inquisitor Selene Infantus. M41,793

BRAEL DUCKED AS a stretch of the defences to his company's right exploded, showering them with shrapnel. The shadow of a greenskin flying machine passed over their bowed heads like a presentiment of doom.

'It's coming back!' shouted Tombek, who had been the first to raise his head. Costes and Perror, huddled around the machine-rifle, were the first to recommence firing at the greenskins that were still racing at them in ragged waves, some on foot, others bouncing on the flatbeds of four-wheeled engines that ran on the same fat wheels as the two- and three-wheeled war machines. The four-wheelers seemed designed to carry their brutish cargo to where they could do the most damage, then tear back through the ruined outlying districts to collect another load.

The machine-rifle roared and coughed oily smoke as Perror depressed the trigger. The makeshift tripod, constructed from lashed-together pikestaves, shook violently as he swung its heavy barrel after one of the retreating motor-wagons. The heavy shells tore into the ground in its wake as it jagged across the narrow street in an effort to evade the gunfire.

A shell clipped one of the rear wheels, which exploded, sending the wagon into a slewing skid before slamming sideways into the wide frontage of what must once have been some kind of warehouse. The force of the impact brought down the wall and half of the roof.

Costes, crouching to one side of the weapon, checked that the ammunition belt would continue to feed through the rifle's inner mechanism without jamming, then slapped Perror's shoulder in celebration.

The walls were lost, Brael was sure. Off to their left, usually obscured by the curve of the wall and the height that had been added to the battlements, the North Gate had taken several hits at once. Shattered masonry and fragments of the gate's defenders had risen in a fluid gout, as if the greenskins had the power to transform the ground in which the city was rooted to liquid. At that moment, large numbers of the attackers had veered away from their original points of attack to make for the ruined gate. Within minutes, the first of them would be inside the city.

Brael's first instinct had been to lead his men to defend the breach, but the reappearance of the flying machines and their explosive payloads had pinned his company to their spot on the wall.

Following Tombek's shout, Brael looked up. There was the flying machine, wheeling in the sky in a parody of a bird's graceful arc.

Brael slapped Perror on the shoulder. When the gunner looked round, away from the firing slit, Brael pointed skywards.

'What to do you think?' he shouted. Perror and Costes exchanged glances then nodded, almost in unison. Under other circumstances, it would have been almost comical, the way in which they had formed a partnership around the looted greenskin weapon.

'We'll need something to rest it on, to raise the barrel,' Costes said. Brael nodded and began tearing at the rubble and rubbish that had been used to augment the battlements. An itch had begun to nag at the back of his mind which, he was sure, had nothing to do with the flying machine's diving approach.

Working quickly, Costes and Perror withdrew the rifle from the firing slit. Resting the tripod on the pile of detritus Brael had pulled from the wall, Perror had only heartbeats left to steady his aim.

'Thank the gods he's coming right at us,' Costes muttered, a moment before Perror depressed the trigger.

The greenskin must have realised what was about to happen. Brael saw the creature tug at the control levers that hung before him. The flying machine began to turn but, being larger than the machine they had encountered outside Grellax, this one was not so quick to change course.

The skin of one wing all but vanished as the machine-rifle's shells tore through it, breaking the wing struts before racing across the pilot's chest and doing the same to the other wing. The dive had become a fall.

'Move!' Brael shouted. He grabbed Perror by the back of his tunic and hauled him away from the gun. Costes, who had also realised where the creature's fall was going to end, had already begun to move.

The wrecked flying machine ploughed into the machine-rifle, shedding fabric and fragments of its superstructure, which seemed to chase Brael, Costes and Perror along the wall. Tombek, Lollak and most of the rest of the company joined them as they retreated at speed from the tumbling, rolling mess.

As soon as the flying machine had exhausted its momentum, they moved cautiously towards it, close-quarters weapons drawn. Perror was cursing it, threatening retribution if it had damaged the machine-rifle.

The pilot was dead, its slab-like head twisted at a fatal angle. Brael saw that several bombs were still attached to the harness in which the pilot had been suspended

beneath the wings. They were long-handled things with
a round charge at one end, the size of a man's fist, and
they looked equally suited to throwing as they were to
being dropped from the sky.

Perror's fears had been realised: the machine-rifle had
not survived the flying machine's impact. While he
cursed, the others fell to stripping the wrecked machine
and its pilot.

Brael let them work as long as he dared before order-
ing them off the wall. Several of the newer members of
the company raised eyebrows – there had been no order,
no call to abandon the battlements, but those who had
fought beside Brael before moved without question.

The shell that vaporised the section of wall Brael's
company had been assigned to defend was as large as a
small house. It had been fired from beyond the horizon
by a cannon as large as the engines that pulled the iron
caravans, before the city leaders had blocked up the termini gates and ordered that the rails be uprooted, in
order to prevent their use by the invaders.

The shell's only victim was the rapidly cooling corpse
of the glider-bomber's pilot. Brael had already led his
men down from the wall and out into the city.

ONCE INSIDE THE *city walls, the invaders abandoned all pretence of strategy. Confident of their eventual victory, their
command structure appears to have devolved upon small
groups, possibly defined upon tribal or familial lines, operating individually, seeking first to destroy then to plunder.*

*[NOTE: though the above is speculation, it is informed by
close study of relevant texts pertaining to ork psychology and
reported endgame tactics. (Cross ref 1119/xenology – psych
sub-list: Orkoid species and sub-species).]*

*Ironically, this lack of overall tactics proved beneficial in the
close-lined streets of Mallax, where large-scale actions would
have been impossible to co-ordinate successfully.*

The fighting moved from street to street. The invaders always pushing forwards, the defenders in barely-disguised retreat.

– Extract: 'Inquisitorial communiqué 747923486/aleph/Samax IV' Author: Inquisitor Selene Infantus. M41,793

'WHAT IN THE name of all that's holy are they?' Tombek hissed the words as he and Brael looked down from the window of a refining works that overlooked the flat, slag-strewn area around the minehead, the buildings that surrounded the shaft and the wheelhouse that stood over the shaft itself.

There were figures moving warily around the wheel-house: greenskins, but unlike any they had seen thus far. They were smaller than the animals that were rampaging through the city, smaller even than men of average height, Brael estimated. They appeared to be armed with lighter weapons than their larger kin: hand-guns and wickedly serrated knives. They wore little or no armour and moved between the slag piles and the buildings closer to the minehead in quick darting runs. It was impossible to estimate how many of them there were above ground.

'They must have climbed up the shaft,' Brael hissed his reply as he motioned for Tombek to slip silently back, away from the window. The rest of the company were waiting for them a street away. Those who recognised the area of the city they found themselves in, after Brael pulled them out of the dogged street-by-street retreat towards the old town, were already muttering their incomprehension.

'Either up the sides or using the chain like a ladder,' Brael continued as they moved quickly down the stairs to ground level.

'Aren't you forgetting something?' Tombek asked as they darted across the street at the rear of the refining works. 'Kobar closed the mine. You were there.'

'I know,' said Brael as he beckoned to the rest of his company from the corner of the street in which they were sheltering. His men moved quickly from door-ways and out over window ledges to assemble around him. 'But you saw them. You saw them come out of the wheelhouse.'

Tombek could only nod glumly and check the heavy pistol he had taken from the dead pilot of the flying machine while Brael briefed the rest of the men. Another of his notions had proved right. Tombek was too stolid, too concerned with the here-and-now to waste time with talk of witchcraft, but the accuracy of Brael's notions was uncanny. Brael always dismissed talk of them as anything other than good luck, but, as Fellick once commented, Brael must have grown good luck along with the animals on his farm to have accu-mulated so much. And this time he had led the company back to the mine like a hunting dog on a scent. He had known that there was danger there, dan-ger that had to be met.

'We all know what's going to happen to Mallax.' Brael surprised everyone by adding a coda to his typi-cally terse briefing. 'And we might not know exactly how it's going to happen, but we know the same thing's going to happen to us. I'm a farmer. I never wanted to be a soldier, but the greenskins made me one. They did the same to most of you. All I've ever wanted to do, since this nightmare began, is to make those animals regret what they turned me into.' Heads nodded in agreement. Brael scanned the faces that sur-rounded him.

'It's been an honour to know you, no matter how long it's been. Now let's go. For Mallax. For Agra.'

'For Mallax. For Agra.' Most of the company quietly echoed Brael's words, then moved off to their assigned positions.

It was probably just his melancholic disposition, Tombek told himself, but he couldn't shake the feeling that he had just heard the company's funeral oration.

FROM HER VANTAGE point at the window that Brael and Tombek had used to reconnoitre the area, Freytha Lodz watched most of the company run out from between the buildings below her and towards the mine's wheelhouse. None of the smaller greenskins had noticed them yet. Brael wanted to get as close as possible to their target before alerting every one of the creatures within earshot with the sound of gunfire – even if that gunfire was covering their advance.

Two loaded muskets of varying vintages were propped beside the window from which she peered. Five others had been assigned the job of covering the advance, each from their own vantage point; between them, they had divided up the company's entire stock of rifles, balls and blackpowder. Those who were racing towards the wheelhouse carried only hand weapons.

Something moved between the buildings off to the right. Freytha shouldered her rifle and brought it to bear. One of the smaller greenskins, armed with a pistol, was taking aim at Lollak's back.

Thinking of Vikor and her mother, Freytha squeezed the trigger.

IT WAS JUST one more gunshot in a city that rang with the sound of death's machinery, but it was enough to alert the greenskins that they were not alone. Brael spared a glance to his right; one of the smaller greenskins lay sprawled between two buildings. Its fellows grouped outside the wheelhouse now turned, bared evilly outsized teeth and brought their weapons to bear.

A few strides more, that's all I would've asked, he thought, then fired his looted greenskin pistol from the hip. A greenskin's face dissolved before it could fire its own pistol.

A glance upwards brought more bad news. The wheel atop the wheelhouse tower had begun to turn. The cage was rising.

A shot kicked up the ground ahead of him. More of the greenskins were running from between the buildings that surrounded the mine. Were they acting as scouts for their larger cousins? The creature that missed its shot at Brael was almost cut in half by Tombek's looted cleaver, held parallel with the ground and swung forward to strike while on the run.

Brael clubbed another greenskin down with the butt of his pistol, now held clumsily in his injured hand. In his good hand he held his own cleaver, which he brought down on the creature as it lay half-stunned at his feet. The larger greenskins were objects of awe as well as hatred, but these smaller animals made Brael's skin crawl.

He turned as something flashed by his cheek: a rust-flecked, serrated blade, wielded by another of the little monstrosities. Suddenly there seemed to be hordes of them, despite the covering fire from Freytha and the others, who were picking off a greenskin with every shot.

Brael brought his knee up into the creature's chest, knocking it back a step, before swinging his cleaver into the chittering, red-eyed mask of its face.

Above the killing ground, the wheel had come to a stop.

Kleeve was closest to the wheelhouse. Bleeding from a ragged cut to his arm inflicted by the last greenskin he had killed, knocking it to the ground with the pommel of his broad-bladed sword and then stamping on its skull until he felt the bone crack. He was only a stride from gaining the wheelhouse door and, a short way beyond it, the shaft and the lift cage. The explosive charge Brael had handed to him from the downed flying machine hung at his belt. There would be more of the smaller greenskins inside, he was sure, but by then it would be too late. They wouldn't be able to stop him using the bomb.

Dropping the sword, Kleeve pulled the bomb from his belt and made ready to pull the cord that hung from the bottom of its long handle. This would prime the charge. He would throw it into the cage the moment he was through the wheelhouse door.

'For Mallax!' he shouted. 'For–'

He didn't hear the familiar ratcheting cough because the first burst of gunfire at such close range reduced his entire upper body to little more than a red mist. The hand holding the unprimed bomb, severed at the elbow, hit the ground heavily. The greenskin filled the wheelhouse doorway, howled something incomprehensible and sprayed the killing ground with indiscriminate fire, killing as many of its smaller kin as Agrans who suddenly cut this way and that in search of cover.

Costes fell awkwardly, his left knee shot from under him. The pain was indescribable, but he managed to unhook the charge that he carried and hurl it to where Perror crouched behind a pile of centuries-old slag. Perror caught the charge, laid it at his feet, then made as if to run towards Costes.

'Wrong way!' Costes shouted through gritted teeth. He jabbed a finger towards the wheelhouse, where two more of the larger greenskins had stepped into view. Thinking back to his journey in the cramped cage, he wondered how many of the beasts, packed in with their oversized weaponry, could make the trip to the surface at once.

For a heartbeat, Perror looked undecided. Then he nodded, picked up Costes's charge, primed it and stood to throw it towards the wheelhouse. It was still in the air when he unhooked his own bomb, primed it and threw it in the wake of the first.

One of the beasts at the wheelhouse door reacted quickly to the movement to its flank, bisecting Perror with a long burst from its machine-rifle. The bombs, however, were already in flight.

THE DOUBLE DETONATION became a triple concussion as Perror's bombs set off Kleeve's dropped charge, filling the wheelhouse with smoke and littering the ground around the doorway with lumps of bleeding alien meat. One of the greenskins – the furthest from where Perror threw the charges – was still twitching, its one remaining eye glowering and livid. Karel, who had seen most of his company die in the mines, drove the wide hunting knife that was all that remained of his previous life deep into the red socket.

Karel was still bent over the no-longer twitching corpse when, bellowing its rage and bleeding from a dozen minor shrapnel wounds, a fourth greenskin emerged from the smoke that hung across the shattered and sagging wheelhouse doorway.

A volley of sharp reports rang out, like fire crackers at a harvest festival. The greenskin took a step back, surprised by the musket balls that ricocheted off its breastplate, and slapped at the two bullets that found bare skin. It roared its defiance to the snipers it couldn't see, then took a step towards Karel, who took a corresponding step back. The hunting knife in the Mundaxian's hand looked absurdly puny when compared to the broad-bladed axe wielded by the beast that stalked towards him.

The pistol that Brael had scooped up from where its smaller greenskin owner dropped it, fingers snapping open when a shot from Brael's own looted pistol punched through its skull from front to back, made a deeper sound. The huge greenskin jolted backwards, hand raised to its face, before dropping to its knees.

Tombek was already running towards it, having kicked away from the smaller greenskin that had been dancing around him, trying to gut him with a long, hooked blade. The greenskin was wearing a helmet that covered the back of its neck, so Tombek had only one good target to aim for.

As if on cue, the creature took its hand from its face. One side of its huge shovel jaw was a leaking mess. Tombek cocked his arm and picked up speed.

The greenskin saw Tombek coming but had no time to react. The cleaver blade struck beneath its chin, severing its windpipe and lodging amidst the dense muscles of its thick neck. The blade also hit a vein, sending thick ichor jetting over Tombek as he jinked to one side to avoid any reflex counter attack from the dying beast.

'Gods, is that it?' Lollak's question hung in the air. Brael suddenly realised that there seemed to be nothing left to fight: the ground before the wheelhouse door was scattered with green corpses of different sizes. Any of the smaller creatures that were still alive must have ducked back into the cover from which they had come. Were they naturally cowardly creatures, unlike their bloodthirsty cousins?

Hearing a now familiar creaking from overhead, Brael looked up. The wheel was turning again.

'Tombek! Lollak! With me!' Brael barked. 'The rest of you, cover our backs.' Brael sprinted for the wheelhouse door, pistol left in the dirt, cleaver held ready to parry the attack he expected to meet him as he jumped through the doorway.

The small greenskin at the winch controls was badly wounded, its body peppered with shrapnel. Another of the creatures lay face-up and blank-eyed a short way off. Seeing Brael, the wounded creature had time to utter a single shriek before its headless corpse dropped where it stood, hand still clutching the winch control lever. The head, propelled by the force of Brael's blow, bounced as far as the other green body before coming to rest.

Brael gripped the lever and pulled back, bringing the cage to a stop somewhere in the shaft below. In the sudden quiet that replaced the sound of the heavy lift chain feeding down the shaft, Brael could hear voices – guttural, animal voices – echoing up from the depths.

'How many of them are down there?' Lollak wondered out loud. He and Tombek had moved to the open pit-shaft gate. Both had unhooked the last of the flying machine's bombs that hung from their belts.

'And how did they get there?' Tombek added. 'Kobar brought the gallery down upon their heads. If they have engines that can drill through that...' His speculation trailed off. Perhaps the greenskins had found another route to the shaft, but Brael doubted it. Mab had spent years studying the layout of the mine and she had been sure that there was only one tunnel, which meant the invaders had tunnelled through the mountain of rock Kobar had dislodged in less than a day.

'We haven't got a hope, have we?' asked Lollak, as if realising this for the first time.

'Not if they get to the surface,' Brael replied. Tombek nodded and primed his bomb. Lollak made to do likewise.

'Save yours,' Brael said. 'I've a sense we'll need it.'

THEY SPRINTED FROM the wheelhouse while the bomb was still falling. The remainder of the company, none of whom was without at least a minor wound, followed their example, racing towards the buildings in which the snipers crouched.

The explosion was muffled, almost lost in the sound of heavy artillery still pounding the walls. It was followed, however, by a much larger concussion that rippled through the ground beneath their feet. Turning back towards the wheelhouse, they saw the tower on which the wheel sat begin to fall in on itself. One girder at a time it began, then faster, like a leaf being crumpled in the palm of a closing hand.

Then suddenly it was gone, dropping out of sight in a cloud of black smoke and soot, taking much of the wheelhouse's roof and walls with it on its way down the mineshaft.

'They must have been carrying some bombs of their own,' muttered Karel.

'That was one of their own bombs,' Tombek added. Brael was astonished to see the large, melancholic Vinaran smile beneath the second skin of filth, blood and alien ichor that they all wore.

'Where now?' Lollak asked. The snipers had left their posts and were stepping warily into sight, scanning the area with their musket barrels. Brael smiled when he saw Freytha emerge from the doorway of the warehouse in front of which they had assembled. Seeing Brael, Freytha smiled back.

Hearing Lollak's question, all eyes turned to Brael.

'Wherever we'll do the most good, I suppose,' he said, unable to think of a better answer. For a moment, the hopelessness of their situation threatened to overwhelm him. No matter where they went, the final outcome would be the same: annihilation.

'We should move, in case the noise attracts a larger force. We don't want to get trapped here.' He forced himself to think constructively. 'Can you move?' he asked Costes, who was being supported by two men whose names Brael couldn't recall – they had joined his company after the first action in the mine. Costes nodded tightly, but his pain was writ large across his face. His shattered knee had been wrapped in strips torn from someone's tunic, but the wound was still bleeding freely.

'When I can't go any further, just leave me with one of those,' Costes said through a rictus of pain, indicating the remaining charges carried by Brael and Lollak.

Brael smiled and nodded. He was about to give the order to move out when the front of a nearby warehouse dissolved in a cloud of ancient brick dust and flying debris. Brael's men scattered, some diving to the ground for cover, others ducking back inside nearby doorways.

Kneeling in a firing position in the doorway she had only just stepped out of, Freytha aimed down the long barrel of her musket at the cloud of dust that still hung in the gap where the warehouse wall had been. Something was stepping into sight. Something big. Something that roared with the same oil-clogged voice as the greenskins' wheeled war machines.

It was built like a man – two arms, two legs, a barrel-shaped body it would take two men to reach around, standing half as tall again as Tombek, the tallest man in Brael's company. Instead of flesh, its hide was of beaten metal plates riveted together in a haphazard manner and daubed with coarsely-executed tribal markings of the kind that adorned all the invaders' machines and other weapons.

And it was not alone:

Two more of the roaring metal creatures flanked the first. In place of one arm, one of the flanking creatures had what appeared to be a double-barrelled cannon, while the other's left arm ended at the wrist, where a circular blade had been attached. This blade was spinning in a blur of serrated teeth. Each of the machines' remaining arms ended as did both arms of the first, in heavy pincer jaws.

Freytha steadied her aim, then fired at the long slit which ran across the front of the machine on the left of the trio. Her shot ricocheted off the plate metal. Alerted to her presence, the machine turned, coughing plumes of black smoke from the engine it wore bolted to its back like a heavy pack, and brought its cannon to bear.

Freytha was already on the move when the doorway in which she had sheltered dissolved. Tracing a zigzag path she found cover behind one of the piles of slag that dotted the area around the mine. The war machine adjusted its aim as it marched towards Brael's scattered company in ragged formation with its fellows. Brael's men now began vainly to pepper its hide with gunfire from muskets and looted greenskin pistols.

Seeing the cannon swing towards the pile of ancient, solidified muck behind which Freytha had dived, Brael jumped to his feet, priming his charge as he did so. But he threw quickly and misjudged the distance. It exploded harmlessly off to one side of its target. The juggernaut's cannon fired again, reducing the slagheap to a crater.

'Pull back!' Brael yelled. 'Pull back!' The machines had moved apart, looking to encircle at least some of the men. The cannon fired again – claiming the lives of two recruits from the mine – and again, this time vaporising a militiaman Fellick had rescued during the retreat from Grellax. After each shot, it needed only a heartbeat's pause before it could fire again.

The pitch of the circular blade's whine changed as it carved through the broad wooden doors of a warehouse into which Brael had seen another of his company flee. The blade withdrew and the pincer-hand reached in. It was greeted by a short scream, suddenly cut off. The pincer shone wetly when it was withdrawn from the doorway.

The first of the machines to come into view slammed a foot down beside a prone figure that lay face down, arms and legs splayed out. As the machine strode on, the body moved. From where Brael now crouched – behind an overturned goods wagon – he saw that it was Lollak. From beneath his body, he drew the last of the looted bombs. Easing himself quickly to his feet, he ran after the war machine that had passed him by.

Brael fired a round at the machine's eye-slit, anxious to keep it from noticing Lollak, who primed the charge and threw it with a delicate underarm action. It flew between the monstrosity's articulated legs and landed directly beneath its body as it completed another step.

Brael caught a glimpse of Lollak hurling himself to one side before the machine erupted. Fire gouted from the engine bolted to its back. Shards of twisted metal were torn free from its bodywork and sent spinning in all directions. Smoke boiled up, around and through its bodywork, emerging in a stream from the eye-slit. One leg was blown away and the machine keeled over, its engine screeching wildly for a moment longer before it too fell silent. Thick, foul-smelling oil began to pool around the inert carcass.

There was no sign of Lollak.

Brael ran past the still-burning metal corpse. Already the sickly-sweet odour of roasting meat hung in the air. Casting about, Brael spotted the prone figure, evidently thrown aside by the force of the blast. As before, Lollak's arms and legs were flung out at odd angles. This time, however, he was not faking.

Brael saw the mess made of one side of Lollak's head by the blast and the rain of flying shrapnel: bloody torn skin, through which Brael glimpsed bone. Lollak's eyes were open, the whites filled with blood and they bulged slightly from their sockets. Blood ran in a thick trail from his slack mouth.

Suddenly, Brael felt very tired. More tired than he had felt since the war began. More tired than he had imagined it was possible to feel. It was over, he was suddenly sure: the war, his life, everything.

The ground shook. Brael turned and saw one of the dead machine's comrades stamping towards him. The spinning blade whined as the machine held it high, ready to bring it down upon him. He knew he should something – run, hide, counter-attack, anything – but, as time seemed to stretch and the screeching blade hung over him for a lifetime, he also knew that nothing he did would make the slightest difference.

From somewhere high above him, Brael thought he heard another engine howl – another of the invaders' war machines, he was sure. Then every hair on his body stood on end. His skin began to tingle and a thin metallic taste coated his mouth.

And then the sun reached down from the sky and hurled the war machine aside.

A burst of blue-white brilliance dazzled Brael and a warm pulse of air seemed to pick him up and hurl him in the opposite direction. He landed heavily, then rolled instinctively to his feet. The torpidity that had seized him as he knelt over Lollak's corpse was gone. Shaking his head and blinking away the blotchy after-images that clogged his vision, he reached for his belt, to find only an old hunting knife he had carried with him since he had left his farm. The looted pistol and greenskin cleaver were lost.

The engine-howl he had heard was louder now, though the note was deeper, as if the mechanism were running more slowly. A figure landed heavily on armour-shod feet in the space where the greenskin war machine had stood. Like the invaders' creation, it stood half as tall again as any man, its smooth hard skin decorated with symbols: crossed arrows, wings on the massive plates that covered its shoulders. Its skin was dark crimson, almost the colour of clotted blood, and though hard and unyielding as the skin of the invaders' walking machines, its clean lines closely mirrored the shape of a man. It had a kind of sheen that reminded Brael of nothing so much as the glaze on fired pottery.

The engine-whine came from a mechanism mounted high on the figure's back and shoulders. Vanes within its two exhausts glowed white hot and the heat washed over Brael as he shook the last of the blotches from his sight. In one hand the figure held a sword, as long as a man's arm and bearing a row of serrated teeth which, Brael was sure, could leap into blurring motion in a heartbeat. In its other hand, the figure held what looked like a breed of pistol. A slight blue-white glow danced around the weapon's barrel.

As if realising that it was being watched, the figure turned. Its mask-like face bore a pair of red, glowering eyes, reminding Brael of the bloody malevolence in the invaders' gaze. On its chest were displayed a pair of spread wings that Brael had seen before: on the wall-hanging in the Sanctum of the Temple of the Holy Varks.

With a shock that almost unmanned him, Brael realised that he was standing before of one of Vika's beloved star gods.

With the same descending note from the engines on their backs, three more crimson-skinned gods dropped from the sky. While still at the height of the surrounding rooftops, they fired a volley of explosive shells at the remaining war machine. The shells ploughed up the ground around the monstrosity, whose own cannon had been cranked as high as possible and was returning fire. One of the invaders' shots struck one of the gods high on the chest, causing his falling trajectory to spin out of union with his fellows. Struggling to regain control of his flight, the figure crashed through the roof of one of the surrounding warehouses and disappeared in a shower of timbers and rubble.

The remaining three pumped round after round into the barrel-chested machine, which staggered back under the multiple impacts before crashing to the ground and lying still, smoke and oil pouring from cracks and punctures in its bodywork.

Eyes flicking wildly around the scene, Brael saw that the survivors from his company were emerging from cover to watch as the gods landed and took up what Brael was surprised to recognise as perimeter positions. A warehouse doorway exploded outwards, causing the gods to shift their positions, ready to meet a new threat. When the god who had been hit by a cannon round emerged, they resumed their earlier stance.

Brael was relieved to see Freytha among the survivors, though one side of her face was painted black by the explosion and red by the blood that ran freely from a long cut across her scalp. Seeing Brael, she shouted to the others who turned and saw him standing before one of the creatures from the sky.

With a rasping, machine-quality, the star god spoke to Brael. Most of what it said was unintelligible, though Brael was amazed to discover he could make out two or three words. Then the metallic tirade ceased and the star god turned away, striding towards the others of its kind, over whom it appeared to have some authority.

Freytha ran to him, as did many of the others, Tombek among them. The tall Vinaran paused briefly over Lollak's corpse.

'Are they? Are they really?' asked Freytha, breathlessly.

'Star gods?' Brael replied, barely able to hold back tears, so powerfully did he feel Vika's presence at that moment. 'I... I think so.'

'Did it speak to you?' asked another of the recruits from the mines. 'I thought I heard it speak to you. What did it say?'

'I'm not sure,' Brael tried to find some meaning in the few words he thought he had understood. 'It sounded like our speech, but there was a lot I couldn't make out. I think he said "High God's Hunting Birds".'

'Could be their name,' Tombek added.

Others joined in the debate, but Brael suddenly felt light-headed, on the verge of tears. He waved what he hoped was a reassuring hand at Freytha, then walked slowly past Lollak's corpse and the still-smouldering remains of the war machine the dead Terraxian had destroyed. He was dimly aware that the star gods were moving around the immediate area, making it secure, perhaps for the arrival of more of their kind – Vika's stories told of whole armies of gods, all serving a god of their own, the high god.

Vika. His dead wife seemed to walk before him, leading their son by the hand and telling him the stories he never tired of hearing. The memory of her voice, the sense that she was there, no more than an arm's length away, was so powerful it threatened to crush him. For a moment, his vision was edged with grey. A high-pitched whining grew to fill his ears.

Suddenly, Vika and Bron were gone. The high-pitched whine resolved itself into the sound coming from the last of the invaders' war machines to fall. Brael had walked towards it unaware, following his wife's ghost. Eyes refocusing on the machine, he saw that part of its upper structure had been torn away by a glancing impact. The eye slit had been torn open; Brael saw green skin and a glowering red eye.

Its pincer arm was a ruin, but still sufficiently strong to enable it to right itself. One knee joint was locked solid. Apparently unaware of Brael's presence, the invader within the barrel-like shell manoeuvred the machine with a dragging, shuffling gait until it faced the star gods, three of whom now stood in a group, while a fourth planted a device in the ground nearby. A light atop the device pulsed with a steady rhythm.

With a distressed grinding, the war machine's cannon was brought to bear on the crimson figures.

Shouting incoherently, Brael sprinted towards the war machine and threw himself into the air. He hit the machine just behind the shoulder joint of the shattered pincer arm. Digging into irregularities in the machine's overlapping plate armour and scrabbling with his feet, he hauled himself more securely aboard and slid his hunting knife from his belt.

The greenskin inside the machine was not about to be distracted by the surprise attack from the flank. It fired off two quick rounds at the armoured figures, determined to have blood, regardless of its own fate. But Brael's cries had done enough. Alerted, the greenskin's target group broke apart, two running to either side, the third taking to the air in a sudden rush of noise. All three of them brought their weapons to bear on the war machine, the suddenly airborne member of the group performing a mid-air pirouette to do so.

'No!' Freytha screamed and took off at a run towards the war machine. 'Don't shoot! You'll hit Brael!'

The war machine was jolting and swinging its body to left and right in an attempt to dislodge Brael, who clung tightly to the uneven, riveted surface with one hand as he held his knife in the other and worked his way towards the eye-slit and the section of the carapace that had been peeled back the way a man might peel back a fruit's skin to reach the flesh inside.

The greenskin inside the war machine must have realised this was his intention, as it threw the machine into ever more frantic jolts and jumps, made all the more irregular by the damaged knee joint. Brael felt one foot slip off the overlapped joint between two metal plates and knew he had only moments left before he was sent flying.

Pushing off with his other foot and hauling with his free hand, he swung round the curve of the machine's bodywork and plunged his knife-wielding hand elbow-deep through the split in its metal skin.

The blade struck something and bit deep. A howl erupted from within the machine as Brael pulled back his arm and struck again. The machine went into paroxysms, mirroring the pain and outrage of its pilot. The pincer arm swung wildly, cuffing Brael across the temple. This, combined with a sudden reverse in the machine's direction sent him tumbling through the air.

The first of the star gods' explosive bolts struck the war machine while Brael was still airborne. He hit the ground heavily, feeling something break as a sustained, ear-bursting volley from the gods' weapons punched into the greenskin's machine, first puncturing, then shredding its metal carapace and pulping the creature within.

Lying on his back, Brael saw one of the gods above him, dropping towards him from the sky. The closer the descending figure came, the greater the pressure Brael felt inside his head. Blood burst from his nose in a rush and his head began to pound. There came a rushing in his ears as the star god touched down, then knelt closer to him. He had holstered his pistol and hung his sword from his belt. Armoured hands reached up to release catches around his neck and he lifted the red-eyed mask from his face.

Golden eyes. Brael thought as darkness rushed in to claim him. Vika was there, with Bron. They were standing outside his farmhouse watching lights trail across the sky. The star god had golden eyes.

Part Four

*'...*IN THE NAME *of the Emperor... in the name of the Emperor... in the name of the Emperor...'*

– Signal detected by Imperial Long-Range Cartographic Survey Ship Beacon of Hope. *M41,791*

IN THE WEEKS he had been there, Brael had got used to the sounds of the physic station – nurses and sawbones moving between the pallets that were arranged in rows across the floor of what had once been a tannery. His bed was on the second floor of the tall, wide old building. Beneath him was a ward for the more seriously wounded. The operating tables were on the ground floor. Sometimes, the screams were loud enough to reach his floor, where they would invade his dreams, and probably those of every other man in the ward.

The scent of old leather and the animal waste-products used to toughen the hides still clung to the walls. It seemed to seep up from the floorboards at night. This didn't bother Brael; it reminded him of home.

The sounds of battle had faded. At first, the physic station had been a chaos of screaming wounded laid across the bare floor in pools of their own blood. Brael learned later that Costes had died here, his life seeping from his shattered knee. The sawbones and nurses could do little more than utter a prayer while applying a dressing. Whether they lived or died was in the hands of the gods.

The star gods, Brael reminded himself.

More of the crimson-armoured deities had landed, Tombek had told him during a visit. They were faster and stronger than any single man and the armour they wore was more war machine than mere protection. The awe-struck Vinaran spoke of vast flying machines that sounded like approaching thunder, spewing more and more of the gods from their bellies, along with smaller flying machines that skimmed over the rooftops, raining bolts of fire upon the greenskins in the streets. On foot, they moved through the city like a cleansing fire, rarely uttering a word, but working together as if they had spent their whole lives dedicated to war.

As he listened to Tombek – and to Freytha and even to Fellick, who had survived the attack, leading a scratch company of walking wounded in the streets around the physic station he had been carried to after the attack in the mines – Brael's broken legs and ribs ached to heal faster. He learned to be let out of the ward so that he might see these wonders for himself. He wondered at night, when sleep eluded him, or during the day, when boredom hovered nearby: was this his punishment for refusing to believe in the star gods?

The greenskins had retreated from Mallax, leaving their corpses for the pit or the pyre (Mallaxian engineers were already speculating on how much energy a burning greenskin might generate) and their damaged war machines for scrap or salvage (there were already plans to create a trackless iron caravan). If not for the countless lives lost, the invasion might have been counted a windfall.

THE IMPERIAL HAWKS' *first wave secured several key points throughout the besieged city. Navigational beacons were placed at the most suitable locations and further units of Space Marines were despatched from their battle barge,* The Carmine Talon. *My party had docked with the* Talon *while en route to Samax IV and I was able to observe the operation from the barge's bridge chapel.*

The Imperial Hawks specialise in fast attack from the air, utilising high-altitude, jump pack-assisted assaults, followed by reinforcement sorties from squadron-strength units of land-speeders, often dropped at altitude and at high-speed from Thunderhawk drop-ships. The effect upon unsuspecting enemies can be spectacular – as was the case in Mallax.

After a year of virtually unobstructed movement south along the length of Samax IV's single main landmass, the invaders had grown complacent, their discipline (always a weak point) lax. Though the defence of the besieged city had been tenacious and impressive by the standards of the native inhabitants, it had presented little real challenge to the aliens. The sudden arrival a company of Space Marines – the Imperial Hawks' Fourth Company – was enough to shock their campaign into reverse. Less than a week after the Imperial Hawks' first assault, the invaders were in full retreat and, as I write, the Hawks are readying themselves for a series of lightning strikes behind the retreating alien line, to capitalise on their disarray and to sow more confusion.

At this juncture, it seems germane to acknowledge that a dispassionate observer might have expected the invaders to make far shorter work of the conquest of Samax IV, given the lack of technological resources and the low level of cultural sophistication on the part of the natives. This may serve to support Harkness's Theory of Orkoid Relativism (cross ref. 999/xeno-anthropology/heretical writings/Harkness, V. [excom. M41,665]) which states that the motivation and tactical sophistication exhibited by this xeno-type may be influenced by the level of resistance offered by their target species. We can assume that the invaders didn't consider the inhabitants of Samax IV much of a challenge.

It is also possible that they had expected resistance on a similar level to that found on reconquered Imperial worlds, given that, in all probability, they had picked up the same Gothic-encoded transmission (albeit using a long-obsolete cipher) as did the survey ship, Beacon of Hope. Whether the aliens detected the signal later than the survey ship, from closer proximity to the planet, will probably remain an unanswered question.

The discovery that Samax IV was unprotected, primitive and ripe for the picking is likely to have served to further encourage a complacent attitude to the inevitability of its conquest.

By this time the troop transports carrying regiments of the Ibrogan Guard had arrived in orbit, diverted at my request from their homeward journey after the suppression of the cultist uprising on Oestragon III. The regiments were set down in the wake of the advancing Imperial Hawks and most were tasked with securing the re-conquered ground. A number of sergeants from the Ibrogan 9th were assigned the task of recruiting and training a local militia to bolster the Ibrogan effort and to act as scouts in their northward progress.

– Extract: 'Inquisitorial communiqué
747923486/aleph/Samax IV' Author: Inquisitor Selene
Infantus. M41,793

'THE STAR GODS aren't alone,' Fellick told him during a visit. 'There are others. Others like us.'

Since early yesterday, Fellick reported, more of the thundering machines had dropped from the sky. Coming to rest outside the remains of the city walls, they had disgorged hundreds, maybe thousands of uniformed men and women. They bore arms similar in kind to those used by the star gods and spoke the same language – a tongue that seemed familiar, though was also very different. If you listened hard, Fellick said, it was possible to get a sense of what they were saying.

'It's as if we all spoke the same language once,' Fellick added. 'Only some of us forgot it and made up bits of our own. One of them showed me a map. There are other worlds like ours, too many to count. These people come from one of them.'

Brael struggled to take it in and longed to see it for himself. The itching beneath the tightly bound splints drove him to distraction, reminding him that it would still be a while before he could join one of the new companies that were being formed from those who had survived the defence of Mallax. Tombek had joined up immediately and, to his immense embarrassment, had been appointed a platoon commander. Freytha had also enlisted. She told Brael that she wanted to lead her unit into Grellax.

'Thank you for finding me there,' she said, before embracing him and kissing his cheek. 'Thank you for giving me a reason to stay alive.'

First Tombek, then Freytha. Karel the Mundaxian also came to say his goodbyes.

'Hope I have half your luck,' he said as he left.

Watching him go, Brael hadn't felt very lucky. While the others went north, to homelands they all thought were lost to the invaders forever, he had no choice but to lay on the pallet like one of the dead.

* * *

MY PARTY MADE *planetfall aboard the drop ship assigned to the Mechanicus support unit attached to the Imperial Hawks Fourth Company and set up an Inquisitorium and Chapel of Penitence in a temple in the old quarter of the city. There the Hawks had discovered the remains of a pre-Heresy pattern vox unit, which we believe was the source of the signal detected by the Beacon of Hope. The ancient device had evidently become an object of veneration and had been maintained in weak, though working order by a cadre of priests upon whom the mark of the mutant was writ clear and unambiguously.*

The priests' cyclopean disfiguration was but the first of a host of mutations, great and small that have since been uncovered and catalogued by my party and myself. If we wish to make Samax IV fit to return to the bosom of the Imperium, our work here has only just begun.

'THERE'S ONE,' BRAEL nodded towards a figure standing at the far end of the ward, where there were no windows. A man, he was dressed from head to toe in black, which made him difficult to make out in the flickering candlelight that lit that end of the room.

'See him?' Brael asked Fellick, who had come to tell Brael that he too was to join a new company.

'They're trying to make me an officer,' he had laughed. 'Seems they're unwilling to take "No" for an answer.'

Fellick shifted on the end of the pallet casually, as if stretching a cramped back.

'I see him,' he said. 'There are others, some in black, who've been paying the new companies a visit. And there are others in red. They've moved into the manufactoria. Some who've seen them say they're actually machines that look like men. Others say they're men who are wearing machines like the greenskins wore those walking war engines. They've got bodyguards of their own and they've forbidden anyone to enter the manufactoria, even those who used to work there. Nobody in their right mind would want to get too close to them, anyway.'

'I've only seen the ones like him,' Brael said. 'They just seem to walk around. They don't talk to anybody and they don't actually do anything.'

'Probably just checking to see there aren't any malingerers,' Fellick suggested.

'That's what I'm hoping,' said Brael. 'A sawbones said the splints could come off soon – in a day or so.'

'Now that's good news,' Fellick grinned. 'Get you back up on your feet and put a rifle in your hand. Maybe I'll have you in my company, if you're up to it!'

They both laughed, then talked for a while about the past, about the men and women they had fought alongside – Tombek still kept an eye out for Massau – but neither of them talked seriously of the future. So much had changed in the past year and had changed again with the arrival of the star gods, the soldiers from other worlds and the unnerving strangers in black and in red.

Agra had been everything they had known, but now it was a struggle to embrace the idea that it was just one world among thousands, perhaps more. The future was a whirlpool of unguessable possibilities that, if stared into for too long, threatened to suck you down.

It was likely, his friend had told him, that there wouldn't be time to visit again.

'See you on the battlefield,' Brael had said to him.

'Not if I see you first!' Fellick had replied. His laughter had been audible through the second and first floors.

I wish I had your faith, Vika, Brael thought of his wife, eyes closed, after Fellick had left. He felt sure that his wife would have been able to accept these changes more easily. The star gods had been part of her world all her life.

And Bron. Brael imagined the look of wonder on his son's face. This would have been even more exciting than watching the lights fall across the sky.

Sensing that he was being watched, he opened his eyes. A woman was looking down at him from the side of his pallet. She wore black. A single metallic icon sat high on her left breast. Her hair was straight and fell to the level of her strong jaw line. Her nose was long and straight, her eyes were dark and her gaze was direct. She showed no emotion as she stared down at him, the way Brael remembered Bron would examine a bug he had not seen before: distant, interested in what the creature might do next.

'My lady,' Brael attempted, without knowing if his words would make sense to his observer. 'My name is Brael Corfe. I come from north of here.'

Still the woman looked down upon him, head cocked slightly to one side. No emotion.

'I had a wife. A son. They died because the greenskins came. I have killed greenskins, before the star gods came, and I want to kill more.'

At this, Brael thought he saw the woman nod – the movement was so slight it was hard to be sure – then she turned and walked away. She wore a slim cloak, gathered at her shoulders by silver-trimmed epaulettes. The cloak billowed as she walked. Brael watched her pass the other pallets without a glance and disappear through the doorway to the stairs.

As was to *be expected, the Adeptus Mechanicus have taken possession of the city's meagre technological assets. They pay no attention to the populace, who regard them and their servitor entourage with barely disguised fear and disgust. Cornelia, my astropath, will remain alert to detect any unexpected transmissions bound for Mars, concerning their discoveries.*

The population of Mallax and what little human life survives beyond its walls is the sole concern of the Inquisition.

SHE RETURNED THAT night. She brought with her a lantern that threw out a beam of bright, pure light and cast a sphere of almost holy radiance around Brael's pallet.

She was not alone. At first, Brael thought it was a child. When it stepped fully into the light, he was shocked to see that it was probably older than him by at least a generation. Its body, however, appeared to have stopped growing after six or seven summers. Its eyes were black pebbles set in the creases and folds that enveloped their sockets.

'Brael,' the woman said. Her voice was soft, her pronunciation of his name tentative, as if she were testing it, trying to match her pronunciation to his. 'Brael Corfe.'

Hearing his name spoken thus eased the fears that had begun to creep through his mind.

'Lucky man,' she continued. Did she know more about him than just his name? 'Talk me. Tell me.'

And so Brael told her about the last year of his life. He couldn't avoid mentioning Vika and Bron, Vika's belief in the star gods and how excited Bron would have been to see them. He told her about the lights in sky, the smoke from the mountains and the rolling tide of death that rushed down from them. He told her about the war, the loss of town after town, city after city. He told her of the men and women he had fought beside: those who had died, and those few who had survived. He told her about Grellax. He told her about Mallax, about the mines, the Holy Varks and the final assault. As he did so, he felt a weight rise up from him. He felt that all that he had done, all that he had endured had been for the good. The death, the suffering had not been in vain. The return of the star gods and their followers had given meaning to it all.

He lost track of time as he talked but the woman's expression never changed. She just let him speak until, from the corner of his eye, Brael saw the stunted ancient beckon to her. Holding up a hand for him to pause, she bent an ear to what it had to say.

The creature's voice was unnaturally high. The words that passed its lips were unintelligible, a stream of non-sense.

'Precog?' the woman repeated a pair of syllables from among the stream that the old/young creature had chattered at her. It nodded.

With that, she offered the runt a warm smile, nodded the briefest of goodbyes to Brael, who still felt there was much more he wanted to say, much more he wanted to tell her, and swept away through the ward, the globe of light causing those asleep on the pallets to stir as it passed over them.

In the dark again, Brael stared at the ceiling, purple after-images dancing before his eyes.

To FACILITATE SWIFT *linguistic assimilation, my acolytes moved among the populace, recording speech patterns, grammatical deviations from standard Gothic and the most prominent dialectical idiosyncrasies. The codiciers in my party began analysing and cataloguing the volumes kept in surprisingly good condition in the city librarium. It is evidence of the Emperor's blessing that the last surviving human city on Samax IV should be Mallax – the city that clung most securely to its distant Imperial roots.*

Alert for evidence of remaining xeno-trace or mutant genetaint, every rumour was investigated, either by formal interview or by psychic scan.

[NOTE: Though some among our ordo frown upon the tolerance and use of sanctioned psykers, such as Gabriella, I

*have, on many occasions found the insights she gained from
subjects, without their knowledge, and therefore without any
attempt on their part to disguise the truth, to be invaluable.
The initial survey of this world was no different.]*

THE SPLINTS CAME off the next day. Delighted, Brael was
anxious to join a new company.

'First you'd better learn how to walk,' counselled the
sawbones who had cut away the bindings and run his
hands down Brael's legs. The nurse who attended him
passed Brael a pair of miss-matched crutches.

So Brael pounded his way around the ward, circuit
after circuit. There were fewer people on the pallets now,
the sawbones and nurses had more time to stand and
joke with each other and with Brael as he passed them
for the hundredth time. The black-garbed strangers also
seemed to have moved on – the cause of some relief
among the medical staff, Brael gathered. They had asked
strange questions in their odd, stilted way of speaking.

There were no more visits from Fellick, Tombek or
Freytha, so Brael just kept walking, cursing whenever he
tripped, refusing assistance whenever he fell.

He discarded the crutches for a pair of battered sticks
after four days. He was walking unaided after seven.

On the eighth day, they came for him: two men, wearing mirrored masks over their faces and a black uniform
similar in design to that worn by the woman who had
visited him.

'Come,' one of them said, his voice muffled slightly by
the mask. Brael found it disconcerting to see his own
face reflected back at him so perfectly from where the
stranger's face should have been.

Brael stood.

'Your things,' said the other stranger. 'Possessions.'

'I have none,' Brael replied. 'I have nothing after the
greenskins. All I want to do is get back to fighting them.'

'Come,' repeated the first of the strangers to speak.

Even though he had discarded the walking sticks, Brael found negotiating the stairs an ordeal. Once at ground level, he was led out of the physic station for the first time in weeks.

Mallax was a ruin, but it was alive. There were people in the streets – Agrans mainly, but many groups of strangely attired men and women passed by. The first time he heard an engine, he tensed, expecting a green-skin war wagon to round the next corner. A short way from the physic station sat a different kind of wagon. The back of the wagon was open and two of the new-comers sat in a covered cab at the front of the horseless vehicle. A uniform, dull grey in colour, on its metal sides it bore the two-headed eagle of the star gods' followers – an icon that had been erected outside the buildings the newcomers had taken for their own offices and workshops. It had also been daubed on walls by grateful Mallaxians.

Brael's escort indicated that he should climb into the back of the wagon. Brael was surprised to find that he wasn't entirely willing to go near it, for it reminded him too strongly of the invaders' engine-driven war machines. Steeling himself, he gripped the side of the vehicle. He felt the vibration of its hidden engine and thought of the much weaker pulse of the Varks in the dimly lit temple.

Setting one foot in a rigid metal stirrup fixed beneath the lip of the wagon's rear edge, Brael climbed aboard with some difficulty, though he again refused any aid. He wanted the newcomers to see that he was fit to return to the militia.

As the wagon rumbled through the streets, a much sleeker machine passed, travelling in the opposite direction, carrying men in ornately-braided uniforms. Brael smiled and waved. They did not return his greeting.

Brael promised himself that he would learn how men saluted each other in the new companies.

The wagon stopped in the shadows of the shattered eastern wall. Seeing the vast breaches in the ancient stone and metal, Brael thought back to the first waves of the greenskins' attack. A high fence that appeared to have been woven out of impossibly thin metal wire had been erected around an old warehouse. Two more of the mirror-faced strangers stood at the gate that led into the compound. At a word that Brael did not understand, the gate was opened and he and his escort passed through.

At first, Brael thought that he had been brought to another physic station. The warehouse contained rows of pallets, half of which were occupied, men on the ground floor, women on the floor above.

Nobody was sure why they had been brought here. They had all, Brael learned, been delivered to the compound by a pair of the mirror-faced strangers. Some – those who had been here the longest – were beginning to take a pessimistic view of their situation. Others still talked of this being a staging post, from which they would be transported to join new companies that had already left Mallax for the front.

'I hope they take us in one of their flying machines,' a boy of nineteen summers told Brael. 'To see the world from the air, like a bird,' he marvelled. 'Such wonders!'

Brael's biggest surprise came when he saw a familiar face across the room.

'Massau?' Brael didn't know whether to greet the slippery guildsman warmly or grab him by the throat. In any case, Massau avoided his gaze and continued to do so for the next three days.

Brael settled down on one of the vacant pallets; there was nothing to do but try to shut out the rumours that circulated through the warehouse, eat the food that arrived three times a day and continue walking to strengthen his legs.

On the fourth day, the warehouse doors were opened and the men and women within were ushered out. There were several wagons in the compound, motors idling. Unlike the open-topped vehicle in which Brael had been driven to the compound, these wagons had metal roofs and windowless metal sides.

Before climbing up into the rear of one of the wagons, Brael turned to the black-uniformed stranger who stood beside the wagon's heavy metal door.

'Are we going to join the new companies?' Brael asked. His reflection opened and closed its mouth in time with his words, but the person behind the mask merely jabbed a finger towards the open wagon door-way. Brael noticed the stranger's other hand move closer to the butt of a pistol holstered on his hip. Brael climbed aboard.

The ride was far shorter than Brael had expected. When the wagon's rear door clanged open, he stepped down into a space outside the city wall that had been blasted by the greenskin artillery and had since been completely levelled by the newcomers. They had created a vast flat expanse of ground, upon which rested a col-lection of flying machines, the like of which neither Brael nor any of his companions could have imagined. There were craft of the kind Fellick had described to him, the kind that carried hundreds of men in their bel-lies. But there were others, much larger, from which trundled vehicles twice the size and weight of the wag-ons from which they had just dismounted. These flying machines were spiked with what Brael took to be weapons, as were the vehicles that rumbled down the ramps from their innards.

Having delivered its cargo, one of the flying machines took to the air and the noise was indescribable. Brael and his companions clapped their hands to their ears, some uttered prayers, one man just dropped to his knees, eyes following the machine as it rose swiftly into the sky, jaw slack with wonder and terror.

Off to one side of the flat expanse sat a jet-black craft that bore no external markings. A line of people could be seen filing up the ramp into its belly. Brael's party was directed to join the line.

'Where are you taking us?' Brael demanded of the mirrorface who pointed towards the squat machine. Brael thought it looked more like an overgrown beetle than anything man-made. When the newcomer didn't answer, Brael repeated his question, louder and in a manner of which he was used to his men taking notice.

In one hand, the mirrorface held a long stick. In a swift, smooth movement, he brought the stick down on Brael's left knee. Still weak, it gave way and dropped him in the dirt. Seeing this, others stopped, looking down at Brael, then up at the mirrored guard.

Several other black-garbed guards moved up to support their fellow, sticks now held ready. The crowd moved back into line. Refusing an offer of a hand, Brael got painfully to his feet and followed suit. Even though the mirrorface had struck his knee, he felt a sick ache beginning to bloom behind his eyes.

The interior of the insect-like machine was almost as black as its outer skin. Long glowing strips buzzed and threw out a meagre light. Eyes adjusting to the gloom, Brael saw that he stood in a vast space, filled with rank upon rank of beds stacked three high. The ceiling was low. There were perhaps five hundred people crammed into this space. A murmur of fear, suspicion and anger began to circulate.

A dull clang reverberated through the metal walls and floor – doors shutting – followed by a hiss and a pressure building in their ears as if they were swimming

down through deep water. Then other sounds, the rising
tone of engines. The floor bucked and swayed gently.
Had the beetle-ship left the ground already?

All I have suffered. All I have done. For this? Brael
asked himself. The ache in his head had resolved itself.
He knew that he would never see his home – his world
– again.

'Why?' he asked, unaware that he had spoken his
question out loud. The only answer he received was the
cacophony of cries and shouts, wails of terror and
despair that grew and resounded around the blank
metal walls.

THE ABSENCE OF *Imperial rigour on this world since the Age
of Apostasy has allowed rogue nature to run unchecked, pro-
ducing deviant gene-strains, among which exists a significant
percentile of latent psychic ability. In some cases, this devia-
tion has passed from the merely latent to the actual and
manifest.*

*The process of tracing all latent and manifest psykers is
ongoing, as is the process of separating them from the general population, and of mining their twisted psyches for the
Imperium's benefit and for the salvation of their souls. The
untapped energies within them will feed the Golden Throne
and maintain the light of the Emperor that shines out across
the Immaterium.*

*The first of the black ships left orbit today, en route for
Holy Terra.*

The ends always justify the means.

In the Emperor's name.

*– Conclusion: 'Inquisitorial communiqué
747923486/aleph/Samax IV' Author: Inquisitor Selene
Infantus. M41,793*

SECTOR 13

Sandy Mitchell

OF ALL THE worlds I've visited in my long and discreditable career, I suppose Keffia stands out as one of the most pleasant. In the abstract, at least; we were there to fight a war, don't forget, so there was plenty to keep the mind occupied, but in the main I look back on my years there through a faint haze of nostalgia.

Being an agriworld, the landscape was almost completely rural, so my overriding impression was one of endless plains of lush greenery cut across by isolated roads, which occasionally intersected at quaint rustic villages where nothing much seemed to have changed since the Emperor was in short trousers. The climate was pleasant too, the small ice caps trickling clear fresh water into all three continents from large polar mountain ranges, while the narrow equatorial band was mercifully free of any landmass worth fighting over. There were a few small island chains, where tiny inbred communities fished and grew tropical fruit, but they were too insignificant to have attracted any enemy attention and were ignored by our side too after the initial sweeps.

All in all I was pretty pleased with life. My inadvertent heroism on Desolatia a couple of years before had won me a little notoriety among the Imperial task force, and I'd been able to capitalize on that quite nicely. Even after all this time there were still sufficient senior officers and Administratum functionaries wanting to shake my hand to keep me comfortably occupied attending receptions and seminars far from the fighting, so that I frequently found myself away from my unit for days on end. A deprivation that Colonel Mostrue, our commanding officer, bore with commendable fortitude, I have to say.

Even while I was at my post things were hardly onerous. The 12th Valhallan Field Artillery were parked well behind the lines, as you'd expect, so I'd had little occasion to face the enemy directly. Indeed, since we were engaged in a protracted campaign to cleanse the planet of a genestealer infestation, there was seldom anything to fire our guns at in any case. The war was a subtle one for the most part, of counter-insurgency and surgical strikes, with the enemy seldom massing in numbers sufficient to justify an artillery barrage. The occasional exceptions to this were renegade units of the local Planetary Defence Force, which would turn out to be riddled with 'stealer cultists with depressing regularity, and turn their guns on the Guard or the local units sent to deal with them until our overwhelming superiority in numbers and firepower had their inevitable effect.

Like most agriworlds, Keffia was sparsely populated by Imperial standards. This made our job of cleansing the place both easier and harder than it might have been. Easier, in that cities were few and far between (I think there were no more than a dozen on the entire globe), which meant that the dense concentrations of population a 'stealer cult needs to really take root and hide in were absent, but harder in that the cult had instead become attenuated, spreading its tentacles widely in small pockets of infestation rather than remaining sufficiently concentrated to root out and destroy in a single strike. The upshot of all this was that we'd been forced into a protracted campaign, cleansing the world province by province, one brood at a time, and we'd already seen three winters come and go since we'd arrived here.

Some, of course, found the slow pace of the campaign frustrating, not least my crony and closest friend in the battery, Lieutenant Divas, who, as always, was chafing at the bit, eager to get the matter over with and move on to the next war.

'We're making progress,' I told him, uncorking the bottle of well-matured amasec which had somehow found its way into my kitbag after the last round of hand-shaking and finger food I'd been dragged off to. 'Both the northern continents are completely clean already.'

'But they were only ever lightly infested to begin with,' he rejoined, finding a couple of teabowls in the clutter on my desk which Jurgen, my aide, had failed to tidy up before disappearing on some mysterious errand of his own. 'The majority of the 'stealers were always down south of here. You know that.'

'Your point being?' I asked, pouring the amber liquid with care.

Divas shrugged, looking uncannily like a bored child getting tired of the current amusement.

'I don't know. We could be here for years yet, if something doesn't change.'

'I suppose we could,' I agreed, trying not to sound too pleased at the prospect. That would have suited me fine, my adventures with the tyranids on Desolatia striking me as more than enough excitement for one commissarial career. (Had I but known, of course, it had just been the prelude to a lifetime of narrow escapes from almost certain death. But back then I had yet to develop the innate paranoia which was to serve me so well in my subsequent century of running for cover and shooting back when I couldn't avoid it. The prolonged period of relative quiet had lulled me into a false sense of security, which a few years later would have elicited nothing more than a vague sense of waiting for the other boot to drop.) So, as I poured the drinks I had little inkling of the fact that the turning point of the entire campaign was no more than a few hours away, and that once again I would find myself caught up in the middle of events over which I had not the slightest control.

The irony was that I'd had my chance to avoid it, but at the time I thought I was being remarkably prudent in not doing so. You see, Colonel Mostrue had never quite shaken the feeling that I'd been less than honest about my supposed heroism on Desolatia, when my attempt to save my own neck had inadvertently stumbled across a swarm of 'nids which would otherwise have annihilated us, and my subsequent panicked dash back to our own lines had drawn them neatly into the killing zone of our guns.

He'd never said anything directly about it, of course, but after that he made a point of creating subtle opportunities for me to prove my mettle, which generally amounted to nudging me in the general direction of trouble and looking out for any overt sign of reluctance to put myself in harm's way again. Luckily my side trips away from the battery had limited his opportunities for such amusements, but on a couple of occasions I'd been left with no alternative but to tag along with a forward observer unit with every outward show of enthusiasm so as not to undermine my fraudulent reputation.

As it turned out, these little expeditions hadn't been nearly as unpleasant as I'd anticipated. On each occasion we'd taken some fire from the cultists as soon as they realized we were sitting out ahead of our own lines calling in their positions to the battery, but to my well-disguised relief the subsequent barrages had taken care of that before they got close or accurate enough to be a real nuisance. To all intents and purposes they'd remained a distant threat, despite the occasional las-bolt putting a dent in the sandbags protecting us. Indeed, in all of these minor engagements I had never even seen the enemy close enough to tell whether they were true hybrids or merely their human dupes.

All that was about to change, though, when the colonel stuck his head into my office the morning after my chat with Divas.

'Commissar,' he said, nailing me with those ice-blue eyes, which always seemed to see a lot further into me than I was comfortable with. 'Do you have a moment?'

'Of course,' I responded, with every sign of politeness, ignoring the faint throbbing of the amasec hangover I'd brought into the room with me that morning. 'Can I offer you some tea?'

'Thank you, no.' He moved aside hastily as Jurgen began to pour an extra bowl. I'd known he'd refuse, of course, which is why I'd offered. My aide was a splendid fellow in many respects, not the least of which was a singular lack of imagination that he compensated for with a deference to authority and a literal-minded approach to following orders which simplified my own life in many ways. But he was hardly the most prepossessing trooper in the Guard, and apart from his habitual untidiness, his spectacular body odour meant that visitors were loath to linger in his general vicinity, certainly not for as long as it would take to drink a bowl of tanna leaf tea. (One of the few Valhallan habits I've

picked up from my prolonged association with the
natives of that icebound world, by the way. It's made
from a plant that grows in the caverns there, and it has
a faintly bitter aftertaste I find most refreshing.)

'As you wish.' I sipped at the fragrant liquid, and
raised an eyebrow in polite enquiry. 'How can I help
you?'

'There's a briefing about the deployment of the garri-
son troops this afternoon at brigade headquarters,'
Mostrue said, clearly fighting the impulse to back away
from Jurgen.

Unlike the iceworlders I served with I had my office
and quarters open to the sweet spring breezes, instead of
air-conditioned to the temperature of a meat locker, and
he clearly found the relative warmth mildly uncomfortable, not least because it let my aide's distinctive bouquet
flourish (another good reason for leaving the windows
open, of course). 'I thought you might like to attend.'

And get palmed off on some risky reconnaissance
mission to the battlefront as soon as we were there, no
doubt. But I couldn't simply refuse; inviting me to
observe the peacekeeping arrangements for the newly-
cleansed continents on behalf of the Commissariat was
a courtesy, at least on the surface, so I thought I'd better
just accept, go along, and hope I could find some excuse
to hang back when the danger presented itself.

I was just opening my mouth to agree, inwardly cursing the colonel, when Jurgen unexpectedly came to my
rescue.

'Begging your pardon, sir, but if you're going to be leaving the battery you'd better reply to the Custodes first.'

'The Custodes?' Mostrue's eyebrow rose, in slightly
exaggerated surprise. 'Have you been up to something I
should be concerned about?'

Quite a bit, as it happened, but I wasn't about to tell
him that. Instead I picked up the dataslate with the

flashing red 'Urgent' icon Jurgen had placed on my desk, and which I hadn't been able to face looking at through the hangover until the tanna tea kicked in, and glanced at it briefly.

'Not this time.' I smiled too, so we could both pretend it was a joke, and nodded to Jurgen. 'Thank you for reminding me.' I turned back to the colonel. 'A few of our gunners are in civilian custody. It seems they got a little over-exuberant in one of the local hostelries last night.' I sighed, with carefully feigned regret. 'So pleasant as this little trip of yours sounds, I suppose I'll have to stay here and sort things out.'

'Of course.' He nodded soberly, always a sucker for the 'duty first' routine, and for once I didn't have to stretch it. Discipline in the battery was definitely my responsibility, so I had the perfect excuse for sidestepping whatever little inconvenience he'd been planning to drop on me.

Of course, if I'd known what sorting out that apparently trivial little piece of paperwork would lead to I'd have gone with him like a shot and taken my chances; but then I'd never have cemented my reputation as a bona-fide hero, and the war for Keffia would have taken another turn entirely.

THE NEAREST VILLAGE to our artillery park, Pagus Parva, was about twenty minutes away, or ten the way Jurgen drove, so I had little time to enjoy the fresh spring air as it wafted in across the kilometres of open fields that lined the road. I'd become quite familiar with the place in the past few months, so I was already well aware that it was somewhat larger than its name implied. It was the bureaucratic centre of the region, sector 13 on the maps of the continent we'd been supplied with by the local Administratum, so boasted a handful of civic buildings as solid and imposing as the temples and libraries of far larger settlements.

In peacetime it had been home to some two thousand souls rather than the handful of hundreds in the surrounding villages, most of them engaged in supporting the scattered farmsteads which clustered around it in some way, but the upheaval of the war and the arrival of so many Guardsmen in the area with pay packets in need of emptying had almost doubled the population. It goes without saying that most of the new arrivals were supporting the war effort by maintaining morale among the troopers in ways which didn't entirely meet the approval of the long-term residents. Or, for that matter, the local Custodes, which had tripled its manpower over the last few months. That had sounded pretty impressive until I'd realized all it meant was that the sector sergeant had been joined by a couple of resentful beatpounders from the provincial capital, who had clearly been selected on the basis of whoever the authorities there had felt the city was most able to manage perfectly well without.

The sergeant herself was another matter entirely, as I knew quite well, having taken care to establish good relations with the local Custodes as soon as we were deployed in the region, and to my pleasant surprise this had developed into rather more than a simple working relationship. Wynetha Phu was a solid career officer in her mid thirties, about a decade older than I was at the time, with a full figure which looked quite good in uniform (and even better out of it, as I'd discovered on a couple of occasions). She was good at her job, knew most of the locals by sight if not by name and reputation, and had turned down the chance of promotion to more challenging duties in the city at least three times that I knew of because she enjoyed the sense of being part of a close-knit rural community. Despite our friendship, she eyed me coolly as I entered the Custodes post from which she exercised her stewardship of the scattered hamlets and villages of sector 13.

'You took your time,' she said. I shrugged, smiling cordially for the benefit of her subordinates, who were slouching around the place trying to look busy, and advanced through the colonnaded entrance hall of the sector house towards the high wooden counter, which barred the public from the working part of the building.

'I know. My apologies.' I adopted an expression of resigned good humour. 'They keep us pretty busy in the Guard, you know.'

'I can imagine, if the ones we've got downstairs are anything to go by.' She prodded the rune, which retracted part of the counter, having recognized her thumbprint, and recoiled slightly as Jurgen followed me through the gap. The nearest constable's jaw dropped visibly as the gap closed behind us with a faint squeak of un-oiled runners. 'Who's this?'

'My aide, Gunner Jurgen.' I performed the traditional back-and-forth hand gesture, which has accompanied informal introductions since time immemorial. 'Jurgen, Sergeant Phu of the Custodes.'

'Pleased to meet you, miss.' He threw her a sloppy salute, which wasn't strictly necessary, what with her being a Custodian and all, but to Jurgen a sergeant was a sergeant and that was that. Besides, she appreciated the courtesy, and reciprocated with a nod.

'Likewise.' The pleasantry was reflexive, but Jurgen smiled broadly anyway, curdling the expression of the constable even more, if that were possible. Wynetha appeared to notice him for the first time. 'Larabi. Go and collect the commissar's men, and sort out the charge sheets.'

'Ma'am.' He acknowledged her order with a manifest lack of enthusiasm that would have got any trooper in the Guard a stiff talking-to at the very least, and slouched off in the direction of the cells.

'You'd better go with him,' I told Jurgen. 'Make sure they behave themselves.'

'Sir.' He trotted off behind the constable, who seemed to move a little faster as his new companion approached, leaving me alone with Wynetha. I'd been hoping for a little friendly conversation, even a mild flirtation or two, but her mind was entirely on business that morning, and I had to make do with a smile and the offer of a mug of recaff.

'Let me guess,' I said, as I scanned the dataslates and let them read my thumbprint to confirm that I'd taken charge of the recidivists in the name of the Commissariat. 'Drunk and disorderly, lewd conduct, and a couple of brawls.'

Wynetha's mouth quirked with what looked like genuine amusement.

'You obviously know your men well,' she said dryly. She sipped her mug of recaff.

'I know these ones a bit too well,' I said, scanning the five names which, between them, made up a good 10% of my workload. That might not sound much to you, but in a battery of over three hundred Guardsmen it was a pretty impressive achievement in its own way. 'Hochen, Nordstrom, Milsen, Jarvik,' and I raised my head to stare disapprovingly at the leading trooper as the small knot of men emerged sheepishly from the cells, 'and the inevitable Gunner Erhlsen.' He grinned at me with the abashed expression I'd become all too familiar with over the last couple of years. 'Tell me, Erhlsen, are you planning to make latrine orderly a full-time career?' He shrugged.

'We serve the Emperor as our talents direct,' he quoted, eliciting a handful of sniggers from among his compatriots.

'Where you're concerned, he delegates to me,' I riposted. The Custodians looked a little surprised at the informality of the exchange, but I felt no obligation to enlighten them. Erhlsen had saved my life back on Desolatia, picking off a tyranid gargoyle, which was swooping on me from behind, and was under the fond illusion that I cut him a little more slack as a result. In actual fact he was completely mistaken about this, but I did nothing to disabuse him (or anyone else) of the notion, being keenly aware that if the rest of the troopers believed that looking out for the commissar's welfare would rebound to their own advantage I stood a much better chance of enjoying a long and successful career.

I swept an evaluating eye over the little knot of troopers. 'All right, Nordstrom. Who started it?'

Of all of them, Nordstrom was visibly by far the worst for wear. The others might have been hung over still, but were at least able to function. Jarvik and Hochen had to hold him up between them, and he seemed to focus on the sound of my voice with a visible effort.

'I'm not sure, sir,' he managed to slur after a moment. 'Start what?' Milsen and Erhlsen exchanged glances and sniggered. If anyone had more clearly been in a brawl I had yet to meet them. Nordstrom's knuckles were bruised and bloodied, his face showing visible contusions, and as his torn, unfastened shirt swung open I caught sight of a dressing patch at the bottom of his ribcage.

'Is that a knife wound?' I asked, unable to keep a sudden flare of concern from my voice. If it was, the ensuing paperwork would take up the rest of the day. But Wynetha shook her head.

'No. It's superficial. It was hardly even bleeding when we found him.'

'And where was that?' I asked. She shrugged.

'An alley off Harvest Street.' No surprise there; it was right in the middle of the area most of the newer residents plied their trade in, a couple of square blocks of taverns, gambling dens and bordellos which had sprung up like mushrooms in the shadow of the Agricultural Records Office to the great discomfiture of the Administratum adepts who worked there (at least, so they said).

'It was those grox-fondlers in the Crescent Moon,' Jarvik said. 'I bet you.' The others nodded, muttering dangerously. 'They put something in your drink, and rob you blind when you keel over.'

It sounded like nothing more than barrack-room gossip to me, but Milsen was nodding eagerly in agreement.

'It's true. They did the same thing to me a couple of weeks back.'

I glanced at Wynetha, who shrugged.

'Wouldn't surprise me if he did get rolled,' she said. 'We're always scraping drunken Guardsmen off the streets around there, and they've usually been picked clean by the time we get to them.'

'I wasn't drunk!' Milsen asserted vehemently. 'Well, not very. Not that much, anyway. I know how to hold my ale.' That much, at least, I knew to be true. Most of the entries in the voluminous file I had on him were for minor infractions involving civic property and small items he'd 'found lying around somewhere' rather than excessive intoxication.

I returned my attention to Nordstrom.

'Nordstrom,' I said slowly, trying to get him to concentrate. 'What's the last thing you remember?'

His brow furrowed. 'Got inna fight.'

That much was obvious, and judging by the condition he was in I'd be surprised if he remembered any of the details. But Wynetha pounced on the opening.

'Who with?' Once again Nordstrom's face contorted with the effort of thinking.

'Dunno,' he said at last. 'Did I win?'

'How about before that?' I suggested. This all seemed like a waste of time to me, but I supposed Wynetha had to at least make an effort to investigate what went on a few hundred metres from her sector house, and the longer I lingered the more I could appreciate her company and the more time there was for Mostrue to leave for brigade headquarters without dragging me along to whatever little surprise he had planned.

'There was a girl, wasn't there?' Milsen interrupted. 'With purple hair?' I glared at him to try and shut him up, but Nordstrom was nodding. The ghost of a smile appeared on his face.

'Kamella.' For a moment a similar dreamy expression descended on Milsen too. 'Amazing tattoos.'

'I knew it.' Milsen looked triumphant. 'The last thing I remember before coming round in the alley is buying her a drink.'

'Ring any bells?' I asked Wynetha, who was also nodding, but with purposeful recognition.

'Sounds like one of the local joygirls. Works out of the Crescent Moon.'

'There, that proves it,' Jarvik said. He glanced meaningfully at his friends. 'Someone should go round there and sort them out.' It was pretty clear from the tone of his voice who he had in mind for the job. I had no objection to that in principle, having found other establishments more congenial for my own recreational purposes, but this was edging into the realm of things I didn't want to know about because they'd make my job more complicated if I did, so I cut in quickly before they said anything which sounded like a positive plan of action. After all, if I didn't know about any potential trouble I could hardly be expected to head it off, could I?

'I think we can safely leave that in the hands of the Custodians,' I said with all the authority I could muster. To his credit Jarvik took the hint and shut up, although I would have laid a small wager that the next time I came to town I'd find the Crescent Moon's windows boarded up at the very least.

'Worth shaking the tree, I suppose,' Wynetha said, to my vague surprise. She looked at the constable she'd addressed before. 'Larabi, keep an eye on things while I'm gone.' She gestured to her other colleague, whose name I never caught, with a brusque jerk of her head. 'You're with me.' After a pace or two she paused, and smiled at me. 'Commissar? It was one of your men who made the complaint, after all.'

I was a little taken aback, I don't mind admitting. And had I realized what I was letting myself in for I would have loaded my collection of defaulters aboard the truck outside and headed back to the battery as fast as I could, and taken my chances with Mostrue. But it seemed like a harmless enough way of wasting a couple of hours on a pleasant spring morning, and there was always the possibility of a little time alone with Wynetha, so I found myself nodding in agreement.

'Good idea, sergeant. It'll save us having to bounce reports and datafiles off each other for the rest of the week.' I glanced disapprovingly at the little group of disheveled gunners. 'And give Nordstrom a chance to pull himself together before we leave.' I could see from the covert glances that the troopers exchanged I'd done the right thing there, reinforcing my carefully constructed facade of being firm but fair.

Then I strolled out of the building to join Wynetha, savouring the sweet spring sunshine for the last time that day.

THE CRESCENT MOON was a seedy-looking establishment at the best of times, which was after dark with the flare of pink and blue luminators flashing to lure the undiscriminating customer inside. In daylight it looked even worse, the peeling paint on the shutters and crumbling

plascrete of the facade was a foretaste of the cheap
wooden furnishings and even cheaper liquor on sale
inside. There were some suspicious-looking stains on
the pavement next to the waste bins that I took pains to
give a wide berth to as Wynetha hammered on the door
with the butt of her laspistol.

'Custodians! Open up!' she yelled, with surprising
volume for a woman so small. After a few seconds of
nothing happening she repeated the procedure, attract-
ing the attention of a small gaggle of passing
Administratum drones that glanced at us furtively and
started muttering to each other that it was about time
somebody did something about that dreadful place.
The door remained resolutely shut.

'Oh dear. There doesn't seem to be anyone in,'
Wynetha said loudly, sarcasm dripping from every sylla-
ble. She turned to the constable, who had drawn his
own sidearm with an anticipatory glint in his eye. 'We'll
have to blow the hinges off.'

Someone had evidently been listening, because there
was a sudden rattling of bolts and the door creaked
open slightly to reveal an unhealthy-looking individual
in badly-fitting clothes and a barman's apron which
might originally have been some kind of colour under
its patchwork of stains.

'Oh wait. My mistake.'

'Yes?' the man said, his hunched posture making his
ingratiating tone sound even more insincere than it
undoubtedly was. 'How can I help you officers?' His
voice trailed off uncertainly as he caught sight of me for
the first time. Whatever he'd been expecting, an Imperial Guard commissar certainly wasn't it. 'And
commissar...?'

'Ciaphas Cain,' I introduced myself, hoping that
something of my reputation had preceded me; a pretty
safe bet given the number of Guardsmen among the

clientele. A slight widening of his eyes suggested that it had indeed done so, but before I could capitalize on it Wynetha took charge again.

'Kamella Dobrevelsky. We want a quiet word.' Wynetha pushed past him without ceremony. 'She works here, right?'

'Yes, she does.' The barman scuttled after us, agitation oozing from every pore. 'But the management is in no way responsible for any actions by members of staff which contravene–'

'Shut it.' The new voice confused me for a moment, until I realized the constable had spoken. Until then I'd vaguely assumed he was mute. 'Just tell us where she is.'

'Upstairs.' The barman's eyes were fixed on the laspistols in the hands of the two Custodians. I glanced around, finding nothing that looked like a threat. The establishment was as shabby as I'd anticipated, looking more like a downhive drinking den than something you'd expect to find on an agriworld, but I guess their customers weren't paying for sophisticated decor.

'Thank you. Your co-operation has been noted,' Wynetha said dryly.

We left the barman goggling after us, and headed for the door in the back of the room with a crudely lettered sign stapled to it saying 'Staff Only.' Behind it a corridor led to the back of the building, presumably to a storage area and, judging by the smell, either a kitchen or a waste dump (in a place like that it was hard to tell the difference), along with a rickety flight of stairs which ascended sharply to the left.

'This must be it,' I said. Wynetha agreed, and led the way up the stairs, which ran into a corridor running the length of the building lined with simple wooden doors. The three of us looked at each other and shrugged. 'One at a time?' I suggested.

'No need.' Wynetha jerked a thumb at the door to a nearby room a few metres along from us. It had a small ceramic plate adhering to it, with a picture of a fat pink pony in a ballet dress, and 'Kamella's Room' written underneath in wobbly letters that were presumably supposed to look like they'd been done in crayon. 'This must be it.' Before I could say anything humorous about her powers of deduction she turned suddenly, and kicked the thin wooden panel from its hinges.

A feminine shriek of surprise and outrage confirmed that we'd found our quarry, and the constable and I followed the sergeant quickly through the wreckage of the door.

'Kamella Dobrevelsky?' she asked, although the question was only a formality. The girl sitting up in the rumpled bed matched Milsen's description perfectly, purple hair tumbling round a narrow face twisted with shock and anger. 'Get some clothes on. You're coming with us.'

'What for?' She began to comply with ill grace, revealing a body entwined with tattoos of a strange but compelling design, just as Nordstrom had said. Despite myself I couldn't resist studying them, taking in how they accentuated the curves of her body, and as I did so I felt the palms of my hands begin to tingle, always a reliable warning from my subconscious that something isn't quite right. She looked up and glared at me. 'Enjoying the view, Ciaphas?'

'I didn't know you'd met,' Wynetha said, switching her attention to me, her tone the temperature of a Valhallan midwinter morning.

'We haven't,' I said. The faint narrowing of the joygirl's eyes as I spoke was enough to tell me that she realized the slip of the tongue had just given her away, and now that the subconscious hint I'd noticed before was hammering against my forebrain it was obvious there was something not quite right about her musculature which the tattoos were designed to obscure. 'But I did tell the barman my name.' I began to draw my chainsword. 'And 'stealers communicate telepath–'

With an inhuman screech Kamella sprang from the bed, faster than I would have believed possible, barging into the constable who was still blocking the doorway. He tried to bring up his sidearm, but was too slow; Kamella's jaw elongated somehow, revealing a mouth full of razor-sharp fangs which clamped down on his throat, shearing through flesh and cartilage, and decorating the shabby room with a bright spray of crimson.

'Emperor on Earth!' Wynetha snapped off a shot, the las-bolt punching a hole through the shoddy partition wall next to its head as the shrieking hybrid turned from the spasming body of the constable back towards us. Beyond it I could hear feet in the corridor outside. Even though I couldn't see the owners, the sound had a peculiar scuttling quality which raised the hairs on the back of my neck. The chainsword cleared the scabbard and I swung it desperately as Kamella leaped again. 'It's a whole nest of them!'

I parried a strike from a hand tipped with talon-like fingernails, feeling the blade bite through chitinous skin, and ducked as those murderous jaws snapped closed a hand span from my face. Wynetha fired again and for a moment I thought she'd missed, until I realized she was holding off the rest of the brood. Clearly I'd have to finish this on my own.

I swept the humming blade back in a counterstrike, taking the hybrid in the thorax, and severing the spinal column. Foul-smelling ichor gushed, reminding me uncomfortably for a moment of the gaunts I'd faced on Desolatia, and the thing that had called itself Kamella dropped at my feet.

'We're boxed in!' Wynetha yelled.

It certainly looked that way. The narrow cubicle was windowless, the only doorway crowded with horribly distorted parodies of humanity howling for our blood. She was placing her shots with care, picking off any foolish enough to show themselves directly with lasbolts to the head or chest, and pumping rounds through the thin wall from time to time to keep them from rushing the narrow space. I glanced around, a desperate plan beginning to form in my head.

'Keep them off as long as you can!' I yelled, swinging the humming blade at the thin wooden wall separating us from the adjoining cubicle. It bit hungrily, whining loudly as wood chips sprayed the room, and in seconds I'd carved a hole large enough to accommodate us. I jumped through, holding my humming weapon up ready to block an attack from the other side of the wall as I emerged, but the room beyond turned out to be unoccupied, and Golden Throne be praised, bright morning sunshine illuminated a shabby bedroom almost identical to the one we'd just left through a window so grubby it might almost have been opaque.

Nevertheless it was the work of a moment to smash the glass with the pommel of the chainsword and dive through, heedless of the drop beyond, while Wynetha sent a fusillade of parting shots through the gap behind us to delay our pursuers.

I hit the pavement hard, heedless of the jolt that drove the breath from my lungs, relaxing to absorb the impact with the instinct hammered into me by years on the assault courses of the Schola Progenium, and turned, drawing my own laspistol. A moment later Wynetha hit the ground beside me, and I peppered the window above us with vindictive enthusiasm, blowing the head of a thickset male from his shoulders. As he fell, I noticed a third arm growing from his right shoulder, tipped with razor-sharp talons.

'How many of these freaks are there?' I asked rhetori-cally, as the barman who'd let us in emerged from the door and levelled a stubber at us. Wynetha took him down with a snapshot to the gut before he could fire, and we looked at one another with grim understanding sparking between us.

'More than we can handle.' More of the grotesques were emerging from the shadows of the alleyways, mov-ing with a co-ordinated purpose that was all the more unnerving for taking place in complete silence. With a chill which raised the hairs on my neck I realised that there were normal-looking humans among them too, carriers of the genestealer taint, doomed to birth more of these monstrous hybrids and with their wills already warped by the telepathic influence of the brood.

I recognised one of the Administratum drones who'd passed us earlier, a piece of piping in his hands, advanc-ing on us with murder in his eyes, a chilling contrast to the prissy bureaucrat of a few moments before.

'Pull back,' I suggested, suiting the action to the word and sprinting in the direction of the sector house, drawn to the promise of protection beneath the spread-ing wings of the aquila on the facade like a penitent to the confessional. (Not that I've been anywhere near one since the schola kicked me out, and I hardly ever told the truth in one while I was there, but you know what I mean.) Wynetha was with me, stride for stride, and our laspistols cracked in unison, striking down the cultists who were angling across the mouth of the street to cut us off. She activated her personal vox as we ran.

'Larabi. Break out the weapons, we're coming in hot.' All I could hear of the reply was the faint echo of static that told me her earpiece was activated, but her expres-sion was enough to keep me appraised of the other end of the conversation. 'We've uncovered a stealer cult. Inform the divisional office and the local Guard units.'

Her voice caught for a moment. 'No, he's dead. Just me and the commissar.'

I missed the next exchange because I was busy ducking a frenzied rush from a hybrid wielding a length of chain. I blocked it with the chainsword, slicing it through, and riposted with a desperate swing that took his head off. Good thing too, it was remarkably ugly, with far too much tongue. When I regained my balance she was looking at me. 'Are your men reliable?'

Well that was debatable really, but under the circumstances I'd expect them to act like the soldiers they were, so I just nodded. Wynetha activated her vox again.

'Arm the troopers.' A pause. 'I don't care how hung over they are, even if all they can do is remember which way to point a gun they're better than nothing.'

'They'll do a lot better than that,' I said, stung at the implied slur on the men I served with. True, they were rear echelon warriors rather than frontline fighting troops – give them an earthshaker or two and they'd flatten a city block neat as you please – but small-arms weren't really their specialty. On the other hand they practised assiduously on the shooting range, Mostrue saw to that, as he did every other regulation, and Ehrlsen at least was a pretty fair marksman, as I could attest from the mere fact that I was still breathing. And don't forget they'd fought off the 'nids on Desolatia, so even if they weren't exactly battle-hardened veterans they'd already proved they could fight up close and personal if they needed to. So all in all I felt pretty confident in their abilities.

'I hope so.' Wynetha took down the last of the cultists between us and the sector house, and we started across the open square towards it. Our boot soles rang on the flagstones, echoes rising from the facades of the encircling Administratum blocks, and small chips of stone began to kick up around us, preceded by the distinctive

crack of ionized air which accompanies a lasweapon
discharge and the deeper bark of a stubber or two.
Despite myself I turned to look behind us, loosing off a
couple of shots myself in the vague hope of keeping our
assailants' heads down, then redoubled my efforts to
reach the sector house.

My worst fears had been realized. The cultists had
been joined by a handful of men in the uniform of the
local PDF, who were armed with standard-issue lasguns,
and several of the hybrids had produced personal
firearms of one kind or another. There were more of
them than I could have dreamed possible, dozens of
twisted monstrosities crowding into the square from all
directions, converging on us with a grim fixity of purpose that clenched my bowels.

'PDF renegades,' I gasped, feeling the air begin to rasp
in my lungs. I couldn't keep this pace up for much longer,
but to falter meant being torn apart by the mob of inhuman hybrids behind us. They surged on like a malevolent
tide, untiring and implacable, uncannily reminiscent of
the tyranid swarms that had forged their foul purpose
and sent them out to infiltrate the Imperium.

'This is just getting better and better.' Wynetha smiled
grimly, and dropped one of our leading pursuers. The
others didn't even falter, flowing around it like water
round a rock. Another group was just clearing the corner of the sector house, angling in to cut us off from our
refuge. A las-bolt, more accurate than the rest, caught
the hem of my greatcoat, tugging at it like an importu-
nate child.

'Aim for the shooters,' I counselled. If we couldn't at
least throw their aim off they'd have us cold in seconds.
If they'd been proper Guard troopers we'd have been
dead already, of course, and I found myself thanking the
Emperor for the habitual sloppiness of the PDF which,
like most professional soldiers, I usually found so

irritating. (Especially while trying to co-ordinate with them on the battlefield. It went without saying that on the few occasions we'd been forced to co-operate with the local forces Colonel Mostrue had been only too pleased to delegate this onerous task to me, and I'd had no choice but to comply with as much good grace as I could muster. Of all the varied duties of a commissar, I've always found liaising with PDF trolls amongst the most irritating.)

We turned in unison, aiming as best we could, but under the circumstances I didn't expect much. At the very best we were only delaying the inevitable until our pursuers closed, but I've always found that when you truly believe you only have seconds left to live each one becomes so precious you become determined to eke them out for as long as possible whatever the cost. We fired as one, expecting little effect, but to my astonishment the renegade troopers were falling, breaking, and running for cover.

'Cowards!' I bellowed, carried away with adrenaline and the reckless bravado of imminent death. 'Stand and fight like men, damn you!'

'Are you mad?' Wynetha was staring at me in astonishment, and I whipped my chainsword up into a defensive posture, ready to take on the first wave of hybrids that was already leaping towards us, inhuman jaws agape. 'Run, you idiot!' Only then did I realize that several of our would-be assailants were falling, bloody craters exploding across their chests, and the distinctive crack of las-fire was coming from behind us now. Instinct took over once again, and I followed her advice, finding the square behind us littered with the corpses of the cultists who had tried to cut us off.

'This way, commissar! Hurry!' Jurgen's familiar voice urged me on, and as I looked up at the sector house, now tantalizingly close, I caught sight of him crouched behind one of the columns supporting the portico, a lasgun raised and spitting death at the horde of cultists behind us. A moment later I noticed another muzzle flash, and made out Erhlsen similarly positioned, picking off one target after another with smooth precision. He caught sight of me and grinned, no doubt enjoying himself hugely.

Larabi was by the doors, the blue of his Custodes uniform standing out starkly against the rich polished wood, blazing away on full auto without even the pretence of expertise, but the crush of distorted bodies was so great aiming wasn't strictly necessary; wherever he pointed his weapon hybrids and human cultists alike fell like wheat before harvesters.

With Jurgen's encouragement ringing in my ears, I put on a final spurt, vaguely surprised to find that a small part of my mind was still able to appreciate the rear view of Wynetha bounding up the steps a few metres ahead of me, and then almost before my senses could register it I was surrounded by the cool marble foyer of the sector house. I turned back to find Larabi closing the doors, while Jurgen and Erhlsen backed through them, still firing on the frenzied mob which was by now cresting the steps outside and bounding over their fallen comrades in a single-minded attempt to reach the narrowing gap.

They almost made it at that, the door stopped, centimetres from closing, blocked by a chitinous arm tipped by three scythe-like talons which gouged a deep groove from the thick hardwood as it flailed around for purchase. The two gunners leapt to assist the constable, putting their shoulders to the wood, but even with all three of them straining every muscle the sheer weight of the tide of bodies behind it began to force the doors open again. I slashed down with the humming chainsword, severing the obscene limb that dropped to the floor, thrashing and leaking foul-smelling ichor, and the door slammed to. Larabi triggered the locking mechanism, and thick steel bolts slammed home, securing it behind us.

'What the hell did you think you were playing at out there?' Wynetha was glaring at me, a complex mixture of emotions on her face. 'Were you trying to get yourself killed?'

There was no point in admitting I'd been so far gone I hadn't even noticed our comrades had opened up a corridor to safety for us, so I just shrugged.

'Well, you know,' I said. 'Ladies first.' The effect was quite gratifying, I have to say; she hugged me briefly, failing to find any words, and turned away, already assessing our situation like the professional she was. Erhlsen and Larabi were looking at me with undisguised admiration, and I was suddenly sure (correctly, as it turned out) that suitably embroidered reports of my gallantry and heroism would be all over the sector before the week was over. I turned to Jurgen, who was taking in the scene outside with his usual phlegmatic manner. 'What's our situation?' I asked.

'Frakked,' Erhlsen muttered, before turning back to the nearest window and beginning to amuse himself by taking potshots at the abominations outside. Fortunately the Custodians tend to the sort of caution I was later to acquire, and the place was constructed to withstand a siege quite comfortably; the windows were narrowed, and placed to provide excellent firing positions.

'Pretty defensible,' Jurgen said, ignoring him. 'We could do with a couple of full squads to cover everything though. We're spread pretty thin.'

'Might as well wish for a Chapter of Astartes while you're at it,' I said, but as usual my aide was immune to sarcasm and he just nodded.

'That would be nice,' he agreed.

'Where are the others?' I asked. Jurgen gestured towards the rear of the building.

'Milsen's covering the back door. He found some grenades in the armoury and he's booby-trapping the entrance. Hochen's with him. Jarvik's up on the roof.'

'What about Nordstrom?' I asked. 'Still sleeping it off?'

'I don't know.' Jurgen looked confused for a moment. 'I thought he was with us.'

'A building this size, he could be anywhere,' I said. Before we could speculate further the sound of las-fire cut across the silence. Drawing the obvious conclusion I glanced across at Erhlsen, but he was in the middle of reloading, and looked as puzzled as the rest of us.

'That came from inside!' Wynetha led the rush back towards the rear of the building. The firing intensified for a moment, then ended with a gurgling scream that raised the hairs on the back of my neck. Too impatient to wait for the counter to retract I vaulted over it, landing heavily, and found myself facing the door to the rear of the building through which Jurgen and Larabi had disappeared to fetch the others what seemed like a lifetime ago, but which my chronometer stubbornly insisted had been little more than an hour.

'Protect the brood!' Nordstrom appeared through the gap, a bloodstained combat knife gripped in his hand, his eyes as vacant as those of the infected humans outside. The full significance of the apparently trivial wound on his chest suddenly became clear to me. I sidestepped his swing, blocking reflexively with the chainsword, and took his hand off at the wrist.

To my amazement he didn't even slow down, spinning to strike at my eyes with the extended fingers of his other hand. I ducked my head just in time, feeling the impact against my skull, barely cushioned by my cap, and heard his fingers break an instant before the crack of a laspistol next to my ear told me that Wynetha was still watching my back. As he fell, she ran past me, sprinting for the end of the corridor.

A las-bolt took her in the shoulder, spinning her back into my arms. I glanced at the wound, noting in passing that it was already cauterized so at least she wouldn't bleed to death, before handing her back to Larabi. Milsen was at the far end of the corridor, his lasgun aimed at us, a dozen or so frag grenades crudely wired to the thick wooden door behind him. A faint scrabbling sound betrayed the presence of our assailants beyond it, still determined to break through. Hochen's body was lying between us in a pool of blood, clearly beyond any medical aid.

'Cease fire, you idiot!' I yelled. 'It's us!'

'I know.' The emotionless timbre of his voice warned me what he was about to do even before my conscious mind registered the blankness of his stare.

'Back!' I yelled to the others, even as he detonated the explosives, blowing the thick wooden door to splinters and himself to perdition. A shrieking tide of malformed malevolence burst through the gap, jaws gaping, talons extended to rend and tear. A volley of las-fire from all of us blasted into the first rank, but those behind just kept coming, barely slowed by the obstruction of their fallen fellows. 'Fire and movement!'

It was a desperate gamble, but one we just made, taking it in turns to shoot down the front rank of hybrids while the rest of our party retreated to the stairwell leading to the roof. Even Wynetha managed to keep firing, her face pale with shock, as Larabi helped her up the staircase to safety. It was a close-run thing, mind, and we'd never have got away with it if the corridor hadn't been so narrow. Even now I break out in a cold sweat at the thought of how things would have gone if the monsters had been able to close a little faster, or our fire had been a little more attenuated.

'Up here, commissar!'

I grabbed the proffered hand gratefully, Erhlsen hauling me clear of the stairwell just as Jarvik lobbed a couple of grenades down among the seething mass of chitin, and Jurgen slammed the heavy steel fire door closed. The dull thud of the explosion shook the metal as I leaned against it and Larabi locked it closed. I gasped, the fresh air of the outside hitting my lungs like pure oxygen, leaving me momentarily giddy from the reaction.

'They seem pretty steamed,' Jarvik said, glancing over the side of the roof, and taking a random potshot into the crowd for luck. I followed his gaze, and the breath seemed to freeze in my throat. We were surrounded now by what seemed to be hundreds of the monstrosities, lapping around our flimsy refuge like the incoming tide round a sandcastle. In that moment I knew we were doomed, that all we could hope to do was stave off the inevitable.

'Look, sir!' Jurgen was pointing at something, a grin of imbecilic delight on his face, and for a moment I thought he'd gone mad under the strain. Then I saw it too, the unmistakable silhouette of an Imperial Chimera, and behind it another... 'It's the Cadians!'

Sure enough the column of armoured vehicles bore the crest of the Cadian 101st, an elite assault regiment that had just arrived in the sector from the victorious campaign in the north. Hard luck for them to be thrown straight back into the fighting, I thought at the time, but as it turned out it was just as well they were the closest Guard unit and the first to respond to the message Wynetha had ordered Larabi to send.

The unmistakable rattle of heavy bolters burst across the square like thunder, scything the milling abominations down where they stood. We joined in enthusiastically from our perch on the roof, pouring down fire from above, watching in undisguised relief as the tide of obscenity broke in disorder. The thudding and scrabbling against the metal door died away as the brood realized it was facing a far greater threat than us, and turned to meet it.

'WELL DONE, CAI.' Divas looked at the gleaming new medal on my coat with barely suppressed envy. As usual, he was the only one present to use the familiar form of my given name, and from the corner of my eye I noticed Wynetha, her dress uniform augmented by a sling which made her look fascinatingly amazonian, grin as she picked up on my thinly-disguised irritation. 'Looks like you got all the fun again.'

'It wasn't the same without you,' I assured him, straight-faced. I glanced across at Erhlsen, who was looking surprisingly subdued considering he was supposed to be another of the guests of honour. 'I expected you to be a bit happier under the circumstances, Erhlsen. Free drink, all the food you can eat...'

'I know. It's these.' He fingered the freshly sewn bombardier's stripes on his sleeve moodily. 'They're kind of... inhibiting.'

'Don't worry,' I assured him. 'Knowing you, I doubt you'll keep them for long.'

'Well, there is that,' he said, looking markedly more cheerful, and wandering off to investigate the buffet.

'What the six of you did...' Divas persisted. 'If you hadn't found the cult they would have infected every Guard unit on the continent eventually. And we'd have lost the war. It doesn't bear thinking about.'

'Then don't,' I said. I was still getting reports in from the purges going on in practically every regiment on the planet, dozens of men executed for the taint they carried without even having been aware of the fact, and it left a sour taste in my mouth. I turned to Wynetha, desperate for a distraction. 'Care to dance?'

'To begin with,' she agreed.

READ TILL YOU BLEED

DO YOU HAVE THEM ALL?

Coming Soon...

LET THE GALAXY BURN!

More action-packed short stories from
the Black Library

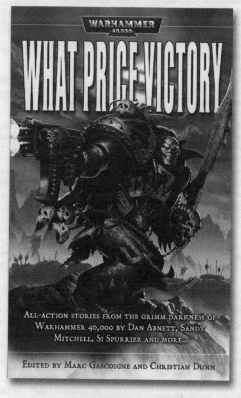

WARHAMMER 40,000

WHAT PRICE VICTORY

ALL-ACTION STORIES FROM THE GRIMM DARKNESS OF
WARHAMMER 40,000 BY DAN ABNETT, SANDY
MITCHELL, SI SPURRIER AND MORE...

EDITED BY MARC GASCOIGNE AND CHRISTIAN DUNN

WHAT PRICE VICTORY
ISBN: 1-84416-077-7

www.blacklibrary.com

HARLEQUIN

Heartfelt or suspenseful, inspiring or passionate, Harlequin has your happily-ever-after.

With new books published every month, you are sure to find the satisfying escape you know you deserve.

Love Harlequin romance?

DISCOVER.

Be the first to find out about promotions, news and exclusive content!

Facebook.com/HarlequinBooks

Twitter.com/HarlequinBooks

Instagram.com/HarlequinBooks

Pinterest.com/HarlequinBooks

ReaderService.com

EXPLORE.

Sign up for the Harlequin e-newsletter and download a free book from any series at **TryHarlequin.com**

CONNECT.

Join our Harlequin community to share your thoughts and connect with other romance readers!
Facebook.com/groups/HarlequinConnection

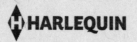